THE
TEXAS
BOYS!

by
Thomas J.
"Texas"
Pilgrim

edited by
Michelle M. Haas

Copano Bay Press
2018

First published in 1878 under the title *Live Boys; or Charley and Nasho in Texas* by Arthur Morecamp (pseudonym of Thomas Pilgrim).

All new material, copyright 2018 Copano Bay Press

ISBN 978-1-941324-14-1

TABLE OF CONTENTS

CONTENTS CONTINUED

Publisher's Note

In hunting down the real Charley and Nasho, all of the usual trails—historical documents, census data and contemporary newspaper articles—went cold. They were mere boys and the author hadn't used their real names, so a thorough investigation was made. I wanted badly to learn who Charley Zanco and his best pal really were, and what became of them in later life. But my research left me empty-handed, leaving me with a lingering curiosity and an ongoing research project for future days.

In keeping with what was selling well at the time, Pilgrim's narrative was marketed as juvenile fiction, targeted at boys entering their teens. J. Frank Dobie, in commenting on the book, gave us assurance that it truly isn't a work of fiction at all. It is far too true-to-life to have been wholly dreamed up by a young Texas lawyer. He called it, rather, a chronicle written by one who had obviously recorded the adventures of another who had lived them. I'm not one to quibble with Frank and certain facts about the author's life make his point very well.

Thomas Jefferson Pilgrim, a Gonzales lawyer by trade, had been sickly since childhood. He died but four years after the publication of this book, having been in the world just four decades. Before his death, he wrote several adventure books under the pen names Arthur Morecamp and Eugene Owl, perhaps living vicariously through reading and writing about the lives of young men more able-bodied to do that which he was unable.

Talking with the young Texas cowboy at the World's Fair about his exploits must have captivated Pilgrim and, fragile though he was in body, his mind and his pen were quite lively and gifted, as this text plainly demonstrates.

The geographical descriptions of the ranch on which Charley and Nasho's boss resided, as well as a description of his operations, seem to point naturally to Thomas O'Connor. This, like the identities of our two young adventurers, could not be proved out, but will remain a research topic until I find satisfactory answers.

Whether you choose to read it as fiction or biography, I think you'll take a shine to *The Texas Boys* early on. It is a book that you'll want to share with your children or grandchildren. Aside from the authentic descriptions of cattle driving and camp life, the book, in its easy-going and conversational way, describes how a boy learns to think like a capable man. Charley is curious, respectful and willing to learn. He's not afraid of hard work. He learns how to solve problems, think on his feet, cheerfully endure privations, stand his ground in the face of adversity and be a frank, honest man. Many of these lessons Nasho already internalized during his tenure with the Indians, though he didn't view them as particular virtues—he viewed them as a means of survival.

The world needs more Charleys and Nashos...and I suppose that's just a more topical way of saying that the world needs more real Texans.

-Michelle M. Haas, Managing Editor
Windy Hill
2014

Author's Preface

I first met Charley and Nasho at the Centennial, and often took a much deeper interest in listening to Charley's narrations of their adventures than in anything to be seen on the grounds. Being a good short-hand reporter, I took down most of these narrations just as they came from Charley's lips, though I had then no expectation of presenting them to my young readers.

As autumn drew on, my physician ordered me South for my health, and I bade goodbye to my little friends with no little regret, thinking it most likely we should meet no more. Fortune, however, turned my steps to the mountains of Texas, where I again met Charley and Nasho, just returned from their daring trip across Kansas and the Northern Texas frontier in mid-winter.

A broken leg, caught in a fall from my horse while bear hunting, laid me up a prisoner at good Mr. Zanco's house for six weeks—weeks that were enlivened by Charley's animated descriptions of their adventures after leaving the Centennial. As before, I took down full notes and, believing from the interest they had aroused in me that they would be acceptable to thousands of American boys, I have hastily thrown them into shape for the press, and here they are.

THE AUTHOR
Kerrville, Kerr Co., Texas
January 31, 1877

CHARLEY ZANCO & NASHO

I live away over in Texas, in Kerr County, on a little
creek called Turtle, up in the mountain. The country
is nearly all mountains up there, and the Guadaloupe River runs through them. I live with Uncle. His
name is Adolphus Zanco, and mine is Charles Zanco. I
am fourteen years old and so is Nasho. Nasho ain't his
right name. He is a Mexican, and his name is Ygnacio de
Garapitas, but we always call him Nasho because it is
shorter. Nasho was born way out on the Rio Grande river, 'most to Mexico, but one day the Kickapoo Indians
came along and killed his father and mother, and took
his poor little baby sister by the heels and knocked her
brains out against the tree that stood in front of their
jacal. Then they set fire to the house and rode off, and
they took all the horses on the place. They put Nasho
on his pony and took him too, and shot their arrows into
the cows and oxen as they rode away. Nasho was only
six years old then. I forgot to say that *jacal* is Mexican
for house. Most of their jacals are made of mud worked
up into rough bricks that are dried in the sun. They call
them adobe, but we say 'dobe for short.

The day the Indians took Nasho off they rode sixty
miles. They were in a hurry because they had been
down on the river stealing horses, and were afraid the
soldiers and ranchmen would be after them. Nasho
said he was 'most tired to death, and so sleepy he could
hardly sit on his pony, but they wouldn't let him stop.

And whenever he would think about his poor pa and ma all full of arrows and bloody, and his little sister with her head all broke to pieces, he would cry, and that would make them mad, and sometimes one of the meanest and worst-looking ones in the crowd would dash at him, and make out like he was going to stick his lance in him; but there was one of them that was finer dressed than the others that was good to him, and carried him in his arms part of the way so he could rest and sleep some, and wouldn't let the mean one hurt him.

At night they went into a deep thicket at the head of a little creek, and made a little fire out of dry sticks that wouldn't make much blaze, and cooked some half-dried meat, and staid there all night. They gave Nasho some of the meat. The good one gave him a blanket to sleep on that they had taken from his pa's house. Next morning they were up before daylight, cooked some more meat and were off again. They were a week reaching their camp way high up on the Rio Grande River in the mountains. Nasho said he was nearly dead, he was so tired, when they got there.

He lived with them seven years. He didn't have much to do, only to herd the ponies and keep them from straying away. He learned to shoot with a bow and arrows, and used to kill birds and rabbits and squirrels, and sometimes he would kill a deer. He said the weather was so cold in winter that he and the other Indian children used to suffer a great deal from it. They didn't have any clothing but buckskins and blankets, and some of their blankets were old and full of holes and let the wind in. And sometimes, too, they had very little to eat and would pick the bones of the deer and buffaloes that had been killed. Sometimes Nasho would go out with a little Indian boy that he liked most of any of the Indian children, and kill a bird or two, or maybe catch a rabbit in their snares or run him into a hollow tree with their dogs, and twist him out, and then they would eat up their game by themselves. They would carry fire with them in a hollow reed that would keep it a long time, and cook their game out in the woods. They knew if they took it back to the village they would have to divide with the other children, and they wouldn't get enough to do them any good. I think they were right, for the Indians had no business to carry Nasho away with them.

Nasho got so he could shoot with a bow and arrow about as well as a white man with a gun, and killed a great many deer and two elk, and sometimes a buffalo. Once when he was out with one of their hunting parties a long way from their winter camp—they didn't stay in one place, but travelled about a great deal, camping wherever they found grass, water and game—he was hunting by himself, and saw an Indian from another tribe riding along on his pony. The Indian had not seen him, so he dodged down into a little hollow, jumped off his pony, crawled through the long grass so as to get right close in the way the Indian was coming and, as he rode by, shot him off his horse with an arrow and killed him. Then he ran up and scalped him, put the scalp in his belt, caught the Indian's pony and led it back to their camp.

The Indian that had been so kind to him, and taken him into his tent, was very proud and happy to see Nasho come back with a scalp in his belt, and told him someday he would be a big chief. That evening when the other Indians had all come back from hunting they made a great feast, and took the scalp Nasho had brought back, and put it on a pole in the center of the village, and they all danced around it for an hour. They called Nasho "the-boy-who-had-killed-a-man." After that he always went out with their warriors both to hunt and when they went on the warpath.

When Nasho was about thirteen years old he came down with a party of warriors to Texas to steal horses. When they got down close to the settlements they separated, and Nasho and two others were to strike in near the head of the Guadaloupe River, and slip down through the country in the night, finding out where the horses were, and then on their way back drive off all they could get. They had no guns, and even left their bows and arrows and lances hid in a thicket where they could get them on their way back. They had only butcher knives, and several lariats apiece with which to catch the horses they wanted to steal. They had killed a cow and cut her meat into long, thin strips, and hung it over their horses so that it would dry in the sun as they rode along. That was all they had to eat.

I reckon they didn't know how close they were to the settlements, or else thought they would keep a sharp watch, but they wasn't sharp enough. Uncle and Mr. Braston was out hunting deer, and saw the three coming half a mile off, just as they got to the head of a ravine. They hid their horses in some thick bushes, and slipped down into the ravine the way the Indians was coming. Nasho was in front, and the other two behind him, one right after the other in Indian file. When they saw Nasho was only a boy they agreed not to shoot him, but Uncle was to take the second one, and Mr. Braston the one behind him on the pack horse, and when Uncle gave a low whistle both were to shoot. Then they were to set Bose and Trailer—Uncle's big dogs—on Nasho's horse, and Uncle was to follow them on foot while Mr. Braston ran to his horse and followed them on horseback. They all came riding along as quiet as cats but watching round on every side.

Uncle waited till the two Indians were right opposite them, and then whistled—*crack!* went the guns so close together you could not hear but one sound—off came both Indians, and out jumped Uncle sicking on Bose and Trailer, while Mr. Braston ran for old George. At the crack of the gun Nasho looked back to see what it was, but when the Indians fell he commenced kicking his pony, and putting his quirt to him, but before he could get fairly started Bose and Trailer had caught up with him, and Bose nabbed the pony by his long mane on one side, and Trailer on the other, and pulled down on him so heavy he couldn't run.

Quick as a flash Nasho pulled out his butcher knife and stabbed poor Bose in the neck, and he hollered and let loose, but before he could stab Trailer Uncle was there and grabbed him around the waist, jerked him off the pony, and took the knife away from him. Mr. Braston came up full jump and caught the pony by his long trailing bridle rope, and tied him to a tree, and tied Nasho's hands behind his back with the end of it. Then they went back and caught the horses of the Indians which had only run a little ways and then stopped to feed, and came back with them to the Indians. They were both dead.

Uncle had shot his Indian through the heart with a rifle ball, and Mr. Braston had filled his with buckshot. They didn't have any clothes but an old blanket and pair of buckskin leggins apiece, and one of them had his leggins sewed on him so tight that they couldn't have been got off without cutting them off. They looked like they had been put on wet, and sewed, and had dried tight on him like saddlers put on the rawhide coverings of their saddles. Each of them had a butcher knife in his belt, and a flint and steel and some punk in a little buckskin bag at his side. They had three lariats apiece coiled round their waists. Uncle said he almost hated to shoot his, he was so unsuspectin'-like, but he knew if he didn't he would get away and steal horses, and maybe kill somebody, so he thought he had better stop him while he could, and to keep from putting him in any misery he just give him a dead shot.

After looking at the Indians a little bit they took their horses and went to the place where they had left Nasho tied, but when they got there he and the pony was gone. They put Bose and Trailer on the track and away they went as fast as they could run. Pretty soon they got out of the bushes and saw Nasho just a-flying across a little prairie to a thicket on the other side. Mr. Braston throwed up his gun to shoot but Uncle wouldn't let him, and they ran him into the thicket, one of them starting around on each side to keep him from coming out. The dogs followed him on and presently Uncle saw him coming towards him to make a break out. He slid off his horse and, as Nasho came stealing out, he took a quick aim and shot his pony right through the top of the neck, and he fell like he was dead.

Uncle ran up as quick as he could and found the pony had fell on Nasho, and lay across his leg so he couldn't get up. Directly the pony got up, for he wasn't hurt much, but only stunned, and Nasho tried to raise up but fell back again. Uncle stooped down over him and found the pony had fell across a rock which had broke Nasho's leg. Mr. Braston came up and they cut some smooth, straight sticks and tied his leg up the best they could. Then they got two poles about twelve feet long, and fastened one on each side of their horses, putting one in front of the other and fastening the poles to the girts with strong strings. Then they stretched a blanket over the poles with long thorns, and put Nasho in the blanket. It sagged down in the middle so he couldn't fall off. Then they got on the Indians' horses, and Uncle went ahead leading the two horses that was carrying Nasho's litter, and Mr. Braston came behind with Nasho's pony, and in this way they went to Uncle's house. The Indians' saddles were mighty poor ones, and didn't have any stirrups, and Uncle said it was as hard riding as he had ever done.

When they got there Mr. Braston helped Uncle in the house with Nasho, and put him on a pallet on the floor, and then went on home, and said he would send the doctor up as soon as he could. The doctor came up that evening and set his leg, and bandaged it up close and tight, and said it would be a month before he could get out of bed. He said he didn't believe Nasho was any Indian, but a Mexican that had been with the Indians a long time until he had come to look like an Indian.

Poor little Nasho looked strange and wild, but he had never cried a bit, nor made any noise, but only asked for water by pointing to the water bucket, and then to his mouth. The next morning some of the neighbors came up to look at Nasho, and to go out to the dead Indians.

Dr. Coleman said it would be a good idea to take the dead Indians to the Comanche Trail, where it curves into the Big Gulch, and hang them up so the other Indians could see them when they came down stealing, and maybe they would be afraid and go back. Uncle didn't like it. He said it was bad enough to have to kill men, but the dead ought to be sacred, and be let alone; but all the rest said it was a good idea and they would do it. They wasn't men like other people, but only Injins, and just the things to make a thieves' gallows of.

Right at the head of Big Gulch, where the Injin Trail comes into it, are two big trees on top of the hill, one on each side of the trail. They cut a long pole and put it across, one end in a fork of each tree. Then they took the Indians and plaited rawhide strings all around them from their feet to their heads so they couldn't fall out when the flesh came off of them, and hung them up to the pole right over the middle of the trail and left them there. They was there still the last time I was up there, for the flesh hadn't dropped off of them, but they had dried up like dead cattle I have seen on the prairies, where the skin had drawn in to the bones and kept them together.

It wasn't a pleasant sight to see them on a windy day swinging backwards and forwards in the wind. I knew they were dead, but I couldn't help but feel like they must get tired standing up all the time, day and night. If they had just stayed at home and let us alone they wouldn't have been killed.

Nasho's Indian Know-How

As soon as Nasho got over his fever he began to talk a little in a curious sort of lingo that Uncle could hardly understand. He could talk Mexican very well, and by a little at a time Nasho quit talking Indian and talked almost altogether in Mexican. Uncle found out that he was a little Mexican boy that had been caught by the Indians, as I told you at first. He said he didn't like the Indians and was glad to get away from them, and if Uncle would let him, he would live with him, and help herd sheep and hunt up the cattle. So Uncle told him he might live with him, and if he was a good boy he would send him to school in the winter with me when there wasn't much to do.

Nasho was a good boy and tried to do just as he was told, and took good care of the sheep when he was sent out to herd them. At first Uncle wouldn't let me go with him, but when he saw Nasho didn't try to run away, or do anything bad, he would send me with him sometimes, and sometimes we would go out after cattle together. He used to tell me a good deal about how he lived when he was among the Indians. If he would only write down what he has seen away out on the prairies and all he knows about how the Indians live, it would be a great deal more interesting than what I am telling you.

There was one place we used to stop at often when we were hunting cattle, where there was soft clay, and while

our ponies were grazing at dinner Nasho would get the
clay, and soften it with water from the little branch, and
make it into all sorts of things—rabbits and bears, and
deer, and horses, and Indians bringing in deer, and little
prairie dogs—and they would look almost like they were
really 'live, sure-enough animals, only they were all the
color of the clay. One day he made a buffalo, and took
some black wool he had brought with him from the old
black sheep, and stuck it over the buffalo, and pulled
some out into threads and made him a little tail, and
cut little horns out of pieces of burnt wood, and stuck
beads in his head for eyes, and he looked just as much
like a little buffalo as could be.

The young lady who was teaching school saw it at our
house one day, and when she found Nasho had made it
she said he must come down to her boardinghouse on
Saturdays and she would show him how to make such
things in wax, which was better to keep than the clay,
and she would teach him to color them too. Uncle said
he might go, and Nasho was so proud he used to work
hard at nights and spare times, making quirts out of
rawhide, and bridle reins out of black and white horse-
hair twisted up together so that they looked real pretty,
that he might make some money to give his teacher to
buy wax and paints for him. He learned so fast that she
was very proud of him and loved to teach him.

One day not long after he had got well so that he could
go about as well as anybody, Nasho asked Uncle to let
him and me go to the place where the Indians had left
their bows and arrows, and get them. Uncle wouldn't
let us go then, but about a month afterward he said we
might. The place where they were was about thirty-five
miles from Uncle's, so that it would take us all day to
get there, and we would have to camp out one night,
but Nasho said he knew the way perfectly well, and it

was in the dark of the moon when the Indians don't come down into the settlements, and besides there was a party of Rangers scouting in the country above us, so Uncle didn't think we would be in any danger. He believes in boys learning to do for themselves.

I thought when we started it would be a very easy matter to go to the thicket where they had been left and pick them up; but after riding all day over so many hills and through so many thickets and hollows that were so much alike, I began to wonder how Nasho would be able to find his way without any trail to go by, and even if he went right and got within a mile of it, how he could tell the exact bush in which they were hidden.

I remember once when I was cow hunting I found a little fawn in a bush where its mother had hidden it. I didn't have time then to stop and get it, but I thought I would as I went back home, so I marked the place so closely by the trees and bushes and rocks around it that I thought I could come right back to it without any trouble. About half an hour afterward I met the rest of the boys, and they sent me back to the pen to take a horse they had found and caught. I was glad to go, because I could get my fawn and take him home, but when I got to the place, I looked everywhere but I never could find the bush where I had left it. So I thought after so long a time, and when he had never been there but once, the chance for Nasho's finding the bush was not a very good one.

But he did. We came to a little open space with thick bushes all round it, and pointing to one that looked to me just like all the rest, he said the bows and arrows were in there, and sure enough they were. I asked him how he knew that was the place. He showed me three young trees taller than the bushes around them, and about the same distance one on each side and the

other on the farthest side ahead of us. In the middle
of the open space was a large rock and an old log that
had been burned almost to charcoal by the prairie fires.
He said he could have found the bush in a dark night,
because it was in a line with the black log and the north
star, and all he would have to do was to go straight
forward. I asked him how he would find the black log
in the night. He said it would show better than one that
wasn't burnt, and besides the white rock would show,
and he could find it from that. He said that the Indians
understood such things so well that when the one who
was ahead stopped there and put his bow and arrows
in the bush, they did so too without asking him any
questions. They just looked round and saw the rock
and log and the trees, and knew that was the reason he
had picked that place because it would be easy to find
again.

I asked him how he could travel so straight. He said
he could tell by the way the sun fell on his shoulder. If
he went to far too the right it would fall over his right
shoulder on his breast, and if he went too far to the left
it would fall over his left shoulder, but he would know
the way anyhow if the sun wasn't shining.

It is strange how animals can travel so straight. I know
once Uncle sold an old steer to a drover and he drove
him off, and about six months afterward he came back.
The next spring the drover came back to buy more
cattle and knew the steer when he saw him, and said he
got away from them in Indian Territory, more than three
hundred miles above there. I know if you take a horse
away from where he was raised he will often get away
and go right back to his old home as straight as a bee.

Well, the bows and arrows and shields were all there.
The bows were made of bois d'arc wood, and the strings
of silk. Nasho said the Indians used to use the sinews

of deer, but they were not good in wet weather, because they would get soft and stretch. Now they buy their strings from the Mexicans.

The bows were about four feet and half long, with a notch at each end to fasten the string to. One of them was wrapped from the middle halfway to each end with sinews. Nasho said that made it a great deal stronger and stiffer, and it would shoot farther and harder.

The arrows were made of young dogwood shoots scraped smooth and even, and feathered near the notch with three feathers so they would go straight. Most of the feathers were buzzards'. Nasho said without the feathers they wouldn't shoot straight or far at all. They had flat, sharp spikes stuck in the end and wrapped with small sinews so they wouldn't come out when they were shot into anything. There were about forty arrows to each bow, in a long case made of rawhide, with the hair on, and with straps to go over the shoulder and carry them by. Nasho's bow wasn't as long or as hard to bend as the others, because he was only a boy. We couldn't either of us bend the bow with the sinews wrapped round it. He seemed very glad to get his bow and arrows again, and said he would make me one like it.

The lances were straight little poles about three quarters of an inch through and eight feet long, with long sharp spikes in the end a foot long, and half an inch wide and tapering to a point. Just below the spikes they had feathers and leather fringes fastened to them.

The shields were made of two hickory sticks about half an inch through, crossing each other in the middle, about a foot and half long and covered tight with two thicknesses of bull hide stretched over the sticks and fastened by strings. On the inside they had two loops to run the arm through to hold them by. All round the edges they had leather fringes and feathers and twisted strings of hair. Then there were little bags of buckskin with paints and tobacco and pipes and other little things. They had strings to go round the waist. Nasho said they were medicine bags.

It was nearly night, so we went back to a little branch where there was some wood and good grass for our horses and made our camp. Nasho told me to make a fire and he would see if he couldn't shoot something for our supper. I got dry leaves and broke some little sticks over them and then some larger ones, and touched a match to it, and we soon had a bright little fire, and pretty soon Nasho came back with two partridges and a rabbit. He said one good thing about the bow and arrow was that they didn't make any noise. We were down in a little open hollow all surrounded with bushes, so that no one would be likely to find us; but if he had shot a gun anyone within a mile of us would have heard it, and known somebody was there, and the sound would have told them where to look for us.

Nasho said he had known an Indian to kill a buffalo with a single arrow.

We cooked the birds and part of the rabbit, and some bacon, and with Auntie's nice bread made a fine supper. I asked Nasho if we had not better put up our horses before we went to sleep, but he said no, he would wake up after awhile and bring them in, and we spread down our blankets and went to sleep. I didn't wake up till morning, but when he called me I found our horses hobbled close to the camp. He had woke up at the right time and brought them in as he said he would. It is strange to me how he could wake up just when he wanted to, but he said the Indians always could.

Nasho said if I would cook breakfast he would see if he could kill something with his bow and arrow. There was nothing to do but cook the rest of the rabbit, broil some bacon on a forked stick and make a pot of coffee, and I had done that and was wishing Nasho would come back when I saw him coming with a load of meat on his back which I knew by the hair was venison. When he threw his load down by the campfire I found he had two venison hams and the saddle.

He said he walked quietly down the hollow keeping a good lookout, as he knew deer would be moving towards higher ground and the open prairie, and pretty soon he saw a buck's horns through the bushes. There wasn't any wind blowing, so he looked to see where the bushes were thickest and, getting on that side, got down on his hands and knees and crept up carefully so as not to make any noise. When the deer would put down his head to feed he would crawl along as fast as he could, and whenever he would raise it he would keep just as still as a stick until he began to feed again. Sometimes the deer would walk several steps before he would take another bite, and sometimes he would bite the leaves of the bushes, and Nasho would be afraid to move because the deer could hear or see him so much more easily when his head was raised this way.

He began to think he would never get near enough for a shot, for the deer travelled away from him nearly as fast as he could crawl towards him; but while the deer was feeding longer than usual he got up in about twenty yards and raised up on his knees, and when the deer raised his head he sent an arrow into him just behind the shoulder. The deer gave one high jump, and fell, and when Nasho ran up he found him lying perfectly still. He cut his throat and then looked to see where he was shot, and found the arrow had gone right through his heart. As he could not carry all of the deer, he cut off the hindquarters, skin and all, and then cut out the saddle, which is the backbone with the ribs on both sides, and then after getting his arrow out, threw his meat on his back and came to camp. The hindquarters of a deer, which are called the hams, are the best part to make venison steaks of, and the back or ribs are the best to stew or roast.

We put some of the ribs on a forked stick to cook for breakfast. While they were cooking and we were eating the bread and bacon and drinking our black coffee, Nasho told me that an Indian hardly ever failed to get a deer when he saw him before the deer had caught sight of him. He said the reason was because the Indian was never in a hurry. When he started out to hunt he noticed what kind of weather it was. If it was a bright clear day and not hot, the deer were more apt to be in the open prairies or on the edge of the woods. If it was warm and in the spring of the year they were very apt to be in low, marshy places to keep the heel flies off of them. In summer they liked thick shady woods where they could lie down in the sand, and in winter they went to the hollows and ravines where the bushes would keep the wind off of them. If the wind was blowing ever so little, the Indian hunter always kept on the lee side of where he expected to find his game.

When he found game he was never in a hurry, but taking care to keep on the right side he watched his chance and crept up whenever he could until he got close enough for a shot. If the deer lay down in a place where he could not creep up to him, the hunter would lie down until he got up again. If the deer saw him and ran off, he would not follow directly behind him, but would make a long circuit, keeping on the lee side of the course he thought the deer would take and come upon it from a different direction. He said he had known an Indian, when game was very scarce, to follow the track of a bear or an elk for two days before coming up with it. He said white men were in too much of a hurry, especially in the settlements where they didn't have much time to hunt, and if they didn't kill anything there would be plenty to eat at home when they got back; but the Indian knew if he didn't kill his game neither he nor his squaw or papooses would have anything to eat, so when he found game or the track of game, he had nothing else to think about but how to kill it, whether it took him an hour or two days, and in the end he hardly ever failed to kill it. I believe Nasho is right about that. When a man hasn't got but one thing to do, he is pretty sure to think all the time about that, and he learns how to do it better than most anybody else; but if he tries to do half a dozen things he is most apt not to do any of them well.

I asked Nasho how the Indians took care of their meat after they killed it, and he said sometimes they cut it into long, thin strips and hung it on strings of hide or lariats to dry in the sun. This took about three days. Then they laid the strips close together and tied hide strings around them so as to make just as tight a bundle as they could, and these bundles they could easily carry on their horses when they moved. In the fall or early in the winter, when they killed buffalo for their winter's meat, the squaws cut up the meat and hung it up around the fires and in the sun until it got perfectly hard and dry. The fat they cut off and melted down in their kettles. Then they took the hard, dry meat, and pounded it between rocks until it was in a kind of powder. They made rawhide bags, turning the flesh side of the hide in, and put in a lot of the pounded meat, packing it just as tight as they could. Then they poured in some melted fat, then more pounded meat and more fat, until it was full. Sometimes, when they could get berries, they would pick a great many and mix them with the meat and fat to make it taste better. When these bags were full they were sewed up with sinews or tanned buckskin, and were heavy and solid, and could be handled just like bags of corn or cotton. I asked him if they did not put any salt in their meat, and he said no. Indians do not like salt.

He said, too, nearly all the work of putting up their meat was done by the squaws, and they had to dress the hides to make clothing and robes to sleep on, and for tents. He said it would take two weeks and sometimes a month to dress a large buffalo hide very soft and smooth, keeping the fur on. The best hides to dress were those killed in November and December. The buffalo were generally fat then and their hair was thick and fine; but in the winter, when they got poor, it was course and rough, and in spring, after they shed off, it was thin and rough and not fit for fine robes.

The Indians once used skins entirely for their clothing and to sleep on, but now they sell their robes and buy clothing and blankets, and sometimes tent-cloth, though most of them would rather have buffalo skins for tents. The Indians that live in the woods make their wigwams of bark and brush, or they buy axes and hatchets from the whites and make log house like the whites, but the Indians that live on the prairies live in tents. They cut eight or ten small poles about ten feet long and place them in a circle with their tops coming together. Then they take the tent covering, in which there are several skins carefully sewed together and which have been put together so as to just cover the tent poles, and wrap it around the poles, leaving a small open space at the top for the smoke to get out, and at the bottom a flap which can be thrown to one side to make a door, or pulled over the hole to keep out the wind entirely. The covering is fastened by wrapping a rawhide strap carefully around it and the poles, and fastening its end to a stick driven into the ground, or a tree or bush. It seems like a very light house, but it keeps out the cold and rain, and the wind cannot blow it down.

When they move, the covering is taken off, the small ends of the poles are fastened on each side of a pony, and the large ends left to drag on the ground, and on them the squaws put their tent covering, their few dishes and pots, their clothing, blankets, provisions, little Indians, puppies, and anything else they may have, and either ride the pony or walk and lead him, while the Indian hunter rides ahead without troubling himself about moving. These poles, weighed down by the loads on them, drag heavily on the ground and make a broad and plain trail, and whenever this is seen it is known at once that they are not on the warpath, for the warriors never take their squaws and lodges with them on a war expedition. Nasho used to tell me a great many things about the Indians, when we were off that way by ourselves, that were very interesting to me, more so than any book I have ever read about them.

When we had finished our breakfast, we packed the hams and the saddle of venison carefully on our horses, and the skin, and started for home. Uncle was glad to see us back again, and Auntie gave us some real nice venison steaks next morning for breakfast.

COONS, POSSUMS AND PANTHERS

The first of November me and Nasho was going to school. We didn't like to go to school much, because we had rather be out of doors on horseback hunting cattle, or helping clear the field, piling the cornstalks into long piles and setting fire to them and watching the rats run out when it got too hot for them, and eating the nubbins of corn that had been left and were roasted by the fire. Sometimes a rabbit would dart out and the dogs would have a chase. They nearly always ran it into a hollow stump or tree where we could twist it out, and Auntie was very willing to have a Molly Cottontail for dinner. Auntie cooks them very nice, but I had rather broil one on the coals, or on a forked stick in the woods than have it any other way.

We used to go coon and possum hunting too at nights. Nobody in the settlement had as good coon dogs as Bose and Trailer. If ever Trailer got his black nose down where a coon had been along that night, he was sure to find the tree where he went up, and when Bose and Trailer treed we were pretty sure to catch the varmint. Nasho and me were both good climbers, though he could beat me a little. Sometimes when they would tree up a tall slim tree that didn't have any branches for a long way up, Nasho would take a strong rawhide strap and fasten around his waist and the tree, but so as to give him plenty of room to move, and then leaning back and throwing his weight against the strap he would work his way up by jerks until he reached the limbs. Then he would take off his strap and climb by the limbs. I could not climb by the strap, but when there were limbs I could go anywhere Nasho could.

Sometimes a coon would run up a great big tree and we would have to let him go. Possums are the hardest to get down. They get way out on a little limb that won't bear your weight and twist their tails around it, and you have to shake until you are out of breath before you can shake him loose. We used to carry a small, sharp hatchet with us, and when a possum tried that dodge the one that went up the tree would take the hatchet with him and cut the limb off, but even then sometimes the possum would catch another limb as he was coming down, and there would be more cutting to do. Possums can't fight, but coons can. One night a great big coon fell into the water and he whipped all the other dogs off, but old Bose swum up and, jumping at him right quick, caught him by the throat, and brought him out. Trailer is the best trail dog, but Bose is the best fighter.

One night Nasho and me were lying on a pile of dry leaves waiting for the dogs to find something, and Nasho was telling me about digging out prairie dogs, when all of a sudden we heard Trailer and Bose both sing out loud and fast, and we knew something was up. We jumped up and ran as hard as we could go toward the sound. It was coming right toward us, and directly Nasho jumped behind a big tree and called to me low to come to him. He said we would wait till the dogs came up, that that wasn't any coon, for the dogs never barked that way on a coon trail, and Bose never barked at all, and now he was yelping like he wanted to split his throat.

We listened to hear if anything was coming, but there was no noise though the weather was dry, and the dry leaves crackled every time anything stepped on them.

Presently we heard something jump on the other side of the very tree we were standing against and—*scratch, scratch, scratch*—it went up the tree as fast as a squirrel. The dogs came up in full cry, and stopping at the foot of the tree began barking like they were crazy. Nasho ran out from under the tree and I followed him, not knowing what was the matter, but when we were out of reach he said, "Panther! Look out, he jump heap."

We began walking around trying to catch sight of the panther against the moonlight, and directly Nasho pointed up to something dark lying close along a limb. It looked more like a bunch of moss than anything else, but Nasho said "See him eyes shine," and getting round a little farther I saw his eyes shining like green glass. I asked Nasho what we must do, and he said "Me stay here and watch him; you go and get Mr. Zanco with gun. Make haste, so he no jump out." I asked him if he wasn't afraid to stay there by himself, but he said, "No, hurry back heap quick."

It was a mile to the house and I didn't much like to go by myself through the woods, without even a dog, but I thought if he could stay there and watch the panther I could go to the house, and I started on a run. I was used to being in the woods a great deal by myself, but not at night, and I got scared a heap of times before I got there. Once I ran almost on to a cow before I saw her, and how I jumped and hollered when she sprang up right before me. Another time a horse jumped out of some bushes right close to me, and I thought sure it was a panther. I saw a black, thick, low something right ahead me and as I thought in the path, and I felt sure it was a bear and that he would be sure to catch me. My heart was in my throat as I came closer to it, but it didn't move, and when I found it was only a black stump, wasn't I glad. I felt as light as a feather and wanted to sing, but I didn't have breath enough, and I was afraid if I made a noise some varmint would hear it and come after me. I think most any boy would have been scared.

I ran into Auntie's room so out of breath I could hardly speak. "Oh, Uncle! The dogs have treed a great big panther, and Nasho is watching him. Won't you take the gun and come and shoot him quick Uncle, please, before he gets away. He run up the tree we was standing against and is way out on a top limb. Make haste Uncle, please."

Uncle put up his book and took down his rifle, and went into the kitchen and got his big butcher knife and we started. I thought he was very slow and wanted to run, but he said we had just as well save our breath, that the panther wasn't apt to jump out with the dogs under the tree, and if he did they would soon run him up another.

"But Uncle, he may jump out and catch Nasho before the dogs can get to him." I wasn't really much afraid of his hurting Nasho, but I wanted to hurry Uncle up.

"Never you fear about Nasho, Charley. He knows how to take care of himself and besides, the panther don't want to catch him. He is a great deal more likely to run from him. Save your breath, my boy, you may need it after we get there. Never hurry when there is no need for it. You will have use for all your breath before you get through the world. Be quick when quickness is needed, but better be steady than fast."

Uncle pretended to be very easy about it, but I noticed he stepped up quicker than usual and we wasn't long in getting there. Nasho was sitting quietly on the end of a log watching up the tree, and as I ran up he put up his finger, as he always did when he wanted me to be still, and said in a low voice, "No scare him, he there yet." I looked and sure enough he hadn't moved, but lay there like a bunch of moss. I pointed him out to Uncle as he came up to us, but he seemed to think it wasn't a panther but only a limb of the tree that had crossed over another one.

After looking carefully he said, "I believe you boys have been fooled. I don't see anything but a limb of a tree."

Nasho moved a little to one side and pointing up said, "Tree no got eyes."

The moon shone bright through a hole among the leaves and moss, and his eyes glistened almost like fire.

"You are right, Nasho, my boy! Trees don't have eyes, and there are a pair up there that belong to a cat, if ever a cat has green eyes."

He bent his head and raised his gun to look at the lock, when Nasho jerked him by the coat and hollered, "Him coming! Mr. Zanco run!"

The way we all got out from under that tree! The panther came down right where Uncle had been standing, and, catching his claw in his coat before he could get out of the way, jerked him to the ground lighting 'most on top of him. Bose and Trailer was on the panther in a second, and all of them seemed to be on top of Uncle. The panther jerked himself loose from the dogs, hit Trailer a slap with one of his paws that cut a gash in his head as clean as if done with a knife, and was off full jump through the wood.

Uncle scrambled up fast, I tell you. Bose was right after the panther and Trailer picked himself up and away he went after Bose. We followed as fast as we could go. I reckon Uncle forgot about not being in a hurry, for me and Nasho could hardly keep up with him. They didn't go more than a quarter of a mile before the dogs treed again, and in two minutes we were all at the tree. It was a good while before we could find him, for he had gone up a big burr oak that hadn't shed all its leaves, and was full of moss, but pretty soon Nasho, who was walking round quietly, said, "See him eyes."

"Where?" said Uncle.

Nasho pointed to the spot, and in a minute I saw Uncle raise his gun. Crack! went the rifle and down came the panther. The dogs were on him in a second, but he made no motion, and Uncle ran up and drove them off. He was stone dead, shot right through both eyes. We dragged him out into a clear place in the moonlight and went to work skinning him, uncle with the butcher knife, and me and Nasho with our pocket knives. It didn't take us all long to strip him. I asked Uncle to let me and Nasho carry the skin. He said we might till we got tired, and cut a little pole and fastened the skin on it so it wouldn't come off. Then we started home, me and Nasho with the pole on our shoulders. It was a long time before I could go to sleep that night, thinking about my run through the woods, and how near the panther came to jumping on Uncle. Auntie has that panther skin now for a foot-rug, and it makes a pretty one too. Uncle rubbed Trailer's head with some grease, and in two or three days he was well, and ready as ever for another panther hunt. I don't believe any of us will ever forget that one.

CENTENNIAL GENESIS

Intended to tell last time about how we came to go, but got to talking about hunting and ran off on that panther hunt. That's always the way with me. At school, when I sit down to study, my mind runs off first on one thing and then another, and I forget all about my lesson. It's like when a lot of dogs are on a hunt, the young ones dodge helter-skelter everywhere, and run over the trail if there is one, while the old ones come along quietly and pick it up and stick to it till they tree. But I am going to tell you what set me to thinking about going this time.

We was going to school, me and Nasho, and of course was at school all day, for we took our dinners, but at night there wasn't much to do and I used to like to hear Uncle talk, especially if any visitor or neighbor came in. One night Parson Theglin stayed with Uncle—he always did whenever he preached in the settlement—and slept in me and Nasho's room, and we had to make a pallet in the shed, but we didn't care about that, because Auntie always gave us plenty of bedclothes. That night he got to talking to Uncle about the Centennial. I believe I can tell now pretty near the very words they used, for I used to listen to them very close, and I believe boys that don't read a great deal recollect things of that kind better than those that do.

Right after supper they took their seats close to the fire with their pipes, for Uncle liked to smoke as well as the preacher. Auntie was busy clearing up the table, but they left a place for her in one corner near the little table that held her work basket and sewing, and Nasho and me was in the other corner. Parson Theglin began:

"Well, brother Zanco, I see by my last *Presbyterian* the Centennial seems to be getting along right sharply. Some of the buildings are nearly done, and they have had so many applications for room that they will have to put up more buildings, annexes they call them—sort of wings—I reckon, to the main houses. And it seems people are coming from the four quarters of the globe to show what they make and sell in their countries. Russia at last has got over her aristocracy and is going to send, and the Chinese, and Turks, and Arabs, and Japanese, and people from Australia—indeed you can hardly name a nation that is even half civilized but what is going be represented there."

"Yes, brother Theglin, there will indeed be a great gathering as you say from all quarters of the world, and a big show of this world's goods they will make when they get together. I suppose if a man had the money he could buy a pretty fair little assortment of what's made best in every country, for I reckon everyone will send what they make best. I was at the Fair in San Antone last year, and there was some fine things there and as pretty a lot of garden truck as I ever saw for the fall of the year. You know, by their irrigating down there, they can raise things any time but I never saw one single farmer that had an average show. One had some corn that it wouldn't have taken more than sixty ears to make a bushel, but I make no doubt his crib was full of corn that would take a hundred to the bushel. It didn't seem quite fair to me. What do you think of it?"

"It seems to me to be fair enough because each man comes there to show his best. He says, here is what I have done, and I can do it again. It won't pay me to take all this trouble every time, because most people don't want such fine work, or rather they don't want to pay for it, but if any of you that see this want such work, you see that I can do it, and I am ready to make just as much as you want. And it stirs people up so to see what other people have done. You see, brother Zanco, most people have got just conceit enough to think that they can do 'most anything anybody else has done. The wiser ones know they can't anymore than a haw tree can grow to be as big as a pecan, but they see that they can do better than they have done, and they try and keep trying and keep improving until they do better than they first thought they could. I never go to Paynod that hearing our best preachers—men that have got more brains than I have, and more of other men's brains in the way of books to put with theirs, and don't have to spend three fourths of the time in the saddle riding over the country, and then when they get home, have the cattle and the oxen and the pigs to look after, and help put up the winter's bacon and maybe take a turn at clearing up the field and mending the fence, taking up all the time in the day and getting so tired that they ain't fit to study at night—I never hear those men that don't have these things to take their thoughts and minds off of the glorious word, without seeing how much better preaching can be made."

Parson Theglin continued: "Putting a new idea into a man's head is like putting yeast into dough—it stirs up everything in reach of it, and don't wait for things to come in reach either; it goes to them. Now it seems to me if I could go there and see all the fine things that every nation has, I should get my head full of ideas that would last me a long time, and stir up and turn around my old musty, fusty ones until they would be nearly as good as new, like an axe with a fresh edge put on it. Of course a man hears a great deal that don't do him any good; but he can throw that away and take only what does, and as I believe that religion has to do with everything in the world, and every man, woman and child in it, I hold that I would be a very poor observer if I didn't find a great many things that would help to make my sermons better. In the first place, the fact that all these different people of different nations come here with their property, shows that the religion of Christ, which teaches peace on earth and good will to all, is gaining ground; for it hasn't been many hundred years since, if the Chinese had landed on the coast of California with their fine silks and their curious works of every kind, they would have been seized, and everything they had taken away from them, and they lucky not to be made slaves of. Of course nothing of this kind has been done in the United States since the Puritans came over, but it was done by the Indians, and worse than that, it was done by Frenchmen and Spaniards in Florida, and Louisiana and Texas, and Canada and wherever one happened to get the better of the other."

But I won't tell any more they said. Auntie came in and they got to talking about what would be there to see, and the strange people, with their curious clothes, and the little taverns where they cooked just as they did at home, until I was nearly crazy to go and see, and forgetting all about where I was, I said right out loud "Let's go, Nasho."

They all looked around at me so straight that I was ashamed, and was going to creep out of the room, but Parson Theglin stopped me. "And you would really like to go to the Centennial, Charley?"

"Yes, indeed sir, that I would, for it seems to me I could see more in a month than I shall in all the rest of my life. And this won't be but once; and if I don't see it now I never will get to see all these things. I would be willing to work for anybody three years after I came back, if they would take me there?"

"Are you not big enough to go by yourself?"

"All by myself?!" My hair 'most stood up just thinking of it.

"Yes, by yourself. Smaller boys than you are have travelled farther, and girls too, as to that matter. Don't you know there are angels whose special business it is to look after little boys and girls, especially those that do right? I'll warrant you if you had the money you could make your way there easily enough, and take care of yourself after you got there, and see all there was to be seen too. Do you think anybody will give you the money to go on?"

"No, sir. I believe Uncle or Auntie either would if they had it to spare; but Uncle has a heap to do to take care of me here at home, and send me to school, me and Nasho. And I ain't got any other kinfolks or friends."

" But you really want to go!"

"That I do, sir. If Uncle and Auntie was willing and anybody would show me how to go, wouldn't I begin about it quick!"

"Did you ever hear about where there is a will, there is a way?"

"Oh, yes, sir. I had that once for my copy at school. But that means for men and common things, and not boys and big things like this!"

"Don't you expect to be a man some day?"

"Yes, sir."

"But how are you going to, unless you begin. A man is nothing but an older, grown up boy. Suppose you were to sit in the house all day every day, do you think you would grow much?"

"No, sir."

"And don't you think you would be weak and feeble, not strong enough to work, and not know how to ride and drive cattle, or climb trees, or plant corn, or feed the hogs and cattle, or do anything? Do you remember how you learned to ride?"

"Yes, sir, well enough. Uncle put me on old Ball, and I was so afraid I cried at first. It didn't seem to me like I could sit still, and I thought if he moved I would fall off, and he would step on me or kick me, and Uncle ought not to have put me on him. But when Uncle led him around I held tight to the horn of the saddle and found I could stick on, and felt very proud, though I was scared all that ride. After one or two times Uncle made him trot, and I was worse scared than before, at his bouncing up and down, but I only held the tighter to the saddle and I found I could stick to him. And when I learned to stick to him when he trotted hard and fast, Uncle put me on by myself and gave me the reins and showed me how to guide him, and it wasn't long before I could gallop him without being afraid of falling. And I was glad then that Uncle didn't take me off the first time when I was so scared, but kept me on until I learned to ride, for I like to ride better than anything else."

"Well, you learned to ride by using the muscles of your arms and legs, and you never could have learned without it. Do you think anybody else could have learned for you?"

"No, sir. I know they couldn't any more than anybody could learn my lessons for me."

"Well, you learned to walk and ride by using your muscles. Now you have to learn your lessons, and you will have to learn to take care of yourself, and get along in the world by using your brains. Do you think you would be able to ride as well as you do now, if you had not began early?"

"No, sir. I know I wouldn't."

"Neither will you be able to use your brains well when you are a man unless you begin early. And the quicker you begin, and the more you use them, the stronger they will grow, and the smarter you will be when you are a man. Just remember every man was a boy once, and had everything to learn for himself. A man's having ten thousand dollars does not make it any easier for his son to learn to walk, and he cannot walk without learning, and it does not make it any easier for him to learn his A B C's, or the multiplication table, or how to write, and he will never know these things without learning. Now I believe it would be a good thing for you to go to the Centennial. I think you would learn more there in a month than you would here in years, and you can learn here besides, after you come back. I think it would start your brain to growing and you would begin to use it more than you have ever done, and would learn to use it to some purpose. In short, I think it would go a long way towards making a man of you, a true man I mean, who is honest and true and good, and not merely a finely-dressed, cane-carrying, cigar-smoking dandy. I don't believe you will want to do the foolish things you will see boys doing because they think they make men of them. I think you will come back a boy, but a wiser and better boy, just as ready to mind your Uncle and Aunt and help them as you are now, and knowing a great deal better how to do it. If I did not think so I should not want to see you go one step."

But Parson Theglin did not have a ready solution for how I was to get about going. "I do not see myself how you are to go, but just remember 'Where there is a will, there is a way,' and we will both study about it, and when I come back next month, you will tell me of the way you have thought out, and if I have any better one

I will tell you. Now do not go around asking people to tell you how you can get to the Centennial. Do not tell anybody you want to go, but keep thinking about it and study out for yourself some way to get there and, my word for it, you will go."

We had prayers then, and Parson Theglin prayed that I might be guided aright and shown the way in which I should go. He didn't just say so, but I knew he meant me, and I felt as if there was something real solemn about it. I think the Israelites must have felt something that way when they got to Jordan and knew they had to cross it and didn't know how.

Nasho had been asleep all the time and I didn't say anything to him about it, but I thought about it a good deal after we went to bed in the bedroom, and the more I thought about it, the more it seemed to me there was a way for me to go. And I went to sleep thinking about it and dreamed that a fine gentleman came along and gave me and Nasho money enough to take us there and back.

CENTENNIAL REVELATION

Next morning when I got up the first thing that came into my mind before I had time to think, was how I was going to the Centennial. I did not say anything to anyone about it, but there was never a day that I did not think of it a great deal, though I didn't seem to be getting any nearer to finding it.

The next time Parson Theglin came was Saturday evening. I had just come home from school, and saw him taking his horse to the crib, and I ran to him and told him I would take him and put him up. He thanked me, and said he would go in the house as he was very tired. I have been studying every way, sir, since you was here, and I don't see any way for me to get to the Centennial, and yet I *must* go, sir, I will never have another chance. My head was so full of it that I had to say that much.

"Well, Charley, wait until after supper, and I get rested a bit, and we will have a talk about it."

"Yes, sir, but Uncle will want to talk to you then, and tomorrow is Sunday, and I am afraid we won't have a chance again. You don't know how bad I want to go, sir. Please tell me if you know any way. I can wait then as long as you wish."

"No, Charley, I am sorry to say, I do not. There is a way, though neither of us have been able to find it, and I am sure it will be found yet. But we won't talk of it just now. Trust me to find another opportunity before I go. I will not go until we do talk it over. Give my horse plenty of corn and fodder he has had a long ride today."

After supper he and Uncle had a long talk, mostly about Church and religious matters. They did not say a word about the Centennial and I was afraid Parson Theglin didn't care much about it, though I felt sure he wouldn't try to deceive me and pretend he did when he did not. About eight o'clock he got up, filled his pipe again, and said he would go out to the stable and see about his horse.

"I know Charley has fed him well, but I like to see him myself before lying down. I can sleep the better for knowing that he is all right. Will you go with me, Charley?"

"Yes, sir. I am sure, though, you will find Blaze hasn't eat up all I gave him. I put twenty good ears in his trough, and plenty of surghum fodder."

When we reached the lot, instead of going to the stable, Parson Theglin climbed up and fixed himself on the fence, and I sat on a stump in front of him. He had broken a splinter off the fence and was whittling it slowly as he spoke.

"Well, Charley, have you found out how you are going to the Centennial yet?"

I felt certain from the way he spoke that he had not thought of any way for me to go, but I was glad to hear him speak as he did, as if it was certain that I was going.

"No, sir, I haven't. I have thought and thought and studied over it, but I can't see any way how I can get there. It will take so much more money than there is any way for me to get. You know I can't earn but little at a time."

"How did you go about thinking up a plan?"

"I just tried to study up some way, sir. I didn't know any other way to do."

"Suppose your Uncle were to send you out to hunt the oxen when they do not come up, would you go riding around through the woods anywhere your horse cared to go?"

"No, sir. If it was a cold wet day like last Tuesday, I would know they had gone down into the bottom, or else up into the gulch out of the wind. If it was a bright, clear day, I would think they had gone out to the prairie, and would go there to look for them. And if a norther was blowing, but it wasn't raining, I would go to some of the hollows where they go to keep out of the wind and pick the grass and the bushes."

"Exactly, you would first consider the weather, decide where they would most likely be, and then go there to look for them."

"Yes, sir. But it don't seem to me this case is like that one. I know where the Centennial is and the road to find it, but I have not got the money to go on, and I don't know how to get it."

"The two cases are more alike than you think for. Think carefully a moment before speaking and then tell me what the weather is in going to the Centennial."

I studied and studied. The weather told me in which one of several places the oxen would most likely be, but the weather don't have anything to do with getting to the Centennial. I will go in the cars of course, and it don't make any difference what it is.

"The weather, the weather...oh, yes, now I see! The weather is the money ain't it, sir?"

"Is what?"

I thought I was thinking out loud. "Ain't the weather the money I must have to go there?"

"That is it. Now what next?"

"It's how much I must have."

"Right again. Do you know how much a ticket costs?"

"No, sir."

"You can buy a ticket from Austin for forty dollars and

you will need about five dollars to pay for your meals on the road. A boy who has camped as much as you have won't need a sleeping car. You can sleep on the seat. Of course it will cost you as much to come back, and you can live there for less than a dollar a day. You will want to stay a month at least, and it would be a good thing if you could stay there three. It would not be time lost or wasted. Now can you tell me how much these three sums come to?"

"Yes, sir. I figured it out in my head. 150 dollars, sir."

"Well, now add fifty dollars more."

"What is that for?"

"For what travellers call incidental expenses; for apples and candy, and papers and toys, and nice things to eat, and car rides, and shows, and everything of that kind."

"But I can get along without these, sir."

"You won't though, and must have more money than just enough to pay your expenses there and back. You may get sick, or have your leg broken, and then you will need money to pay a doctor or surgeon. A prudent traveller always allows pretty liberally for the incidentals. You will need then 200 dollars. Now what's the next thing?"

"The same old trouble, sir—how to get it."

"Do you expect anyone to give you this amount?"

"No, sir."

"Could you borrow it?"

"Oh, no, sir. I would be afraid to if I could."

"Why?"

"Because, sir, it's more money than I ever could pay back again. I couldn't borrow money if I didn't see how I was to get it to pay back."

"Right, Charley. Stick to that through life. Never borrow money at all if you can help it, but never unless you know just how and just when you can repay it. Better do without what you want yourself than force someone else to do without on your account. Then as you do not expect someone to give it to you, and cannot borrow it because you do not know how you could pay it back, how are you to get it?"

"I must make it."

"When you start after the oxen, why not go on foot?"

"Because, sir, I would get tired directly, and I cannot travel as fast as a horse, and the oxen would outrun me if I found them on foot. Old Coley can run nearly as fast as a horse, and I can't see through the brush afoot like I can on horseback."

"Then you take a horse because you and the horse can do more than you can by yourself."

"Yes, sir."

I was thinking how foolish I would be to start after the oxen afoot when I had a pony in the pasture or lot, and how the oxen would laugh at me when they saw me coming afoot and run away from me just as easy as could be, and going over the whole thing in my mind, when I wondered why Parson Theglin didn't keep on, and looked up to see he was whittling away as quiet as could be and didn't seem to have any notion of saying anything else. So I said "Well, sir, now what?"

"That's your question, my boy, not mine. I am not going to the Centennial."

"But you said, sir, you would help me if I couldn't find any way to go. And I can't, sir."

"Have you tried?"

"Yes, sir. All the time."

"How? Riding around through the woods anywhere your horse wanted to go?"

I saw what he meant and fell to studying again. I took my pony to go after the oxen because I could travel faster, see farther, and run faster than afoot.

"But I can't go there on Bullet."

"Can't go where?"

"Oh, sir, I didn't know I was talking out loud. I was just thinking why I took Bullet to hunt the oxen, but I can't ride him to the Centennial."

"Why not?"

"Because, sir, it would take me so long."

"Men have walked from New York to San Francisco, and that is a thousand miles further than your trip."

"But then, sir, I must have something to eat on the road, and a heap of times there wouldn't be grass for Bullet, and I would have to buy corn and fodder for him."

"Make him pay for his own corn and fodder, and carry you too."

"How, sir?"

"That is your lookout, not mine. If I was going I would find a how."

"But you said, sir, you would help me to find a way."

"Exactly. I said I would help you, not find it for you. I suppose you will want me to go with you next thing."

"Oh no, sir, I don't expect that, but if you would only tell me how to go."

"If you cannot find out how to go, you will not be able to go by yourself, or take care of yourself after you get there."

"Yes, sir, but I am only a boy."

"And you will never be anything but a boy if you do not begin some time, and now is the time unless you intend to throw away the best opportunity for educating yourself you ever will have, and be only a cowboy and clod hopper all your life. What is your head good for if you cannot put it to some use? Why, you might almost as well have fried brains as lively, active ones like such a boy as you ought to have. Cannot ride to the Centennial, hey? What's the longest trip you ever took?"

"Last summer the time I went up to Brown and Coleman counties with Mr. Negus. He wanted help and told
Uncle he would give him two dollars a day if he would
let me go and take two horses with me. And Uncle said
I might go and take Bullet and Aunt's mare that she
rides, but I must be very careful of her and not run her
much. We was gone three weeks, camping out all the
time, and Mr. Negus said I made just as good a hand
as any of them. I roped a big steer and tangled him up
in the rope and threw him down and held him down all
by myself, while Jim Langdon got down and tied him;
on Bullet I mean. And two or three nights when we had
poor pens and had to stand guard over them, I stood
guard with rest."

"Then you know all about driving cattle?"

"Yes, sir."

"And when you were in Brown County you were gone
three weeks?"

"Yes, sir. I wished it had been longer, though I got tired
sometimes and wished I was back to one of Auntie's
good suppers, and nice soft beds. But I would a great
deal rather have stayed longer than come back sooner."

"And you were nearer the Centennial then than you
are now."

"Yes, sir."

"And suppose you had kept on three months without
turning back."

"But Mr. Negus' cattle don't range that far off, and
nobody wouldn't go where their cattle didn't run."

"What are the boy's brains good for? He found somebody that gave him two dollars a day and fed him, and
he didn't have to feed his horse, and was gone three
weeks and liked it, and now talks about not going where
cattle don't run. Did you ever hear of cattle going where
they did not want to go?"

"Yes, sir, many a time."

"How did they go?"

"Somebody drove them."

"What for?"

"Because they wanted to bring them home or drive them to market."

"What market?"

"Kansas, sir, mostly, though sometimes they drive them to San Antonio or maybe Rockport."

"And going to Kansas is going away from the Centennial, isn't it?"

"Oh! Yes, sir! Now I see! Now I see! I must hire to somebody to drive beeves to Kansas, and then go on from there to the Centennial. I will be making money all the way to Kansas, and I can leave my horse there and get him when I come back and ride him back to Texas, and it won't cost me much. Ain't that the way, sir? How strange I didn't think of that at first! You are very kind to me, sir, to take so much trouble to make me think for myself when it would have been so easy just to have told me I must drive beeves to Kansas. If I had been any account I would have thought of that at first. I am afraid I never will learn to think."

"Yes, you will. You have not tried much yet. I mean tried steadily and persistently, taking the weather into consideration and not riding around wherever your horse wants to go. For what we call the mind is very much like the horse we ride. If we train it to work steadily it will soon learn to go just where we tell it, but if we let it alone it will be turning around and leaving the path we started it in, and going first here and then there and never getting where we started to go. It is steady persistence that wins, my boy. Try, try again, and keep trying, and after awhile you will win. It takes some men thirty years. And the reason that most men do not win and

never amount to anything in the world is because they
have nothing they are determined to do and just wind
about here and there, or they get tired and quit, and try
something else, and get tired of that and try something
else again and thus waste their own lives. Be sure that
what you want to do is the right thing for you to do, and
worth doing, and then never give up, and sooner or later
you will win. We'll go in now, Charley. It is getting late. I
will trust you for having taken good care of Blaze."

That night at prayers I couldn't help but think that
God was a little like Parson Theglin, only ever so much
larger and better, and he would have time to think
about me a little, and take care that I didn't get hurt or
go wrong, only I must help myself too; and before I laid
down I asked him to help me go to the Centennial, and
to learn to think, and to keep trying when I wanted to
do anything.

I wanted so bad to ask Uncle that night if I might hire
out to go to Kansas, but I did not get a chance. I was
certain though he would let me go, for Parson Theglin
wouldn't have made me think of that way if it had been
one Uncle wouldn't have liked, and there wasn't any
other way for me to go, and I was just as certain I was
going as that I was lying in bed thinking of it. And there
wasn't a happier boy in Kerr County that night.

Work Begins In Earnest

I felt sure all the time I was going to the Centennial, but I knew now how I was going and I was a heap surer than before. The greatest thing in the way now was horses. If we had three horses apiece we would get $75 apiece a month, and we could make enough at that to take us from Kansas there and back to Kansas again. But we had only one horse apiece, me and Nasho, and how to get the others was the trouble. We could only get $25 or $30 apiece a month if we only had one horse. There must be some way now to get the other four horses we needed, though I couldn't see how it could be. We didn't have any time but Saturday to do anything in, and then Uncle almost always had something for us to do.

Well, I went to Uncle and said to him, "Uncle, we want to go to the Centennial very bad, me and Nasho. We have been wanting to go ever since that night you and Parson Theglin talked about it, but I haven't said anything about it because we didn't know how we could manage to go, but we can do it now this way. We can hire to somebody that is driving cattle to Kansas and leave our horses in a pasture there and go on to the Centennial with the money we make, and stay there a month, then come back to Kansas and ride our horses home again. We can learn so much Uncle, there will be so much to see. I do hope you are willing for us to go."

"Yes, Charley, I am willing for you to go. When you first spoke of it that night I thought it was only a boyish whim that you would soon get over, but if you are in earnest about it, as I believe you are, why you can go. You are very young, you and Nasho, to take a trip like that alone, but I am satisfied if you will behave yourselves and do what is right you will get along. I will do anything I can to help you along. You won't need much money because on the drive you will be fed. You have a horse and saddle apiece and some clothes, and Auntie must try and make each of you another good suit before you go. Your clothes and blankets will be all you will want."

"Oh, Uncle, I just now thought of it! We can kill deer and dress the skins. You know what a good hand Nasho is, and Auntie can make us a nice suit out of buckskin and we will wear it to the Centennial to show the people what Texas people used to have to dress with and what two Texas boys can do now."

"A right good idea, Charley, my boy!" said Uncle slowly with his eyes set to one side a little as if thinking about it. "A right good idea. I believe this is setting you to thinking. I despise anything like rowdyism even in dress, but well-tanned buckskin makes a neat suit. I have seen the President of the Republic of Texas dressed in it and he looked just as well as the fancy French minister with his fine rig just as if he had gotten out of a bandbox. You and Nasho kill the deer and dress the hides, and I'll ensure that Auntie will do her best in cutting them out and putting her best stitching in them. I will give you all the Saturdays I can."

"Maybe we can make some money driving cattle or getting up stray horses. We want two more horses apiece, and they will cost us at least thirty dollars apiece, and I don't see how we are going to get that much money, but we are going to try.

"All right, my boy. I'll help you all I can, and where there is a genuine working will, there is nearly always a way. Remember that and keep your wits about you, and I'm sure the way will be found."

I hadn't said anything to Nasho about it, but Monday morning as we were going to school I told him about it and asked him if he didn't want to go. He said yes, if I went, but he didn't seem to think anything more about it than he would going on a cow hunt. He's a curious fellow, Nasho is. He don't ever get excited like most boys. If the house was to catch fire over his head I don't believe he would get excited a bit, but he'd be sure to get out.

One night when we was on a cow hunt and stopping at Mr. Hansom's, the stable caught fire where some-body had been smoking. There was a very fine horse in it and two men ran in to get him out. They jerked and pulled and tried to drive him out, but he was scared and wouldn't budge a step. Nasho ran in quietly and said "You no right, me get him out," and wrapped his big handkerchief, which he wore round his neck when he was coon hunting, round the horse's head so as to blindfold him, and then patted him on the head a min-ute or two, and led him out without any trouble.

Mr. Hansom was so glad to save his fine horse that he gave Nasho ten dollars, and all of them said that Nasho had more sense than any of them. I have always heard that the Indians don't say much, especially the young ones, and they must think a heap before they speak, and I think Nasho must have learned a good deal from them.

I told him we would want two horses apiece and I didn't know where we would get the money to buy them.

"We make the money," he said. "We kill more deer and we dress their hides nice, and we catch heap wild turkeys and take Uncle's wagon and go to San Antonio and sell 'em, and we drive cows for somebody. We find way to make the money."

We talked about it all the way to school, and my head was so full of it and of some way to get the money that it was hard to keep my mind fixed on my lessons. It would keep running off on other things. Yet I never did want to learn more. I studied my geography more than ever, for I wanted to learn something about the countries and the people that would have something to show at the Centennial. I thought maybe Miss Masover, our teacher, would be able to help me learn what I wanted to know most, so I told her what we were going to do, and asked her if she would tell me what I needed to know most, and to learn it fastest. I asked her, too, not to say anything about it, and she said she wouldn't. I knew she wouldn't.

She said she had two or three books that would tell me a great deal about the different countries and the people, and she would lend them to me and I must read them. And then she made me tell her all about our trip, and how we were going, and how we expected to get the money, and seemed to feel just as much interested as if she was going herself. Seems to me women care a heap more about people they like than men do. Uncle is just as kind to me and Nasho as he can be, but he don't think about a heap of little things about us like Auntie does.

When I got through she said "Well, Charley, there is another way in which I think you can make some money. I will help Nasho make the very prettiest things he can, and when you go to San Antonio you can take them and sell them and get more money that way."

I thanked her for her kindness, and then it was time for school to take up and we couldn't talk any more. It seemed to me as if everybody was trying to help us when they saw that we was in earnest, and trying to do all we could ourselves.

That evening we hurried home from school, and telling Auntie we was going down in the bottom and wouldn't be home till late, we took the little axe Uncle had bought for us, and the hatchet, and went down in the bottom. We hunted about until we found a good place in an open thicket where there wasn't any trees, where the hogs would be likely to come, and cut down some poles and, out of them and dry logs and branches we cut off of other trees, we made a pen about six feet square and four feet high which we covered with logs and brush.

Before we covered it up we dug a trench on the south side about a foot deep and four feet long running into the pen with each end about the same distance apart outside of and in the pen. This trench we covered with small sticks and two or three boards we found that had been washed up in a rise of the creek, and put heavy chunks over them so that the turkeys couldn't raise them up. Then we covered the top and baited it with corn, and strewed corn around in front of it, so they would find it if they came near it, and then smoothed the ground off a little with a brush-top and left it. It was in the night before we got through, but the moon was shining bright so we could see well enough to work, and we never thought of being afraid.

You may well ask: "Well, but Charley, I don't understand what that trench is for in your turkey pen. If I understand you, you began your trench about two feet from the pen, ran it under the bottom log, and let it come out about two feet on the inside. What is that for?"

We made it begin about three feet from the log on the outside. Why you see, the turkeys find the corn leading to the trench, and they run along picking it up and when they come to it and see the corn in it, and we put it pretty thick, they just draw themselves up like a hog getting through a hole under a fence, and go in. They come out on the inside of the pen, and when they raise their heads and find they are in a pen they begin to run round and round and are caught.

"Why, Charley, haven't they sense enough to go out the way they went in?"

No, sir. You see they keep their heads up all the time and never think of looking down for a way to get out. Sometimes a whole gang will go into a trap this way. You can catch partridges the same way, though they are more likely to get out than turkeys.

"Well! I would have supposed anything would have sense enough to get out the way it got in."

I reckon it's being in a trap that makes them forget and turn foolish. They never do get out.

On our way home, the dogs treed a possum up a little haw tree and Nasho ran up and shook him out, and I kept the dogs off so they wouldn't bite him all up, and we took him home. Auntie was glad to get him, but he wasn't very fat, and we put him in a pen to feed for Christmas week. We fed him on bread scraps from the table and corn, and he got as fat as a pig. I have never eaten anything here at the Centennial better than baked possum and sweet potatoes.

After that we made two more turkey traps, and every other night we would go down to see if we had caught any. It was two weeks before we did, and we began to think we wasn't going to catch any, though Nasho said in his dry way "Plenty turkey here—see him tracks we catch him by and by."

On Friday evening we went down and there was twenty turkeys in the pens. We stopped up the holes so they couldn't get out, and next morning Uncle went down with us with the wagon, and we made a hole in the top of the pen so me and Nasho could get in. We caught them one by one and tied their legs together with strings we had brought with us, and when we had them all fast we then handed up to Uncle who put them in the wagon. Me and Nasho made a pen to keep them in, and fed them on corn and millet heads and sugar millet seed till they got right fat.

Afterward we caught thirty-five more, so that we had fifty-five. We gave Auntie five. When we went down for the last ones we found a bee tree, and when we had put the turkeys in the pen at home we came back with axes and cut down the tree and smoked the bees out, and got thirty pounds of honey. The bees nearly all lit on the branch of a low tree nearby, one on top of the other until they made a great big brown lump like a knot on a tree, and Uncle put a blanket under them and cut off the limb easy so it wouldn't disturb them and let it fall into the blanket and hived the whole swarm. He took it home and put it in one of his hives, and that made twenty hives he had. We caught one hundred partridges, which we put up in a big trap like a chicken coop to fatten and keep.

THE PECAN HUNT

On Wednesday night, soon after we had gone to bed, there came up a hard norther. I was thinking how cold it would be for us to do anything the next Saturday, when all of a sudden I happened to think we could make something out of the norther. All the pecans near us had been gathered, but when me and Nasho had gone after the bows and arrows the Indians had left, we found a little bottom of pecan trees in a ravine where I was certain we could gather ten or fifteen bushels. So the next morning by daylight I was up and asked Uncle if me and Nasho could not take the wagon and go up there and gather the pecans. He said we might, so we ran out and got up the horses, and fed them and put the harness on while they were eating and Auntie was getting breakfast ready. We were to be gone until Saturday night, so Auntie cooked us some bread to take with us and ground us some coffee, while we were eating our breakfast. It was twelve miles to the place, and we were in a hurry to get off, so we would have more time to pick in. As soon as we were done eating we hitched up the horses, put in our provisions, a frying pan and the little coffee pot. We took cow hunting ropes and hobbles for the horses and were ready to be off. I told Nasho to get in and let's go.

"We no got gun; maybe see deer."

I was too busy thinking of the pecans and had forgotten the gun. We got it and the powder horn and shot bag and put it in the wagon.

"Charley," said Uncle, "if you will be right careful of it you may take my rifle. I wouldn't let any other boy have it, but I know you will take care of it."

"Yes, indeed, Uncle, that I will, and I think I'll get a deer too, with Carry True." (That was what Uncle called his rifle.)

Uncle handed me the rifle, powder horn and bullet pouch, and told us to take care of ourselves. Then we started off. I hollered back, "Don't be uneasy, Uncle, if we don't get back until late Saturday night. We want to have all the time for picking pecans we can!" The dogs both followed us.

We reached the grove about eleven o'clock and, picking our camp, we unharnessed the horses, hobbled them and set to work. Nobody had been there to gather, and the hogs hadn't found it, and the ground was strewed with pecans. They were nearly all large fine ones with thin hulls. We worked until dark and thought we had about five bushels. We had brought wheat sacks to put them in, and small bags that would hold about a peck, with strings to fasten them around our necks, to pick in.

We kept the sacks in the wagon because they were too heavy to move when full, and as fast as we filled our bags we emptied them in the sacks and tied them up.

A little before dark Nasho said we would quit and he would make a fire and get supper while I tied up the horses and fed them. Close to where I found the horses I saw a big covey of partridges, and told Nasho I would go back and shoot some with the shotgun.

"No, no. Maybe so deer close by, and when he hear gun he run off. No must shoot."

I saw he was right, so I went back with a short, stout stick and throwing into the bunch killed three, which we had for supper. Then I tied up the horses and fed them. While supper was cooking Nasho took the water gourd to the hole to get some water, and I saw him stop and look close at the bark of a tree on the way. He beckoned me to come to him, and showed me scratches where the bark had been rubbed off.

"Bear do that," said he. "Last week, maybe so he come again. He heap fond of pecans."

We were up next morning by daylight, and Nasho said he would take the gun and go look for a deer, while I got breakfast. I thought he ought to have let me go, but I didn't say anything and began stirring up the fire to cook with. I had cooked the meat and had the coffee on, and was busy feeding the horses when I heard old Bose growl low like he does when something is wrong. I looked the way his head was pointing, and saw a bear coming slowly and steadily up the hollow in which the grove was. He had seen the wagon and horses but didn't seem to care anything for them. I went round the wagon so he couldn't see me, made Bose be still, got the rifle, and took a stand by a tree where I could get a good rest on a windfall.

He came along as straight as if he thought it was his own property and nobody had a right to trouble him. I tried to be as cool as I could, but my heart thumped hard, and my hand shook so I couldn't hold the gun steady. When he got in about fifteen yards he stopped and looked as if he didn't like the look of things at his camp. As he halfway turned to go off, I took the best aim I could and fired. I saw him fall, but he got up again and started off. Bose was after him in a second.

I remembered Uncle had told me never to go up to game that had been shot until my gun was reloaded, so I began to load as fast as I could. When I got the bullet well home and the cap on, I ran after them as fast as I could. The bear was trying to get away but wherever he would turn, Bose would run up and nip his hindquarters, and he would whirl around and try and catch him. I ran up in a few feet of him, and as he turned to try and catch Bose I took good aim and shot him through the head. He fell, and I knew I had got him that time. I was mighty glad, for it was my first bear.

Just then I heard two guns almost at the same time, and I knew that must be Nasho. After looking at the bear awhile I went back to camp, and just then Nasho came up with a hindquarter and ribs of a deer. He said he had found five deer, and had crept close to them and shot and killed one, and without waiting to see about that shot he fired the other barrel at another, and going up found he had killed two—both big bucks.

"Me hear gun too. What you kill?"

"Come and see," I said, and took him to the bear.

When he saw him he shook my hand and said "Me call you Strong Heart now. You kill bear."

We cut some ribs out of the bear and fixed them over the fire to cook while we finished skinning him. Then we went to our fire and got breakfast, for we were both as hungry as wolves. We cut the bear into quarters so we could handle it easier, and cut some poles and made a scaffold over the fire and put the meat on it so it would be in the smoke. Then we hitched up the horses and drove up to where Nasho had killed the deer. We hung them up in a tree so they would be in the smoke too, and then set to work picking up pecans. It was nearly dinner then, and we were a little tired too, and we didn't get any more pecans picked up than the day before. We feasted that day on deer ribs and bear meat.

That evening when we stopped for supper Nasho said, "Wolves smell meat tonight, and come. We hide and kill maybe so two, three." He tied his rope to some of the entrails of the bear and getting on his horse and tieing the other end of the rope to the horse's neck rode off, about a quarter of a mile from camp, and then rode in a circle clear round the camp, and came to the place where the bear was killed.

Then he came to camp. There was a low sunken place, about twenty yards from the place between that and our camp. We took our blankets and made our bed there, leaving the dogs to take care of camp, though it was so close we could easily see anything that happened there. Besides, we knew if the wolves came there or anything happened the dogs would make such a noise we would be sure to wake up.

We intended to lay awake until about twelve o'clock, but we had worked so hard we was tired and went to sleep. I woke up all of a sudden and found a pack of wolves snarling and fighting over the entrails. Nasho had waked up too. We both took good aim at the crowd, for they was all mixed up so you couldn't see any particular wolf to aim at, and fired together. Then Nasho fired his other barrel. The wolves all ran off, though some of them stopped a few hundred yards off and sent up a howl. We found three dead and another got up and staggered off. Nasho ran up and, picking up a rock, knocked him in the head. They were all large, full-grown gray mountain wolves. We went back to bed and slept till morning. The first thing, we fed the horses and got breakfast and then set to work to skin the wolves. This didn't take us but a little time, and then we went to work picking pecans again.

By dinner time we had picked up all there were, and thought we had about thirteen bushels. After dinner we took down our meat, packed it in the wagon, with the hides of the deer, the bear and the wolves, and started home. It was sundown by the time we got there. Uncle was glad to get the meat and very proud that I had killed the bear, and we had done so well. It took two hours to

put away the meat in salt so it wouldn't spoil, and get
the hides packed up right, and then we went to bed
tired out but well satisfied with our pecan hunt.

Roping Wild Bill

There was a wild horse that sometimes came down into Kerr County that nobody could catch. He was a beautiful blue roan about fourteen and a half hands high, with head and legs of a deep mouse color, and long hanging tail and mane almost black. Some of the best riders in the country had tried to rope him, but they never could get near enough. He ran away from their fastest horses as easily as from a cow, and he was always watching so they couldn't surprise him. They tried to run him down, first one running him and then another on a fresh horse, but he didn't seem to get tired, and everybody had at last given up trying to catch him. Nobody knew where he came from. He wasn't a regular mustang, for the mustangs had all left the country long before; yet no one who had ever seen him would think for a minute that he had ever been in a pen. He must have run wild when a colt.

One Saturday when we was on a cow hunt, me and Nasho, one of the boys that I met told me that Wild Bill, as everybody called him, had come into the country again. I had never seen him, but had often wished I could, and as we rode along I got to studying if there wasn't some way we could catch him. He was a very uncertain horse about his range. He had been seen way over on the other side of the Brazos, and as far west as the Nueces, and he came and went just as if the country belonged to him. Sometimes he would stay in our range a month, and then again he would just pass through and be gone again. There wasn't any use in us trying to run him down, that was certain. We had just as well try to catch an antelope. I thought maybe we could watch him a day or two and, when he was quiet, drive some gentle horses up as close as we could without scaring him. Then if he went to them as he was most sure to do, we could, maybe, by being very careful, manage to work the bunch into the big beef pen at Seiders'. I asked Nasho what he thought about it.

"No good. He got too much sense to go in pen."

"But we could go there and cut brush and build long wings on each side of the pen, and he won't see them until he gets inside of them and then he can't turn back, for we'll be behind him."

"No can do it. He too sharp for that. Me know better way dan dat." And he told me how he thought we could catch him. I thought so too, so when we came back that night I told Uncle that Wild Bill had been seen up near Seiders', and me and Nasho thought we could catch him if he would let us go Monday and try.

"You would run down every horse on the place and then hardly get in sight of him."

"No, Uncle, we are not going to run him. We know we never could catch him that way. I'll promise you that. Please don't ask us how, but just let us go Monday and stay until Wednesday night."

Uncle thought about it a minute or two and then said, "I don't like you boys leaving school to go horse hunting. I am afraid you will get so you won't care anything about your books, but I'll let you go this time. Remember, you musn't run your horses. It wouldn't do a bit of good, but only break them down for nothing. I have no idea if you can pen him, and if you had him roped I don't believe you could do anything with him. But you may go and try."

"And may we take Auntie's mare for Nasho to ride? His pony is lame."

"Yes, if your Auntie is willing."

Auntie was willing, so Monday morning we started early with our blankets and provision enough to do us until Wednesday night. We took good strong ropes about thirty feet long, and a stout halter to put on him if we did catch him. We met Mr. Seiders near his place driving up some horses, and he told us he had seen Wild Bill that morning with some horses only a few miles off. We was glad to hear that, for we were afraid we might have to hunt for him all the days we had to stay, and then maybe not find him. Finding him wasn't catching him by a heap, but it was the first thing toward it.

It wasn't long before we came in sight of the bunch Mr. Seiders had told us about, and we stopped at once so as not to scare Wild Bill if he was with them. Sometimes he would run off at once if he saw anybody, and again he would let you ride pretty close to him, but if there was three or four together and they began to separate, he always ran off. He knew he could run away from any one man, but I reckon he thought if three or four got around him they might get close enough for one of them to catch him.

The horses were out in the level open, but from the time of day—it was nearly dinner time—and the direction in which they were feeding, we 'most knew they were going to El Hoyos Insondable to water. This was a water hole about a mile off that everybody knew. It was on the level, but only a few yards from a deep hollow with high bluff banks. It was nearly round, about thirty feet across, with rocky banks, but smooth as if it had been cut out of solid rock, and didn't seem to have any bottom. One day when we camped there three of us tied our stake ropes together, and a rock to the end, and let them down into it, but we never found bottom, and they were nearly a hundred feet long. It never got any fuller, for it couldn't without running over, and there wasn't any branch that run into it, and it was never any lower. Close to it, and between it and the steep bluff, was a big spreading tree with thick branches. A little below that the bluff wasn't steep, and there was a path where cattle and cow hunters went up and down from the gulch to the prairie.

We took a circle round so the horses wouldn't see us, and got into a little hollow that ran into the Big Gulch below the water hole. Then we rode up to the path, and nearly to the top of the Gulch, and hitched our horses. Nasho went to a place where he could be hid and watch the water hole, and I took my stake rope and went to the tree, climbed it, and fixed myself among the branches, where I couldn't be seen easy but had room to use my arms and a clear space below me. I tied my rope fast to the tree so as to give me about twenty feet to use, and fixed a noose in the other end that would stand open well if I dropped it. It wasn't long 'till I heard Nasho say in a low voice, "They comin'."

I coiled my rope up so it would run out free, caught it up in my left hand, fixed my noose in my right hand, settled myself well in the branches and waited. Directly they came up along the path that led to the water hole. There were two or three six months' old colts in the bunch and they were running and frisking around, but the others came straight to the water and drank. Then they scattered about a little and stood around as horses often do after drinking. Wild Bill didn't seem to be much thirsty and didn't drink much. Two or three of the horses came up to the tree where I was and rubbed and scratched themselves against it. I kept hoping Wild Bill would come up too, but he didn't. You see, our first plan was to find Wild Bill by himself, or try and work him off by himself, and get in the way he was going without letting him see us and tie the mare to the tree where he would see her and come to her, but when we found the horses near the water hole we thought maybe he would come to the big tree to scratch himself and give me a chance to catch him.

The horses began to feed off and I was so disappointed, for I knew when they left that chance would be gone, when I saw Bill raise his head and look up in a way that made me know something was up. I was afraid at first somebody was coming and would scare him, but I saw in a second it wasn't that, for he wasn't scared. In three or four minutes I saw another bunch of horses coming from another direction, with Mr. Seiders' gray stallion in the lead. As soon as he saw Wild Bill, he neighed and ran up to him and tried to catch him by the neck. Wild Bill was ready for him, and the fight began. They reared up and struck at each other with their forefeet and tried to whirl and kick each other, but they were both too sharp for that, and always managed to get out of the way.

Once or twice Wild Bill caught the gray by the neck and shook him like a dog does a rat, but he would break loose again. I could see their big eyes flash, and they neighed and screamed all the time, or rather gray did, for Bill didn't make much noise. He had such a thick mane that the gray couldn't get a hold on his neck. As they kept fighting, rearing up and whirling round to dodge each other, they kept getting nearer and nearer the bluff until they was in ten feet of it, but neither of them seemed to notice it. I came very near shouting loud to scare them away, but thought I would wait until the very last. Just then the gray made a quick jump and caught Bill by the neck close down to the withers and give him an awful bite. I heard his teeth pop when they came together. Bill jerked himself loose and ran against the gray so hard he almost knocked him down, right on the edge of the bluff. The gray nearly got on his feet again and, in throwing his head round, saw where he was. He made a terrible effort to save himself, but just then Wild Bill struck him again and over he went head over heels. As he fell he gave the most horrible scream I ever heard. It seemed to go right through me and 'most freeze me up, and even now when I think about it I shut my eyes and stop my ears and try to keep it out.

Wild Bill turned around and gave a little low neigh as much as to say he was satisfied. Then he started straight for the tree to scratch his neck where the gray bit him. My heart nearly jumped into my throat when I saw him coming, but I fixed myself for him. I was never as much excited in my life, not even when I killed the bear. I knew I wasn't in any danger, but I was so afraid he wouldn't come close enough, or I would miss him, or something would happen that I wouldn't catch him. Just as he got under me I dropped the noose squarely over his head. He made a big jump and started to run, but the rope brought him up. I was so glad I wanted to holler as loud as a dozen boys, but I was afraid it might scare him and he might try harder to get away and break the rope. He set himself back and pulled until the root of his tail nearly touched the ground but he was fast. Then he jumped forward and ran as fast as he could, but the rope jerked him back so hard it nearly turned him a summersault. I was glad and scared all the time for fear he would break the rope.

Directly Nasho came up at a gallop on Bullet. Wild Bill was pulling back as hard as he could. Nasho rode up behind him, touched him with his foot and, as he jumped forward, threw his rope and caught both forefeet. Then he tightened up his rope, whirled Bullet, put spurs to him, and as Bill raised his feet for another jump, he jerked them from under him and down he came on his head. He surged and jerked and tried to get up, but it wasn't any use. Bullet had him stretched out so he couldn't get his feet under him. I slid down the tree, got the halter and rope from Nasho's saddle and ran up and caught Bill by the nose with one hand and the ear with the other, and turned his head straight up. He tried harder than ever to get up, but it was no use. We had him. Then I put the halter over his head and fastened the rope to the tree. I was sure of him now, and I was so glad I hardly knew what to do.

Wild Bill was mine.

There were twenty men that would have given two hundred dollars for him, and one man in San Antonio had offered five hundred for him, but they couldn't get him now. Me and Nasho had done what a heap of the best cow hunters had tried to do and couldn't. It was Nasho's plan, but he had agreed I was to catch him and have him if we caught him. How to get him home was the next thing.

Taming The Infamous Wild Horse

Nasho left Bullet and went down and got the mare, and I held Bill until he got back. Then he took the rope again, and I took the rope I had caught him with off from the tree and his neck, and fastened one end to the halter and gave the other end to Nasho. Then I let the halter rope already on him loose from the tree and got on Bullet as quick as I could. Our plan was to ride on each side of him so he couldn't run hard against either rope before the other would stop him. If he ran toward me, Nasho would check him; and if toward Nasho, I would, and in this way we thought we could, partly by leading, and partly by driving, get him home. Nasho loosened the rope round his feet so that when the horse got up it would come off, and then rode about fifteen feet on the other side from me and whistled to him to get up. He didn't move. He hollered to him, and rode up closer and clapped his hands, and jerked the rope so it would hit him, but he wouldn't budge.

"He sulk now, make much trouble."

He tried again, but the horse wouldn't move. All in a minute I thought I would ride him, and said, "Nasho, let's saddle him while he is down and I'll ride him."

"No, no! No good! He quiet now, but he pitch like mule when he get up."

I was afraid he would, but I had been the first one to catch him and I was determined to be the first to ride him, and now was as good a time as any. How proud I would be to ride up to the house on him! He couldn't do anything but throw me, and it wouldn't be the first time I had been pitched, and I would fix him so he couldn't get away if he did throw me.

I got down and unsaddled Bullet and took the bridle off. I tied my rope to the tree so if he jumped up he couldn't get away. Then I walked up and dropped the blanket on him. He winced a little, but didn't try to get up. Then I let the stirrups fall over his sides, but he wouldn't move. We had a good deal of trouble to get the girth under his belly, but at last we did and I girted the saddle as tight as I could. Then I took my bridle reins off my bridle and fastened them to the halter, for it wasn't any use to put the bridle on him. It's always the best way to ride a wild horse with a halter. Then I cut a stout stick nearly as big as my arm and about two feet long, and fastened the end of my rope about the middle of it, so that if he threw me and ran off the stick would catch in the bushes and hold him. I cut another one about fifteen inches long and wrapped it in a piece of saddle blanket and fastened it tight to the horn of my saddle in front of it, so he couldn't throw me out of the saddle so easy if he pitched. I coiled up my rope and laid it over the horn of the saddle so I could throw it loose if I wanted to, and was ready to get on him.

I tell you I was scared. I was 'most certain he would throw me, but I was going to try him anyhow. I almost wished I hadn't said I would ride him. Nasho fastened his rope to the tree and then unsaddled the mare and saddled Bullet. I let his rope loose from the halter, gathered up my reins, put my foot in the stirrup and swung myself in the saddle as well as I could with him lying down. He jumped up quicker than anything I ever saw except a buffalo, and started off in a run. I was glad of it, for I had a heap rather he would run than pitch, and I got my feet in the stirrups and settled myself well in the saddle.

When he had run about a mile I looked back and saw Nasho coming, but he was a good way back. Wild Bill was too fast for Bullet. He kept straight on in a long swinging gallop that got over a heap of ground in a hurry. Uphill and down, jumping hollows, through the brush, he never stopping for anything. I looked ahead and saw a creek and was afraid it had steep banks. As we got nearer I saw a little to the right a path that I knew went to the creek, where there was a crossing, and tried my best to pull his head around so he would get in it, but it was no use. I might as well have pulled against an elephant. We kept getting closer to the creek. The bank was a bluff, but I couldn't stop or turn Bill. I caught my reins up tight, clinched to my saddle, shut my eyes, and over we went.

The bottom was deep mud, so it didn't hurt us. Bill gathered himself up, turned down to the crossing, galloped through the water up the bank and into the bottom. By good luck he took the path, and by dodging down to his neck to miss low branches, and twisting around every way to keep others from dragging me out of the saddle, I managed to stick to him till he got out on to the prairie again. I got some hard licks from swinging branches and bushes by the path, but I was very glad to get off with that.

Running through the bottom had checked him up a little but as soon as he got out, he struck out in his long gallop again. I knew by the sun and the way he was going we must have come ten miles, but he didn't seem the least bit tired. All right, old fellow, I thought. This is better than pitching. I can stand it as long as you can.

It was glorious riding, I tell you. A broad, open prairie, not level and flat but running in long, easy swells, the ground was smooth and hard and no holes, and the grass not high enough to be in the way, and not

many gullies. I felt like I could ride that way all day. He
didn't shake me much more than if I had been sitting
in a chair. I would have liked it a heap better if I could
have done anything with him, but I could neither stop
or guide him. He didn't have any idea of anything but
going straight ahead.

I had just looked at the sun and thought we must have
come nearly ten miles more, when I saw timber ahead
and I knew it was on some stream, a good big one by
the looks of it. It must be the Colorado. I began to get
scared, for we might strike it at a bluff, and where it
was swimming, and I knew I couldn't stop my horse. I
was a good swimmer, but I didn't like the idea of jumping into swimming water on a horse I couldn't manage.
I thought about throwing my rope down and jumping
out of the saddle, but I knew I was most sure to get hurt
that way, and there wasn't any bushes to catch the stick,
and I had ridden him so far I didn't like to give up now.
We kept going like a flash, it seemed to me, and my
heart was beating faster and faster—I believe it would
have come out of my mouth if it could have got through
my throat, but it stuck there and nearly choked me.

I had a heap rather he had commenced pitching, but
he just kept straight on. I couldn't see the water; the
bank must be bluff closer and closer. Oh! how my heart
beat when I saw a steep bluff forty feet high, and the
blue, still water at the bottom. I would have jumped out
of the saddle if I could, but it was too late. I caught my
reins tight, clinched to my saddle, jammed my hat on
my head, shut my eyes, and over we went. It seemed to
me an hour before we struck the water. We must have
turned a complete summersault but we hit the water
feet foremost and under we went. Ugh! how the cold
water made me shiver. I thought we never would come
up again, but we did. I was 'most stifled and strangled,

but I held on to my reins and clinched to the saddle. My horse just stopped a second to blow the water out of his nose and struck out for the other bank as if nothing had happened. He swum high out of the water and straight as a boat could pull. If there hadn't been anything in the way he would have made the other bank without any trouble, and I reckon would have run twenty miles further. But we wasn't to get out so easy.

Out in the middle of the river where the current was strongest, a young cottonwood tree had drifted and lodged. The butt end and roots had caught on a bank that came up to the top of the water, and the branches had lodged against an old snag sticking out of the water that held them. The current was carrying us right down against the branches. I had taken my feet out of the stirrups and got my knife as quick as I could and cut the strings that fastened the stick in front of my saddle so I could get out easier. The horse did his best to swim upstream enough to clear the treetop, but it was no use. We kept getting nearer and nearer until we struck it and lodged. My horse reared and pawed with his forefeet, and tried to turn round so he could swim away, but he couldn't. The current kept pushing him against the branches, and he had to keep working to keep from being sucked under and drowned. I had stuck to him till now, but I couldn't do any good there so I slid out of the saddle and swum to the branches and caught hold of one and drew myself out of the water.

Poor fellow! He was scared now sure enough, and whimpered to me and looked at me as much as to ask me not to leave him. I was so sorry for him I just determined I wouldn't leave him as long as he could keep his head above water or I could swim a lick. I crawled along the branches to him and patted his head and spoke kindly to him, and he kept up a low whinnying as if thanking me. He wasn't a bit afraid of me now. I felt so sorry I believe I cried. But being sorry didn't do any good, and if I couldn't get him out of there pretty soon he would give way and be sucked under and drowned.

I couldn't see any way to get him loose. I couldn't swim out into the river and pull him away from the tree for he was stronger than I was, and he couldn't swim away himself. He had tried it two or three times. I couldn't pull him up along the tree because he was tangled in the branches and couldn't get out. I was just about to give it up and it seemed as if my heart would 'most break to sit there and see him drown right before my eyes asking me to help him, when I happened to think of what Parson Theglin had said to me about steady thinking. I couldn't get him loose, that was certain, but maybe I could get the tree loose. I crawled to him again, patted and rubbed his head and told him I was going to get him loose, and then began to work my way along the tree toward the butt end. As I got away from him he whinnied to me so pitiful I could hardly help but turn back to him, but I looked round at him, stopped a moment and hollered to him "All right, old fellow, I'll come back directly and help you out."

He seemed to know I was trying to help him, and hushed. I got down to the end of the tree and found it had caught by some roots against a big rock around which the sand had washed so as to make it look like a sandbar. The roots wasn't big ones, and wouldn't have held it if some grapevines that were wrapped round the trunk hadn't caught too, and help hold it.

I had my camp knife in my belt and got it out. It wasn't very long, but it was heavy and sharp, and I cut the grapevines and then commenced on the roots. It didn't take me long to hack two of them in two, and the rest broke, and the butt end began to float downstream,

I crawled back as fast as I could to the other end, and cut the branch that was holding my horse. Then I got the rope from the horn of my saddle, and swum to the snag that was holding the tree, for I couldn't crawl any further on the branches, and wrapped my rope around it.

The tree began to move downstream slow, and as the branches gave way from the snag, they raked and scraped me terribly but I hung on to the snag and my rope. It was taking the horse with it but when he got to the end of the rope, it stopped him. The branches jerked him under once, and then swept round him and left him free. I called him, and he whinnied and turned and swam to me. I coiled my rope up as he came, and when he got to me, patted and rubbed his head a second or two, and got into the saddle and turned his head across stream again. He could make it now without any trouble, and the bank was low so we could get out.

Just as I was thinking our trouble was over I looked again at what I first thought was a lump of clay, and saw it was a calf's head. It had bogged. It wouldn't do to land there. So I turned his head downstream again. He looked round as if to ask me what that was for, but didn't pull a bit. I could manage him without any trouble. A few steps below the low place there was a big bluff, and we had to swim down the river a quarter of a mile. I would have turned him across the stream again where the bank was low, but it looked like it might be boggy, and I knew he was tired, and it was a heap easier swimming downstream.

I got out of the saddle and held to his mane with one hand, and the reins with the other, and tried to help as much as I could by kicking for myself. It seemed to me a long time, though I know from the distance it couldn't have been but a few minutes before we came to a little

flat place running out into the water, and a path from it
going up the hill. I knew it was a stock watering place,
and turned his head to it. In a minute we were out on
dry land again, and glad to get there too, I tell you.

I rode up the hill and found we had come out in a little
valley where the grass was good. I turned him down to
an old dead tree and got off of him. He rubbed his nose
against my face, whinnying as if he was trying to thank
me forgetting him loose. I patted his head and neck and
talked to him as if he had been a boy, and knew what I
was saying. Then I unsaddled him and staked him out
to get some grass. He was hungry, and went to eating,
though every little while he would come up for me to
pat him, and rub his nose against my face.

I got my matches out of my pocket, and made a fire
to dry my clothes and saddle blanket. They were in a
bottle corked up tight, and hadn't got wet. It's the best
way to carry matches I ever saw. Uncle told me about
it, and told me too, always to carry them in my pocket,
and not in my saddle pockets, for if my horse got away
I would have them with me.

I was hungry, for I hadn't eat any dinner, but Nasho
had our provisions, and there wasn't any house near.
I looked around to see if I could see any birds, and in
moving about a rabbit jumped up almost from under
my feet and ran off. I followed him, and saw him go into
a hollow in a tree close to the ground. I cut a little green
stick with a fork at the end, and twisted him out directly.
It didn't take me long to skin and wash him at the river,
nor to cook him either. I found some salt in my saddle
pockets in a bottle, and there was plenty of red pepper
growing along the river bank, and I made a good meal
off of him.

By the time I had finished my dinner my clothes and
saddle blanket was dry, and I put them on. The sun

wasn't more than half an hour high, but I wanted to get across the river before night, and find a house where I could stay all night, for I didn't have any provisions or blankets, and it's lonesome camping out by yourself. I rode down the river a mile and found a ford and crossed, but didn't see any house. Then I rode up the river two miles above where I had swam it, but still didn't find any house, so I thought I had as well camp.

I stopped at the first open place where there was grass and wood, unsaddled my horse, staked him out and gathered up wood enough to keep up fire all night. In getting up wood I started another rabbit, and caught him like the other one. I didn't want any supper, so I just cleaned him and hung him up in a young tree where nothing could get to him. Then I saw some old, black moss, and got a lot and made me a bed of it. By this time it was dark, so I tied my horse up close so he couldn't hurt himself with the rope, but left him room to lie down if he wanted to, and after petting him a little went to bed. I wasn't any more afraid of him than I am now, and he wasn't afraid of me, or the saddle, or the rope, or anything about me. I waked up cold once or twice in the night, and put on more wood, and went out and petted my horse a little and then lay down and went to sleep again. The moss made a soft bed, and the saddle blanket was plenty of covering with the fire. I was a little bit afraid of panthers, but I was too tired to keep awake.

I woke up early next morning, staked my horse so he could eat grass, and began cooking my rabbit. It was cold, and I put on a good deal of wood and it made a blazing fire. Directly I happened to look up and saw my horse watching something. It was Nasho. Wasn't I glad to see him! He had followed my trail all the way but was stopped by the darkness only half a mile from the river, and had camped as I did, though he had provisions and coffee, and our blankets. It wasn't many minutes before we had a pot of coffee on, and some bacon cooking, and while we ate breakfast he told me how he followed the trail after he lost sight of me.

Once a bunch of horses had got in the path and he couldn't see my horse's prints at all, but he kept on the way I had been going and pretty soon he struck them again. He said sometimes on the prairie he could scarcely see the tracks, but generally he kept on as fast as his horse could travel. When he got to the bluff where we had jumped off he didn't know what to do, but turned down the river to see if he could see anywhere I could get out, intending to go down and look for the tracks, when he happened to see my fire and came to me.

"Me mighty glad to see you, for me tought you was gone up when me see tracks go over bluff."

I told him I was mighty glad to see him too. There ain't many American boys that would have followed me up as he did. Nasho'll do to trust every time if he likes you.

After breakfast we started back, and that night we reached home. Uncle was very much surprised to see me come riding up on a strange horse, and a heap more so when I told him how we had caught him and what a ride I had had. He said I ought not to have got on him, and it was a wonder I hadn't been killed, but I heard him tell Auntie that those boys would do to go to the Centennial, no fear about their not being able to take care of themselves. From that day to this I have never had the least bit of trouble with my horse, and I wouldn't take ten thousand dollars for him. I don't want to take any more such rides, but I wouldn't have missed that one for a heap.

COMMENCING COMMERCE IN SAN ANTONE

The week before Christmas we asked Uncle if we
might go to San Antonio and sell our pecans and
turkeys. He said yes. We took the wagon bed and
put long slats to it for side boards and over it so as to
make it a big coop. We had one already made for the
partridges. One wagon would near hold all our stuff,
so we borrowed Mr. Lowry's and brought it to Uncle's
so as to get an early start next morning. Auntie cooked
bread enough to last us there and back, and ground
coffee, and we took some dried beef too.

Next morning we hitched up the horses to the wagons, one span to each, and started. One wagon had
fifty turkeys and twelve dozen partridges, and the other
fifteen bushels of pecans. We took old Bose with us to
keep the hogs and cattle away from our horses while
they were eating. We had to take corn and fodder for
them, for there ain't much grass on the road in winter.
Neither of us had ever been there, but Uncle told us the
road and we knew we could find it. It was the main big
road all the way.

I 'most forgot Nasho's wax figures. He had some of
the best and prettiest he had ever made, for Miss Masover had helped him a great deal and he had taken a
heap of pains with them. One of them was a Mexican
on a black horse roping a white bull. The Mexican had
on a red jacket, and yellow pants with buttons down the
sides and open from the top of his shiny black boots,
and a red sash around his waist, and a broad brimmed

hat, and everything was just as natural as could be. He was whirling the rope around his head, and his horse was wheeling on his hind legs to get out of the way of the bull that was running at him with his head down to hook him. They were both fast to a little stand that could be set on the mantle or a table.

Another one was an Indian woman sitting over a little fire cooking a lizard stuck on a stick. Wrapped up in her blanket was a little Indian baby. Off to one side was an Indian coming to camp with a deer on his back. They were all as poor and scrawny as could be, and looked 'most starved, as they must have been to eat lizards, but they were going to have plenty to eat now that the hunter had come back with game. There were some trees back of the camp and big rocks with moss growing over them and all just as natural as if they had been actual little people, and trees and rocks. Then he had men and women dressed in Mexican fashion carrying baskets of all kinds of vegetables and fruits, and chickens, and turkeys, and parrots, and cages of birds, and everything was just like life and colored just like what it was made to represent. Miss Masover gave us a letter to one of her friends in the city, that she said would help us sell the wax figures so as to get more for them than we would by ourselves.

We started early Tuesday morning, and Thursday, about ten o'clock, at the eight-mile hill, we came in sight of San Antonio. It made me think of what I had read of oasis in the desert. We were travelling over a rough country with a good many rocks and not much timber, and scrubby too, and only now and then a house, and all of a sudden on getting to the top of a long hill there was a city almost under one's feet, it looked so close. It was a pretty sight, the big white houses thick together, and the church steeples looking like arrows pointing to heaven, and the pretty little houses shining among the trees around them. In the spring, when the trees are all in full leaf, it must be a great deal prettier.

We drove right into the city to the main Plaza. The last mile there were houses all the way, and the road was through a lane. Alongside of it, part of the way, was a ditch full to the brim of clear running water. Some of the houses on the road were the finest I had ever seen. They had large yards in front of them, laid off with trees and evergreen shrubs and flower beds in all shapes and forms. Some of them were of brick, but most of them were frame, painted white, with green shutters, and nearly all had fences in front of them of palings with fancy cut tops. One had a wire fence, but it wasn't pretty. It looked like no fence at all, and like anyone could go into the house that wanted to.

Sometimes right next to the yard of a fine, large house with a beautiful yard would be several little huts, just one room and a dirt floor, and nothing in the little pen of a yard but two or three poor dogs without any hair on them. They were mostly Mexican jacals, where the poor Mexicans, called *peons*, or greasers, lived, and the dogs were Mexican dogs called *pelones*. A peon is really a Mexican who owes another man and has to work for him till he pays him, and that is not allowed in Texas, but all poor Mexicans are called peons or greasers. Sometimes we would see Mexican women washing at the ditches, or maybe cooking something over a little fire out of doors.

When we got into the city, we found a great many people coming and going in wagons and carriages and on horseback, and we had to keep a good lookout to prevent getting run into, or running into somebody. Bose got under my wagon. Everybody seemed to be in a hurry. Most of the wagons that was going in had corn, or fodder, or wood, or chickens and turkeys, or something else to eat that was raised in the country, while those that were coming out had all sorts of packages out of stores. Once in a while one would have a new plow or harrow or cultivator. A good many of the farmer's had their wives or daughters with them, and one or two looked like the whole family had come in for Christmas.

The Plaza was full of wagons coming and going, and a good many standing still waiting for somebody to come and buy. When I saw so many wagons with turkeys and chickens, I was afraid there wasn't much chance for us to sell ours, but when I saw so many people I knew it would take a great many to do them all, and ours was prime fat.

Pretty soon a man came along with a pencil behind his ear, and seeing our loads stopped and asked us where we was from.

"From Kerrville, sir."

"Did you come by yourselves?"

"Yes, sir."

"Where did you get so many wild turkeys?"

"We caught them in pens, and the partridges in traps."

"Why you are lucky little fellows. You will be rich when you sell them."

"Oh no, sir, we want more money than that!"

He seemed so kind, and to feel so much interest in us, that I just thought I would tell him all about it, so I told him we was going to the Centennial, and had been working to get money to buy horses to drive cattle with, and how we caught the turkeys, and about killing the deer and bear, and catching Wild Bill. He listened with a great deal of interest, and asked us a great many questions, and wanted to see the wax figures, but they was packed up so close and carefully we couldn't get at them there. I told him we had a letter to Mr. Gamble about them.

"Well," said he, "Charley, you go with me to Mr. Gamble's store, and we will see what can be done in the way of helping you to sell them. We must make them bring a good price. Your little friend here, what's his name?"

I told him, "Ygnacio, but we called him Nasho for short."

"Well, Nasho will stay with the wagons until you come back."

I carried the box, for it wasn't very heavy, and we went to the store. It was full of books and pictures, and piles of paper and toys, and pretty things.

When the box was opened they all said it was fine work, and as pretty figures as they had ever seen, though they have a great deal of that kind of work in San Antonio. A lady who came up, asked who made them. I told her Nasho.

The man who had come with me then told them something about us, and that we wanted to sell our things so we could go to the Centennial. While they were talking, I gave Mr. Gamble the letter from Miss Masover. He read it and then shook hands with me, and asked me a good many questions about her, and then invited me to come to his house and bring Nasho with me and stay all night. I thanked him, but told him we would have to stay with our wagons. Then the gentleman who came with us said, "I tell you what, Gamble, we must have a raffle, or an auction, and sell these things for these little fellows, and make them bring a good price."

"But, Mr. Penseler, I have got just such things on hand now, and they don't seem to sell much."

"Will you auction them off if I send the people here?"

"Yes, with pleasure."

"At what hour?"

"Eleven o'clock will be as good a time as any."

"All right. You be ready and I'll engage to have the people here. And be sure you make them bring the last cent."

Then he stepped into a store with bolts of goods piled up on boxes in front of it, and clothes and boots and shoes stuck and hung wherever there was any place for them, and come out in a minute with a square piece of red flannel with a broad yellow stripe pinned across both sides. "Now Charley," said he, "you fasten this to a stick and put it in front of your wagon where it can be seen all round, and you and Nasho drive your wagons right where I found you this evening, tomorrow morning as soon as you get your breakfast, and you won't have any trouble in selling what you have. What do you ask for your turkeys?"

"Fifty cents for the hens, and six bits for the gobblers."

"You ask six bits for the hens and a dollar for the gobblers"

"But that is more than they are worth, sir."

"Not a cent. They are fat on corn and stuff, and besides turkeys don't get caught that way every day."

"I don't like not to do as you say, sir, but everybody sells them that way, and it don't seem to me to be right to ask more."

"I am glad to see you are honest, though I would have sworn to that anyhow. Everybody asks all they can get, and you must do the same. It is not everybody wants to go to the Centennial bad enough to work as you little fellows have done for it, and you must have all you can get—you will want it when you get there. I wouldn't tell you to do anything that was wrong, Charley. There ain't so many honest men in the world that we can afford to spoil any that are coming on and make rogues of them. Will you do as I say?"

"I wish I could, sir, but indeed I can't. It don't seem to me it would be right. Please don't think I am setting myself up against you, sir; indeed I am not, but you know everyone must do what seems right to them, and it don't seem right to me to ask more than other people. It would seem like we wanted to swindle people."

"You look like swindling people, don't you, bless your green little heart! All right, Charley. I don't want you to do what you don't think is right but think about it to-night and see if I am not right. Remember, people don't have to buy of you. You ask your price, and if they are not willing to give it, they can go somewhere else. When you come to buy your horses whoever sells to you will ask all he thinks he can get. At what wagon yard do you stop?"

I told him.

"That's a good one. Watch your wagons tonight. Ah! I see you have got Bose along. I'll warrant nobody will steal anything without his knowing it. Put up your flag when you get up in the morning and after breakfast drive where I told you, and my word for it by ten o'clock you won't have a turkey or partridge left. Then drive back to the yard and leave your wagons and look about town, and at eleven come to Gamble's and watch your figures sold."

CHARLEY & NASHO MAKE HEADLINES

As it was nearly dark we went to the wagon yard and put up. There were a great many others in the yard, but we did not believe they would try to steal from us, and if they should we knew Bose would wake us up.

Next morning we were up by the first peep of day, fed our horses and got breakfast. I put up our flag the first thing on getting up. While we were eating, a little fellow came along with a bundle of papers under one arm, and a single one in his other hand, and seeing our place came up and handed me a paper!

"Got your name in the paper, country-kin. Look for the blue mark and read, turkey-stock'll be active this morning. The early-bird catches the worm. The sooner you git your gobblers to the plaza the better. Good luck to you, and when you get to the Centennial just tell General Hawley to save his private box for me and have the military ready July 4th. Give you a letter to the General if I wasn't in a hurry. Goodbye."

I hardly knew what to make of him, he was so free and easy, but I asked him if he wouldn't have a cup of coffee and some breakfast.

"Thank you, I will try your coffee. Don't upset your coffee pot. I don't hold a quart." He drank half a cup of coffee and put down the cup with a smack of his lips.

"Better set up a coffee stall when you get there, young one. There's no defalcation about that coffee, for I know coffee, I do. None of your boarding house stuff, that. If the little greaser don't know how to make good bread just let me have him a month before you start and I'll put him to school in that line where his education won't be neglected. It runs in the breed to mix flour stuffs and get its best out of an oven. But my customers are suffering for their morning's ration of intelligence. It's all they'll get during the day, most of them, and they'd be in bankruptcy before dinner without it. They suspends regularly every Monday morning, but come out again shining at breakfast Tuesday. Adios, Señores."

With a low bow and a wide sweep of his cap he was off on a trot, screeching like a cat fighting: "Ere'syer morning paper! All the latest news! Two genuine Texas Lions in town! Turkeys active this morning. Tell's you where to see the show, the Herald does, only ten cents!"

I didn't understand more than half he said then, though I did afterward, but I didn't forget a word of it. It's curious how people can remember and keep thinking about what they can't understand.

When he was out of sight, I could hear him long afterwards. I picked up the paper and looked for the blue mark. I found it on the inside page, what they call the local page, Mr. Penseler told me afterward, and there a big blue mark right over an article that had in big type this heading:

TWO REGULAR TEXAS LIONS
IN THE CITY
LAST NIGHT.
THEY ARE EXPECTED ON THE MAIN PLAZA
THIS MORNING.
GET YOUR AMMUNITION READY
AND BE ON HAND WHEN YOU SEE THE
RED FLAG.

Yesterday evening while on his rounds for news for the many thousand readers of the *Herald*, one of its reporters was attracted by the sight of a wagon full of wild turkeys whose youthful driver, of fourteen or thereabouts, was evidently in the city for the first time. Near him was a second wagon full of pecans, engineered by a little Mexican of about the same age as his Saxon comrade, but who, though evidently not city raised, seemed as indifferent as a savage or a man who had just bought out our good town and was resolving which one of his wife's relations to give it to. Drawing near and entering into conversation, he found the little fellows had fifty wild turkeys which they had caught in pens, twelve dozen partridges—fairly trapped, no nets, gentlemen sportsmen—fifteen bushels of pecans, half a dozen deer and one bear skin, and a lot of wax figures which the little Mexican had made. All of the above were the result of their own labors.

Questioning them as to their object he soon found that they intended going to the Centennial, and were trying to raise money to buy horses so that they could hire to drive cattle to Kansas. From there they would go on to the great Fair, come back to Kansas and ride their horses home again. The reporter felt so much interest in the little fellows, so frank, honest, shrinking and yet straightforward and manly were they, that he interested himself in assisting them to dispose of their hard-won booty, for the bear had been killed by Charlie only after a severe fight. Taking him over to Gamble's the box of wax figures was opened and found to contain some of the finest statuettes ever exhibited in San Antonio. The writer claims to know something of this work, for he has seen hundreds of exhibitions of it in its home in the Mexican Capital, but more thoroughly correct imitations of the objects represented both as to form, color and everything that goes to the making of *tableau vivants*, he has never seen. A gayly-dressed cavalier lassoing a bull, an Indian hunter returning with the spoils of the chase to his famished camp just in time to forestall a meal upon disgusting reptiles, market men and women, birds and flowers are among the subjects so accurately represented. He was astonished to find such delicacy of design and skilful execution in one so young, and whose life one would rather suppose from his appearance to have been passed among the Kickapoos, though he was neatly attired and not without much latent intelligence, than amid work like this, that might well have come from pupils who had spent years in Mexico's superb art-school; but on further inquiry he ascertained that the young artist had had the inestimable advantage of the teaching and skilful assistance of one who was last season one of the most admired belles of our gay city, but who is now teaching the young idea to shoot among the mountains of our northern frontier. To her other favors she had added that of a letter introductory to Mr. Gamble, our enterprising and public-spirited stationer. He at once became interested in the little fellows, and promptly acceded to the suggestion of our reporter, to have an auction for the sale of the statuettes. It will come off this morning at eleven o'clock sharp, the popular J. Mangum Rolemoff having volunteered his valuable services to assist in offering them to the public. Aside from their artistic merit, for which we vouch our critical reputation, the occasion is certainly one which appeals most strongly to those of our free-spirited fellow-citizens, and they are legion, who take pleasure in assisting honest industry, all the more when it presents itself in the shape of two orphan boys, for they are such, who, at an age when most boys would care for little else than marble and top, or gun and horse, are doing men's work to gain the means to take them to the World's Fair next year. They are not going out of idle curiosity, but with a desire more to be expected in mature men than such striplings, to reap the advantages of such an education in the practical exhibition of the world's deeds as no books can give, and as is not likely to be again offered to any American boy now conning his worrisome lessons. We sincerely trust every article will be made to bring its true price, many times enhanced by the nature of the boy's ambition and the beautiful and lovely woman's generous heart, that have so lavishly been expended on these treasures. Aside from the pleasure of their possession as articles of beauty, they can never fail to remind their fortunate owners of the power of determined will, however immature and undisciplined, and they can and will be made such an ever-present and stimulating encouragement to other boys more favorably situated as can be drawn from no books with their tales of the heroic past. These little fellows are only working for a commencement. When they start on their cattle drive to which all this work thus far has only been preliminary, their labor will only have begun. Many a weary mile must be passed over, many a long day of broiling sun and stifling dust, many a painful night when weariness has become torture to exhausted frames, many a pitiless storm during which frightened cattle will be rushing round them in wild confusion, like the bison herds of the prairie, must be endured ere they reach their distant goal. And into all this they venture alone, animated only by that sublime thirst for knowledge which has written the names of many of its possessors high in the temple of fame, and handed them down to the ages as worthy of all honor because they sought that wisdom which Israel's sage King deemed more to be desired than all of earth's treasures.

These beautiful statuettes will be on exhibition at Gamble's from 9 a.m. until the hour of sale. Don't miss your only chance, for the sake of your own future gratification, and the honor of the Lone Star.

We are about to forget to call the attention of our readers, many of whom, as is so often the case in art centres, are as ready for a feast gastronomical as intellectual, preparing for the last by the first, that they will find the choicest turkeys of the season, their wild gamy flavor added to and improved by careful feeding, on the south side of the main Plaza, at a wagon flying a red flag with a bar of yellow. Don't offer these noble little fellows less than a dollar each for their superb wild fowls or your dinners will be sauced with the Paschal Lamb salad of bitter remorse. But it's no use suggesting this. Parsimoniousness is not a feature of our game city. And if you want the finest nuts of the season, nuts that gathered sweetness and richness from sun and air until their stems would no longer hold them, nuts that will never call into requisition the iron-hearted nut-crackers or break the little folks' teeth by their obduracy, just call on Señor Don Mexicain El Pequeño, and he will furnish you with a dessert the gods might envy. Three dollars a bushel, remember; no one can afford to offer less.

SELLING OUT

By the time I had finished reading the paper break-fast was over, and we hitched up and drove to the main Plaza. We saw people in every direction, coming and going to market with baskets on their arms. Directly a man came along with some greens sticking out of his basket, and hollered to us in a pleasant voice, "Hand us out a gobbler Charley; one of your best, and here's your dollar." I told him I didn't ask but six bits, but he said, "All right, my boy, the other quarter will buy you a lunch some day at the Centennial."

He took his gobbler and left, but it wasn't but a few minutes till another one came, and then another, and then they kept coming in a regular string, and in an hour we had sold all but one, which I kept, and all the partridges but one dozen, which I wouldn't sell, though several persons wanted them. Almost everybody wanted gobblers, but most of them gave us a dollar apiece for the hens as well, though two didn't give but four bits, which I told them was all we asked.

My wagon was now empty, all but the deer and bear skins, but Nasho hadn't sold but one bushel of pecans. We were talking whether we hadn't better go to some of the merchants and sell them all together, or go round among the houses with them, when we saw two men coming from different directions, and both in a hurry. They wasn't Americans, nor Mexicans, nor Dutch, and they didn't speak very plain English. The first one that got to us said, 'most out of breath, he had walked so fast: "Mine goot boy, I takes all your pecans at dwo dollars a bushel. De down ish full of pecans. You can't git so much from anybody else."

Just then the other one came up and said, "I gifs you dwo dollars and a quarter a bushel, Charley."

"Dwo and a half."

"Dwo and six bits."

"Three dollars I gifs. Stay, my friend," and he called the other one to him, and they talked a minute and shook their heads and came back to me together. The last one said, "Dis man agree for me to take all your pecans at dwo dollars and a half a bushel."

Now I had heard from some men at the wagon yard that common pecans were bringing two dollars and a half a bushel, and ours were uncommonly fine ones, and I thought they were worth three dollars, and I was 'most certain too that the two men had agreed to buy them together, so as not to give so much for them by bidding against each other, so I said, "The other man offered me three dollars."

"No. I don't gif no such brice. Dey is worth no more dan dwo dollars and a half."

"Very well, sir," I said. "They are worth three dollars a bushel."

"Nobody ish fool enough to give you no such price," said the second man.

"Then nobody needn't buy them."

"Come, Charley, I'll do petter by you ash nobody else. I gifs you dwo dollars and sixty cents, and dakes dem all. You mosh stay here all day before you can beddle dem by the bushel, and den you don't git no more ash I offer you."

"Three dollars a bushel." They went off together again and talked a few minutes and came back, and the one who had offered two dollars and sixty cents said, "I gifs you dwo dollars and six bits, my goot boy. Dat is awful big brice."

I didn't like his trying to beat me down, and just turned to Nasho and asked him to watch my team while I went across the square. I hadn't more than started before he came to me and said, "You makes one goot merchant, mine sharp poy. I gifs you dree dollars. How many has you got."

"Fourteen bushels, but I'll keep one bushel."

"Dat ish too many. I don't want no more ash den bushels."

"Well, I will sell you ten bushels."

"Come on den."

I took Nasho's wagon and drove to his stand at one of the street corners, and measured him out ten bushels. He gave me three ten dollar bills, and tried hard to get me to buy some fruit and candy from him, but I wouldn't. I wanted some, but I intended to buy from an honest man. In driving along down the street another fruit man at the other corner stopped me and asked what I had to sell. He thought my price was too high, but when I showed him what fine ones they were he took the other four bushels, and gave me two five dollar bills, a two-dollar one and two fifty-cent pieces in silver. Just then I saw Mr. Penseler going along and called him. When he came up I told him I had a turkey and a half bushel of pecans for him, and wanted to know where he lived, so I could take them to his house. He didn't want to take them, but I told him he must, and he got on the wagon and we drove to his house and left them. Then I went back to where I had left Nasho, and stopped on the way at Mr. Gamble's store and left a dozen partridges and a half bushel of pecans for him, and then me and Nasho drove to the wagon yard and put up our teams.

Just as we got through, Mr. Penseler came to the yard
and asked me if I wouldn't like to go to the Alamo. I
told him yes, because I had often heard Uncle tell about
it. He had a brother killed there. When we got there
and while we were walking about in the old fort, I tried
to think how everything must have looked nearly forty
years ago, when there were one hundred and eighty-
two dead Texas soldiers, and sixteen hundred Mexicans
lying in and about the old walls, and what a terrible
sight it must have been when Santa Anna, the Mexican
General, had all the dead Texans burned. They went
out and brought in great loads of dry wood, and spread
a lot on the ground, and put a row of bodies on it, and
then another big lot of wood and then more bodies,
until they had made several big piles. Then they set fire
to them, and put on more wood as it burnt out until nothing was left of the bodies but ashes. Old Santa
Anna was mad because they had fought him so long
and killed so many of his men. He had four thousand,
and they fought him eleven days, and killed nearly ten
Mexicans apiece, but not a single one of them got away.
They even killed Col. Bowie in his bed, but he fought
them to the last.

Mr. Penseler showed me where it was. There was one
woman and her child in the fort, and the Mexicans
didn't kill them. She lives in Austin now, but her child
is dead. Uncle always says if it had not been for the
fight at the Alamo, all the Americans in Texas would
have been driven out of the country. Old Santa Anna
himself was afterward caught at San Jacinto with his
whole army all that wasn't killed, but Gen. Houston,
instead of burning him or hanging him, sent him out of
the country. I tell you, reading about things is not like
seeing them, or the places where they happened. I had
often heard Uncle tell about the massacre of the Alamo,

and didn't think a great deal about it, but when I was there inside the walls where the firing never stopped for eleven days, and where that morning before daylight one hundred and eighty-two men that had been well and strong an hour before, were left on the ground all dead, besides the hundreds and hundreds of Mexicans, it did seem like a terrible thing to me.

A man can't do any more than give up his life for anybody, and they gave up theirs for their friends and country. I don't think we ought ever to forget them, or that they died for us. I have heard some people say many of them were bad men who had to leave their own States because of things they had done there, or to keep from paying their debts. I don't know anything about that, but they was sent there to keep the Mexicans back, and they done it till they died. Gen. Lee couldn't have done any more. Mr. Penseler told us there was some talk of the old Fort being sold to some men for a livery stable. It seems to me it would be like selling a graveyard. It is all the grave they had.

Wax Figures & Counterfeiters

When we left the Alamo we went to the bookstore and watched Mr. Rolemoff sell the wax figures. There were a great many people there, some of them ladies. When the clock struck eleven he got upon the counter, and making a very polite bow, said—I won't pretend to give the very words he used, but it was pretty near like this, for it was the first auction I had ever been at and I listened close:

"Ladies and gentlemen, you are aware of the very unusual circumstances that bring me before you this morning. The beautiful works of art which I have the honor to offer you, aside from the origin which so greatly enhances their value, speak for themselves so much more eloquently than I could do that I will not enter into particulars, and with such an audience as I have the honor of addressing, it will be unnecessary for me to dwell on their merits, or use the ordinary tricks of the trade, to draw out the full value of the goods presented. I here offer you (and he held up an old market man with a basket full of vegetables and fruit on his back) a figure which is somewhat familiar to the most of you, not only in reality, but in imaged resemblance. Whether you have seen any better work of this description you will be the fitting judges. For myself, I have only to say that I entirely coincide with the views expressed by the *Herald* of this morning in its local upon this subject. What have you to say about this charming little statuette?"

"Two dollars and a half."

I looked to see who it was that bid, but before I could find him in the crowd, somebody else said, " Three dollars."

"And a half."

"Four."

"And a quarter."

"Half."

"Six bits." They bid so fast I couldn't keep up with them, but the auctioneer seemed to see everyone.

"Four dollars and six bits have been offered, some gentleman I am sure will make it five. Oh, thank you, sir! Five dollars, five dollars, five dollars, fi-v-e dollar-s. If you are through, we will not dwell. Once more...Five dollars...Going, going, gone! Mr. Herkimer takes it. I will here say, ladies and gentleman, that the sale will not occupy more than half an hour, at the expiration of which time you can obtain your purchases at the counter. Our gallant little frontiersmen wish to leave the city immediately after noon, and we request that the goods will be settled for at once on that account."

Then he put up the man roping the bull, and it brought twelve dollars and a half. Altogether they brought fifty-five dollars. In a few minutes after the sale was over, Mr. Gamble handed me the money, and I thanked him for his kindness in helping us so much. I was going to give the money to Nasho, but he told me to give him five dollars and keep the rest. Mr. Penseler told us to come back there at half past twelve and we could take dinner together. Then we separated.

I wanted to buy a nice shawl for Auntie, and went to a store where I saw such things hanging out and asked to see some shawls for ladies. I told him I didn't want a very fine one, but a good, warm, pretty one. He showed me some, and I picked out one and asked him what it was worth. He said six dollars, and I told him I would take it, and got out my money and handed him a ten dollar bill. He looked at it, and turned it over, and looked at it again close, and then told me to wait a minute, and went back to the other end of the store.

Directly he came back again with a gentleman who I felt sure owned the store. He came up to me and said, "My little man, where did you get this money?"

"I sold pecans for it, sir."

"Who bought them?"

I told him I didn't know his name, but I knew where he kept. He asked me how I knew he gave me that particular bill, and I told him, because I sold him ten bushels at three dollars a bushel, and he gave me three ten dollar bills, which I put away in one pocket. He asked me then if I had any more pecans, and I told him I had had four more bushels but had sold them to another man. He asked me if I knew what kind of money he had paid me in, and I told him he gave me two five dollar bills, and a two dollar one and two fifty cents, and I had put it with the rest of the pecan money. He asked me if I had got any money since, and I told him we had just sold some wax figures and got the money for them, but that I had put it in another pocket by itself.

"Where did you sell the wax figures?" he asked me.

"At Mr. Gamble's. Mr. Rolemoff auctioned them off."

"Ah! You are the little boys who came in from the mountains with pecans and turkeys and wax works?"

"Yes, sir."

"Are you sure you haven't mixed your money?"

"Yes, sir. When Mr. Gamble gave me the money it was in a roll, and I didn't unroll it, and when Nasho said he only wanted five dollars I didn't take it out of that money, but out of the pecan money, and put the other by itself.

"Let us go up to Gamble's and see about this. This is a counterfeit bill. Do you know a man who tries to pass a counterfeit bill can be put in the penitentiary?"

"No, sir. But I didn't know it was bad money. It wasn't my fault; I didn't make it, and didn't know it wasn't good."

"I am satisfied you are not to blame, but I want to find out who is. It is somebody who knew what he was doing, and was willing to get you into trouble."

We went to Mr. Gamble's, and the gentleman with me walked up to the counter and said, "Gamble, how much money did you pay this little fellow this morning?"

"Fifty-five dollars."

"Was it put up together any way?"

"Yes, in a roll."

"Would you know the roll again if you were to see it?"

"Yes. There were two twenties, a ten and a five, the last on the outside, and it had been pasted in a torn place. I happened to notice it in putting it up."

"You could swear to the package if you saw it?"

"Yes, if it has not been disturbed. Furthermore, I recollect distinctly that the two twenties were National Bank Notes of the First National Bank of Springfield, Mass. In looking over the money in the drawer last night I happened to notice them, and wondered through how many hands they had passed in getting here, and what each man got for them in turn, and I forgot to take the cash out of the drawer last night, so they were there this morning. The ten I don't know anything about, but I could swear to the way they were rolled up and the patched five dollar bill."

"Excuse me, Mr. Gamble, you know I do not doubt you for an instant, but there are a good many patched five dollar bills."

"Yes, sir, but they are not patched with buckskin."

"No. At least I never saw one that was. Let's see your roll, Charley?"

I pulled it out of my pocket. I had wrapped a string so it wouldn't come loose and maybe so get torn.

"There was no string on it when I handed it to Charley, but that is the exact way in which it was done up. Begin at the end Colonel, and in the first turn you will find the buckskin patch."

The Colonel, as Mr. Gamble called the gentleman who was with me, asked one of the clerks to take the roll from me and undo it, and tell him what were the kinds and denominations of bills in it. He unrolled it and showed the buckskin patch. Then he spread the money out, took up one bill at a time and said, "One five dollar greenback, one ten dollar Indianapolis First National Bank note, one twenty dollar Springfield First National Bank note, another twenty dollar Springfield First National Bank note."

"All right," said the Colonel nodding his head. "Now we'll go to the man you got the money from."

As we started out Mr. Gamble handed me a nice pocketbook, and said, "Here, Charley, is something to keep your money in."

I thanked him and put it in my pocket. When we got there the Colonel asked me which was the man, and I pointed him out. He commenced cursing him for trying to cheat me, and told him he had a great mind to put him in the penitentiary, and would if he didn't give me a good bill in place of the counterfeit. The fellow was scared and took the bad money back and gave me another bill which the Colonel looked at and said was good. He gave the man the bad one and told him the best thing he could do was to burn it up, for if it was ever traced to him again he would go up for the penitentiary sure.

I thanked the Colonel very much for his trouble in helping me, and went back to the store and paid for the shawl, and the clerk gave me a hood which he said the Colonel had bought as a present to go with the shawl. I asked him if the Colonel didn't own the store, and he said no, that he was a lawyer.

Then I went to another store and bought a nice pipe for Uncle, and one for Parson Theglin, for both of theirs was old and broken, and some tobacco to go with the pipes. Then I bought a good, strong pocket knife with three blades for Nasho. When I got back to the store I found Nasho and Mr. Penseler there. Mr. Penseler took us to a restaurant and we had a good dinner. He wanted us to stay and see more of the city, but we told him we wanted to get home. I thanked him again for being so kind to us, and as we were leaving he asked, "Have you sold your skins, Charley?"

"No, sir."

"They have the heads and feet on, haven't they?"

"The bear has. We skinned the head and left the claws on the skin of the feet."

"Well, don't sell that, but get the skins of every kind of animal you can, taking care to skin them as nicely as you can, and dress them well and take them to the Centennial with you. You can put them in the wagon, and you will get a great deal more for them there than you can here."

He told us where to leave our deer skins to be sold by the time somebody from Kerrville should come down, and then we left him. We got our wagons, gave Bose some dinner and started home. Uncle was very much pleased when I told him all about our trip, and was very proud of his pipe, and so was Auntie of her shawl and hood. Nasho had bought a fine knife for me, and some pencils and paints and a pretty box for Miss Masover. It made me feel very much ashamed to think I had forgotten her when she had been so kind to me, and the first time Parson Theglin went to San Antonio I got him to buy a real pretty book I had heard her say she would like to have. Nasho brought Auntie a pair of fine chickens, and Uncle a pair of Berkshire pigs.

A Bear, A Horse Thief & A Job

New Year's day of 1876, me and Nasho went out to hunt up a yoke of oxen for Uncle. I was riding Bullet, and he his pony. We were going up Big Gulch, and on turning one of its elbows we saw a big black bear in front of us. We knew it was the big bear that had been seen several times, but nobody could kill. He always whipped off the dogs and got away before the men could come up. "Oh, Nasho!" I said. "Let's go home and get the guns and come back and kill him."

"No, no good; when we come back he gone and no can find him. Maybe so he get in hole in rock, no can get him out."

He was walking about quietly turning over big rocks to get the worms and frogs and things of that kind that live under them, and did not see us. We drew back around the elbow again so he wouldn't see us, and I asked Nasho what we must do. He didn't say anything but seemed to be thinking about it.

"I'll stay here and watch him, and you go home and get the guns and dogs and come back and we'll kill him."

"No. No good. Sun gettin' hot; he go in hole pretty soon and no can get him out. Tink we rope him."

"Our horses can't hold him, and he'll catch us."

"One horse no can hold him; bof' can. Tree yonder; get him dere and tie him fast and he choke heself."

I didn't like the job. I was afraid he was too strong for our horses, and would jerk them down and hurt them, and maybe so catch us. It was a bad place to rope in too, for the Gulch wasn't more than fifty yards wide there, and there were a good many big rocks in it, and the sides were steep and rocky. But I was willing to try. We girted our saddles tight, and fixed our ropes.

"Carley, we bof' run at him togedder, you on one side, me on oder, and bof' rope him same time. Keep you rein tight and look he no catch you."

He didn't see us until we got in fifty yards, and then only raised his head and looked at us. We kept riding on, but instead of running, he started towards us. Nasho stopped. I thought he was afraid. I was too, but I wouldn't stop. I spurred my horse into a quick gallop, and as I turned to pass by him threw my rope, but my horse was afraid of him and shied so I missed him. The bear whirled and ran after me. Nasho wasn't afraid, but had been waiting for this and ran up behind and threw his rope over the bear's head. He checked his rein and his horse set himself to meet it. The bear was so heavy he jerked him to his knees, but the check pulled the bear over head over heels. He got up and ran for Nasho. Nasho whirled his horse and ran. I came up behind and roped him and jerked him back, but he was going so fast he pulled Bullet down on his nose. He was scared though, and was up in a second. Just as the bear got up and started to me, Nasho had whirled and pulled him back.

We had him now between us. He pulled and reared on his hind legs and caught the ropes between his paws and bit at them and growled terribly. We kept pulling apart, and now and then, as either of us got a chance, jerking down. This would make him terribly mad. Directly he stood on his hind feet and, catching my rope in both his paws, commenced walking towards me. Nasho made his horse pull as hard as he could, but he couldn't hold him back. I spurred my horse to make him jerk loose, but the bear held too tight. He came along the rope like a man pulling overhand.

"Carley, Carley, ride little closer. Me jerk him down."

I saw Nasho riding towards him, so as to get a start, and then he turned and ran his horse against the rope. I spurred my horse up a little so as to slack my rope, and he jerked the bear down, but he didn't turn loose and was up again in a second and coming to me the same way. Nasho jumped off his horse, picked up as big a rock as he could manage, got on him again, and running up to the bear threw the rock on his head. He just shook it a little but didn't stop. He was getting pretty close to me, and my horse was terribly afraid. He pulled back till he set down on his haunches and snorted, but he couldn't budge the bear.

Nasho ran his horse almost at full speed by the bear and past me, and jerked the bear a summersault. He tumbled almost under my horse's nose. I whirled Bullet, and ran and jerked the rope out of his paws, but he was up again in a second and coming after me. We ran towards the tree, but he was so close to us we couldn't ride around it and get a hitch as we wanted to. Nasho turned his horse to one side and with a quick jerk pulled the bear down. By the time he was up I had my rope tight on the other side. He grabbed Nasho's rope and began pulling up to him as he had to me.

There was a big rock between me and the bear. I rode up to it, jumped down and wrapped my rope around it so it would hold. He didn't go but two or three steps before it stopped him. He pulled his best and snarled and bit at the rope, but he couldn't pull the rock. Then he whirled and ran towards me. I got out of the way. I expected he would break the rope, but it held and jerked him over. He ran back to the rock, and catching it with his paws, turned it over, tearing it out of the ground, but the rope didn't come loose. We both turned towards the tree and he followed us, foaming and panting like a dog, for it was all he could do to drag the rock. When we got to the tree Nasho rode around it quick and then kept on, and when the bear got to it, he stopped his horse and made him pull hard. This caught the bear close up to the tree. He pulled his best, but the turn round the tree made it a heap easier for the horse to hold, and he held him. This made the bear furious, and he jerked and reared on his hind feet and bit at the rope and snarled more than ever, but Nasho watched his chance, and when ever he could, tightened his rope a little more, until he got the bear's head close up against the tree.

"Carley, hold my rope tight; no let him loose any."

I rode up and caught his rope, wrapped it quick around the horn of my saddle, and pulled my horse back. The bear got his head away from the tree a little, but I watched my chance and jerked him back again. Nasho jumped off his horse and ran to the bear, keeping behind him so as to keep out of his sight. He pulled out his butcher knife and, when he got close enough, grabbed the bear by the hair with his left hand and with the right stabbed him as hard as he could. The bear could only get his head and shoulders round, but Nasho had to jump back to keep him from catching him with his paws. He pulled terribly, but Bullet held him. I began to ride around the tree, keeping my rope tight and in this way wrapped his body close to the tree, so he couldn't turn. Nasho ran up on the other side and, reaching round the tree, sawed away on him until he cut his throat. The blood spurted out in a stream.

I kept him tight against the tree until his head fell and his paws dropped, and I knew then he was safe, and unwrapped my rope and threw it down, and the bear slowly sunk to the ground. We set to work and skinned him, being very careful to skin his paws so as to leave the claws on, and not cutting the head off at all. While we were skinning him the oxen came in sight. As soon as we were done, Nasho drove the oxen home, and I staid to watch the meat until he and Uncle came back with the wagon to take it home. Everybody said Nasho was a very brave boy, to run up and stab the bear as he did, for if had got loose it would have caught him, and it would have been all up with him then.

We were very careful in dressing the bear skin because it was a very large one, and had fine black fur, and the hide wasn't full of holes or cuts.

You ask, "How do you dress skins, Charley?"

Well, first stretch the skin tight on the ground by running a rail or pole under the middle, and cutting little slits in the edges and putting pegs through them which you drive tight into the ground, pulling them outward so as to stretch the skin as tight as you can, or you can hang it over the fence and fasten a rail or heavy stick to each side, though this don't stretch it even, or nail it against a door; but the first way is the best. You leave the flesh side up, and scrape, and rub, and pick at it until you get all the flesh and fat off. Then you take the brains and spread over it and rub them into it. This makes it soft. You keep it in a shady place where it won't harden, and every day rub and work it with a sharp bone edge, or an old dull drawing knife, until you have worked nearly half of the thickness off. It will help a great deal to put some of the brains in water and let them steep, and every day take the hide up and moisten it in brain water, and then rub and work it dry.

The best way to rub it is to put it over a smooth cottonwood log with two legs in one end, so as to raise it about a foot and a half from the ground. This keeps it smooth and makes it easier to work, and you ain't so apt to cut it. You can put a little alum and saltpetre on it and work it in to keep the bugs off. If you don't mind it being yellow after you have got it perfectly soft and pliant, you can smoke it over a very slow fire. This makes it more waterproof and keeps it from getting hard if it should get wet. It is a heap easier to dress skins without the hair, because you can work from both sides.

Little skins, like coon, and squirrel, and polecat don't need near so much work. A bearskin is one of the hardest of all, because it is so thick and heavy, and you have to be careful not to hurt the fur. We left the head on that one, but took out the tongue and all the meat to keep it from spoiling. We dressed some very nice skins of coons, and squirrels and polecats, and one more deerskin which I killed one night in the bottom when we were coon hunting.

We had money enough now to buy the horses we wanted, and Auntie had our clothes made. She made each of us a nice suit of buckskin, with fringe down the legs, and the jackets embroidered. Nasho's pants had big buttons all down the legs, and was open at the bottom, and he had a red silk sash he had bought at San Antonio to go round his waist. Each of us had a coonskin cap, with the tail on to hang down behind.

One night when we came home from school we found Col. Hunt was at Uncle's and going to stay all night. He was driving a span of fine gray horses. He is one of the biggest stock owners in Texas. We took the horses out and watered and fed them. After supper Uncle introduced us to Col. Hunt, and said he was buying cattle to drive to Kansas. I asked Col. Hunt if he wouldn't hire us; both of us wanted to go to Kansas. He said we was too young, that it was too hard a trip and he never liked to see boys go there. They always saw so much that was bad, and wanted to act like men, and spent all they made and came back worse than they went. We told him then what we wanted to go for. He said that was a different case, and that he would like to help us, and he would see about it. He asked if we knew how to drive cattle, and I told him we had driven a good deal for boys.

"Tell the Colonel about catching your horse, Charley," Uncle said, and I told him all about it. He said he thought boys that could do that would do to drive cattle. He asked me if we had horses, and I told him we had one apiece and money to buy two more apiece. He said that would be enough. Then he told us it would be a long, hard trip, that it would take two months to go through, and he was going to start by the tenth of February, and the nights would be cold, and we might look for a good deal of wet weather, and asked as if we thought we could stand being on guard two or three hours every night, and maybe all night when it rained and stormed. I told him I knew it would be very hard, but I thought we could stand it, and would do our best to make good hands.

Next morning when we went to the lot to feed, we found the old muley steer had jumped over the fence at a low place and broken it down, and Col. Hunt's horses were gone. We told Uncle and asked him to let us go after them. He said we might, and Auntie hurried up and gave us some breakfast while our horses were eating. Col. Hunt said his horses were raised on the Nueces, and would be most likely to go that way. He would have gone with us, but there wasn't any horse up but ours, and Uncle told him we would be pretty sure to find them.

By good luck one of them had a short rope about fifteen feet long on, with a hard knot in the end. They were both shod all round and their tracks were the same size. They had started off right down the road, but after a while had stopped to feed a little as they went. We knew that they would be apt to travel pretty steady because they were going home, and followed the trail as fast as we could. It was no trouble in the road, because where it was too hard for their feet to show much, the rope end made a plain trail. When we had gone about ten miles they left the road, and the trail was hard to follow. Sometimes we would lose it altogether, but we would ride on in the direction it was going and strike it again where there wasn't so much grass and the ground was softer.

We found there was another track on top of theirs, and we knew from its looks it was made by a horse with a man on him. We was afraid then that somebody was trying to steal the horses and hurried on. About twelve o'clock we found the tracks went into a pen. When they came out again we knew from their looks that the man had caught them and was leading them. The track led through the woods a while and then it took an old dim road and kept straight ahead.

It was about two o'clock before we came in sight of them. It was a negro was leading them. I told Nasho if he wouldn't give them up when we told him we were after them and wanted them, and if he started to run, we must rope him and jerk him off his horse, and I would catch the horses and run with them. The negro was riding a pretty good horse, but I knew he couldn't catch me on Milco—there wasn't a horse in Kerr County could do that. Nasho said all right, he would rope him, and fixed his rope, but let it hang by the saddle so it wouldn't be noticed.

We rode up to him and asked him what he was going to do with those horses. He said it was none of our business. I told him the horses belonged to Col. Hunt, and had got out of the pen last night and we were after them. He said Col. Hunt never had seen them horses, that he had bought them in Northern Texas and was taking them to his home on Old Caney. I told him I knew the horses, and that they were Col. Hunt's, and I wanted them. He said with an oath he would like to see me get them. I rode up and reached out my hand as if I was going to take the rope he was leading them by, when he pulled out a pistol and said, "Look here, white boy, you get killed fust thing you know, where nobody'll ever find you. If you know what's good for you, you leave here mighty quick."

He began to cock his pistol, but just then Nasho's rope fell over him, and before he could do anything he was jerked out of his saddle. His pistol went off and the fall made him drop it. I hollered to Nasho not to let him get up, and he kept pulling him along on the ground, and I jumped down and grabbed his pistol. Then I took after the horses which had been scared by the noise of the pistol, and ran ahead. I caught up with them directly and, reaching over from my saddle, got hold of the rope they were tied with. They were tied together so I could manage them easily. I turned back and rode up to Nasho. He still had the negro down, and wouldn't let him get him up, for every time he tried he would jerk him down again. He got a terrible hard fall when Nasho jerked him out of the saddle, and it seemed to have stunned him a good deal. I told Nasho to let him get up, and handed him the pistol, as I had my hands full with the horses, but not to shoot him. Then I told the negro to take the rope off, and he did it.

We started off and left him sitting in the road. His horse had run way ahead and was still going nearly out of sight. We hadn't got fifty yards before we heard a pistol go off, and the bullet come whizzing by our heads. We both ran. He fired five times more, but we were out of reach directly, and none of the bullets hit us.

After the fifth shot we both reined up, and Nasho said, "Me go back and kill him now. He no got any more shoot."

I told him he mustn't, we had the horses and that was all we wanted.

"He try kill us. It right now for we to kill him."

I told him that he musn't; if he did Uncle wouldn't let him stay with us any more, and he would be hung for it too.

He said, "Injin no do dat way. Man try to kill Injin, Injin kill him when he get chance."

I told Nasho to keep on, and rode back and told the negro I would leave his pistol at Mr. Ochse's store at Kerrville, and he could get it by going there. He only cursed me, and I rode back to Nasho. It was in the night before we got back to Uncle's. Col. Hunt was very glad to get his horses again. He had been uneasy about them all day for fear somebody had stolen them and we wouldn't be able to get them. He wanted to give us fifty dollars for catching them, but we wouldn't take it, because he was staying with Uncle and the horses had got out of his pen. He said we were the bravest boys he had ever seen, that very few men would have tried to take them away from an armed negro if they had no arms, and it was a very fortunate thing that one of us didn't get shot. He said if he had been along without any pistol he would have just followed the negro until he met somebody, or came to a house where he could get a gun, and then taken them away.

"But Mr. Hunt, when he saw you was following him he could have left the road and not gone by any house or settlement."

"Well then, I would have left the trail and gone for a weapon or assistance and come back and followed him up."

"Yes, sir. But he might have suspected what you had gone for, and left his horse and saddled one of yours and led the other, and by going into the mountains on a rocky ridge it would have been very hard to have followed the trail, and he might have gotten away altogether."

"There is a good deal in that, Charley. If it was to do over again and I knew the risk I would not let you go, but as it is I am thankful to you and your brave comrade for getting my horses back. They are great pets of mine and never tried to leave me before, the rascals. You ought to let me pay you for your trouble and labor."

"Oh, no sir, we don't want anything. We are glad to have gotten them for you."

"Well, my boys, you may count on driving to Kansas for me if you want to. I don't want you to go now because it is too early and cold, and the trip will be a great deal harder for you. I will have other herds going later when the weather will be more pleasant, the grass will have come out, and the country you travel over will be much prettier. You come down to my Casa de Bueyes ranch by the middle of March at the farthest. I will pay you full men's wages from the time you leave home until you leave me in Kansas, and the regular half-rate wages to come back on, and send you with one of my best bosses, who will treat you well. If you can buy horses cheap here, buy them, and if you can't I will sell you good ponies at a reasonable price. If you buy your own horses get them in good fix before you start, for its hard work on them. And you must remember you will have a hard trip. We never take any extra hands, and every man has to do a full hand's work."

I told him we were very much obliged to him, and felt
sure the boss couldn't have any reason to complain of
us.

The next morning early Col. Hunt left, but before
going he told us if we were at Casa de Bueyes by the fifteenth of March we would see him there, and if we got
there later he would leave instructions with his manager
about us. He thanked us again for getting his horses
back for him and then drove off.

Buying Horses on Credit

I reckon you think we are never going to get off, but we are most ready to start now. It seems to me it very often takes longer to get ready to do anything than to do it. When Mr. Braston was going to build his gin and press, he was in the bottom every day for weeks walking all through it backward and forward picking out the best trees for his timbers. Then it took a long time to cut them down, haul them up with the big log wagon, and hew them down right. But when he had got his timbers and boards and irons all on the ground, and the holes dug, it didn't take but a few days to put them up.

You see, it took us a long time to get ready because we had to make all the money to buy our horses. And I wanted to tell you everything that had been interesting to me, and some of the things I have told you about—gathering the pecans, and Uncle's killing the panther, and catching Wild Bill, and getting back Col. Hunt's horses—were as interesting to me as many things that happened on our trip.

After Col. Hunt left, Uncle wanted us to keep on going to school until we were ready to start, but we told him as we were going away to be gone so long, he ought to let us help him all we could in getting in the crop before we went, and at last he said we might. When we took our books to carry home, Miss Masover told me I must read at night, and rainy days and odd times when I could, and learn as much as I could before going, and said she would keep me in books. I told her I would. I do like to read books that tell me things I want to know. Before I thought about going to the Centennial I didn't care so much, because it seemed to me a long time before I would be a man and have to use what I was learning; but that talk with Parson Theglin showed me that I was getting to be a man all the time, and I saw that the more I learned before going the better I would understand what I saw, and the more I could learn there. I wanted to know as much as I could about the countries and the people that would have something to show there, and I had to study geography and history to learn those things. I wanted to write letters to Uncle and Auntie while I was gone, and I tried to do my best to write plain so they could read them without any trouble, and I wanted to spell my words right, and had to study spelling a great deal to learn them.

I know people used arithmetic in almost every kind of business, and though I didn't expect to ever be a merchant, I wanted to be a good businessman as far as any business of mine might go, so I studied arithmetic a great deal. If Uncle wanted to lay off so many acres, or a half or quarter acre, I could do it for him. I could tell how much corn or wheat the wagon bed or the crib would hold, how big 'round and deep he must dig the new cistern to hold a hundred barrels of water, how much seed it would take to sow three acres in wheat, how much his corn and cotton seed ought to bring him, and how much he would need to buy his groceries, and cloth and other things.

I found by reading at nights and when the weather was too wet to work, and sometimes when we would come up too early for dinner, though it wasn't but a little bit at a time, I could learn a great deal in time, and I knew I wouldn't have any chance after we started.

There was a good deal to do about the place. The fence needed a little mending, and the field had to be cleared of corn and cotton stalks, and there was three acres that had been belted, and the logs had to be rolled together and burnt. Me and Nasho did a heap of that work. We couldn't lift much, but a book that Miss Masover had given me showed me how to rig pulleys and levers of all sorts so that we could make the oxen do the lifting and pulling. Uncle said we could do as much work as 'most any two men. Then the ground had to be plowed and harrowed. And all the time the cattle had to be looked after more or less, and the hogs killed and the meat salted down.

Soon after Col. Hunt left, we went down to San Antonio again with Uncle to get some things he wanted, and we found a drove of ponies there for sale. Bullet was a work horse, and I didn't want to take him away because I knew Uncle would need him, so I bought two, a brown and a bay. Nasho bought a gray and a sorrel. They were all good, stout, chunky ponies, and in pretty good fix. Whenever you see a horse so short between his last rib and his hip joint that you can't more than lay your hand broadways in the hollow there, you may know he can stand a heap of hard work. He is not apt to be a good riding horse, or to run very fast, but he'll have bottom sure. I called my brown horse Bob and my bay Monkey, because he was such a queer looking little fellow, and so fond of playing with the other horses. Nasho don't name any of his horses.

We didn't have money to pay for our stock, because we wasn't expecting to buy when we left home, and hadn't brought it with us. Uncle said he would try and arrange to get it for us, and went off to see about it. While he was gone the gentleman who had helped me about the counterfeit money came to the pen. I went up and spoke to him and he seemed glad to see me. He said he had come down to buy a pony for his little boy, and asked me to pick him out one that I thought was gentle and a good riding pony. I looked among the horses very carefully, for I wanted one that would suit him when we was gone, and at last I found a very pretty little chestnut sorrel that I was certain from the looks of his head and eyes was gentle, and I knew from his make ought to be a good riding pony. His mouth and head showed he was young too, so I told the man who had the horses I wanted to ride him to try him. I got him in a corner and caught him without roping, and got on him bareback and rode him up to the gentleman. I wanted him to see that I was so sure he was gentle I was willing to risk him myself. He turned to Nasho and asked him what he thought of the pony.

"He good one. Carley pick right. Give him plenty eat."

I rode him about and found he had a good *sobre paso* walk, and a quick, easy gallop. When I came back with him I told the gentleman he was gentle and a good riding horse, and I thought he would suit him. He couldn't stand as much as some of the others, but he would have plenty to eat and not much to do, and would keep fat. He thanked me for picking him out, and I showed him the horses me and Nasho had bought. He asked me why I didn't take them out of the herd, and I told him Uncle had gone to try and get the money to pay for them; that we had the money at home, but hadn't brought it with us. He asked me when I would be in San Antonio again and I told him early in March.

"Well," he said, "Charley, I'll loan you the money to pay for them if you will give me your note for it to be paid by the fifteenth day of March."

"I am very much obliged to you, sir, indeed, and I'll be sure to pay you by that time, because I have got the money at home. But I don't want but two of the horses. Nasho wants the other two."

"Yes, but I don't know anything about Nasho, and can't lend him the money."

"But he has as much money as I have."

"Yes, but maybe he will not want to pay me!"

"Oh, yes, sir, he will. I'm sure of that."

"Will you go his security?"

"You mean, sir, that I will agree to pay it if he don't?"

"Yes, that is it exactly."

"Yes, sir, I'll do that, for I know he has the money and I'm sure he'll pay it."

"Very well, I will pay for the horses."

He paid the man for them.

"Now come up to my office and we will fix the note."

We left the horses tied, and went with him. He sat down and wrote two notes. I remember them perfectly well because it was the first time I had ever promised to pay money that way, and I couldn't help but be a little afraid I might lose my money and not be able to pay him when it was due. They were in these words:

SAN ANTONIO, TEXAS, FEBY. 8, 1876

I promise to pay to C. H. Vandervere or order sixty-five ($65) dollars on the fifteenth day of March, 1876, money borrowed.

CHARLES ZANCO.

SAN ANTONIO, TEXAS, FEBY. 8, 1876

I promise to pay to C. H. Vandervere or order fifty-five ($55) dollars on the fifteenth day of March, 1876, money borrowed.

YGNACIO DE GARAPITAS.

My horses were the best and cost the most. Then Col. Vandervere—I knew that was his name from the note—said, "Now Charley, how are you going to make yourself security for your friend? You know I am trusting you and not him. I couldn't collect the money from either of you because you are only boys, and boys can't give notes that can be collected by law if they won't pay them."

I thought a moment, and then took the pen and wrote under Nasho's note:

> If Nasho don't pay the money, I will.
>
> CHARLEY ZANCO.

"But, Charley, this note is signed Ygnacio de Garapitas, and you say if *Nasho* don't, etc. Nobody knows who Nasho is."

"Oh yes, sir, I see. I ought to have written his full name."

"Is there anything else wanting?"

"I don't see anything else, sir."

"Ygnacio de Garapitas says he will pay this money on the fifteenth day of March, 1876, but you do not say when you will pay it if he fails."

"Yes, sir, I see now. I ought to have said on the fifteenth day of March, 1876."

"Yes, that is right. But we call the day a note is due its maturity, and instead of saying the fifteenth day of March again, we say at maturity. Do you understand?"

"Yes, sir."

"Well, we have spoiled this note. What must we do about it."

"Tear it up, sir, and make another."

"Why tear it up?"

"Because, sir, if we didn't I would be promising to pay you one hundred and thirty dollars instead of sixty-five."

"Exactly. Learn to do things right, Charley. If people would always be careful and know first exactly what they meant in dealing with each other, and second, put everything down on paper exactly as they meant, there would not be much work for the lawyers. My word for it, Charley, the way to win lawsuits is never to have one."

"I don't see how I could win a lawsuit if I never had one."

"What is it you win by a lawsuit?"

"The money or other thing we go to law about."

"Well, now if you make your agreement in the beginning so plain that there can be no misunderstanding it, don't you see that the other party will not be likely to go to law about it?"

"Yes, sir, because he would be sure to lose."

"Yes, and not only have to pay you but the costs of going to law, and probably his lawyer. Now if you prevent a lawsuit by making everything too plain to go to law about, you get your money or property, and that is all you could do by a suit."

"Yes, sir, I see now. I don't win the suit because there won't be any, but I get all that I could get by a suit, without it."

"And save much time, trouble and expense. Now sit here, Charley, and write another note and make yourself security."

I sat down and wrote:

SAN ANTONIO, TEXAS, FEBY. 8, 1876

I promise to pay to C. H. Vandervere or order fifty-five ($55) dollars on the fifteenth day of March, 1876, money borrowed.

YGNACIO DE GARAPITAS.

If Ygnacio de Garapitas don't pay this note at maturity, I will.

CHARLES ZANCO.

"That's right, Charley. I must get to work now. Remember what I have told you, and whenever you come to San Antonio come and see me."

He handed me the first note and I put it in the stove where there was a little fire, and burnt it up. Then we told Col. Vandervere goodbye and went back to the horse pen. Uncle was there. He said he had not got the money but he would go to his merchant and get it from him. I told him about the note. He said I ought to have asked him about it first, for I might have got cheated. I told him I would not have given the note if I had not known Col. Vandervere, but I was certain he was honest and would not cheat me.

That evening we started home and got back all right with our horses.

Becoming Cowboys

On the first day of March we were ready to start. The field was all cleared and planted, and the corn had been hoed out the first time. Our horses were in good fix, for we had fed them a good deal of corn and they had had very little to do. We had put new rigging on our saddles wherever it was needed, made hobbles for our horses, and had two good stake ropes, thirty-five feet long, and a good picket-pin—a piece of iron about eighteen inches long, sharp at one end so it could easily be driven into the ground, and a head at the other with a ring and swivel. Picket-pins are a great help on the prairie, because often you can't find a bush to tie to, and then you can pick a clear place, if there are bushes, so that your horse won't tangle up. We had two short ropes to neck our loose horses with, so that it would be easier to lead or drive them.

Our saddle blankets were made of moss. It is the best thing I have ever seen for a saddle blanket because it is soft, and thick, and cool, and don't scald a horse's back. Sometimes a wool blanket in very hot weather will scald a horse's back so that it gets sore, and it is very hard to cure it, if you have to ride him. A saddle blanket ought to be washed every month in summer to get the sweat and dirt out, because they make it hard and stiff and it rubs the horse's back. If a man has a good saddle that fits his horse well, and don't pinch or rub him, and keeps a good, clean, thick blanket, and when he gets off his horse to stop, if it is very hot, will after unsaddling him rub his back dry with his blanket, his horse will not get a sore back. If it gets rubbed a little and he will keep it well greased, it will get well in a very few days. Axle grease is a good thing to put on a sore back. If his back gets rubbed badly he must cut a hole in his blanket so that neither it or the saddle can touch the sore place, and then by keeping it well greased it will soon get well. He must never let his horse lie down in the sand or gravel, when he is hot and wet with sweat, as it is almost certain to make his back sore. It is a great deal easier to keep a horse from getting a sore back than to cure it after it comes.

We had wallets to put our clothes in, but we didn't take many with us. One change of underclothes, two extra pair of socks, and an extra shirt apiece, were all we wanted. We wore flannel overshirts. They are warm early in the morning when it is cool and damp, and in the middle of the day they keep the hot sun off better than cotton, and the sleeves are not in the way like coat sleeves. We had leggins made of duck, doubled and boiled in oil, with a leather belt at the top to fasten round the waist, and bound with leather at the bottom to keep from wearing out against the stirrups. Boiling in oil makes the duck waterproof. We had blue soldier overcoats to put on herding at night if it was cold, or when it rained.

Then we had a piece of oil cloth about six feet long and five wide to spread down on the ground at night to keep the damp out, and a rubber blanket to put over us to keep the rain overhead off. We never needed the last much going, because whenever it rained we had to be up with the cattle. Then we had two other blankets apiece, so we were well off for bedclothes. In cow hunting we hardly ever took but one blanket apiece, because we didn't want to load our horses so heavily, and we

could sleep on our saddle blankets, but on the drive
you have to keep a horse saddled all the time, so you
can jump on him in a minute if the cattle run. Then we
had a little bag apiece made of waterproof stuff to carry
provisions in, and a little coffee pot, and a cup apiece.

The night before we were ready to start Uncle talked
to me about our trip. He told me it was a long trip for a
boy of my age, to be left to myself with no one to go to
ask what he should do in many cases, such as he had
never been placed in before.

"Auntie and I," he said, "Charley, have tried to teach
you what was right, and what is right here will be right
in St. Louis or in Philadelphia. If you will follow that I
have no fear but that you will find friends to help you
wherever you may go. Here is one rule I want you to
particularly remember, my dear boy: 'Do unto others as
you would have others do unto you.' Follow that, and
it will not only tell you what to do but will make you
friends in doing so. Never allow yourself to do anything
that you think may be ever so little wrong—you know
how soon a wide gap is made in a fence when the first
rail is thrown down. You must write to us, Charley, when
you get through with the cattle, and after you get to
Philadelphia. I have done very little in the way of letter-
writing, but I will let you know how things are going on
at the old place, and if you get sick or anything happens
to you, be sure and let me know, and Auntie and I will
find some way to help you."

Early the next morning we saddled our horses, packed
our blankets, wallets and camp tricks on one of our led
horses, and tied the other two together. When Auntie
came to tell me goodbye I couldn't help but cry a little,
because I felt so sorry for her; she seemed to feel so
badly at my going away. I didn't seem to mind it much
on my account; it was for her I felt so bad. She has been

just the best Auntie in the world to me. After I got in the saddle Uncle shook hands with me and whispered, "Remember Uncle's last advice. Do unto others as you would have others do unto you."

Nasho went first, leading the packhorse, then came the two necked horses and Monkey by himself, for though he was so playful and full of tricks, he never tried to run away, and I came behind on Comanche to drive the loose horses. We had tied up the dogs to keep them from following us. When we got to the bend of the road I turned for one more look at the old place, and saw Auntie still standing where I had left her, wiping her eyes with her apron. I couldn't help it. I just galloped back, and jumped down and kissed her until she stopped crying and then I got on Comanche in a hurry and just gave him the reins until I caught up with Nasho.

That evening, about sundown, we stopped at a house and bought some fodder for our horses, for there was hardly any grass, and then found a good place and camped. We had brought corn enough with us for two feeds. The next morning we were off by sunup and got to San Antonio by dinner time, but we didn't stop there long. I went to Col. Vandervere's office and paid him the money me and Nasho owed him and got our notes. He said the horse I had picked suited his little boy exactly, that he was as gentle as a dog and rode easy.

After we left San Antonio the country was all prairie, and the nearer to the coast we got the smoother and flatter it was. Some of the grass was coarse and rough, and not much account, but a good deal of it was green and short, and fine, called the mesquite grass. This is the best grass in Texas for horses, and very good for cattle too. You see cattle haven't got any upper teeth, and can't bite short grass like horses. Horses will get fat on mesquite grass in winter because it comes up fresh and green when all the other grass is dry and dead.

It took as five days to get to Casa de Bueyes. We camped out every night. We had bought a six-shooter between us at San Antonio, but we didn't see any game on the way to shoot except mule-eared rabbits, and we didn't care anything about them. We got to the ranch late one evening just as the hands were coming in from the day's work. They had been road-branding a herd that was making up to start to Kansas. There were a good many Mexicans with baggy leather breeches and great broad brimmed hats and red sashes round their waists. Nearly all the men wore leather leggins and broad hats to keep the sun out of their faces, and flannel overshirts and big handkerchiefs tied loose round their necks. Sometimes we would have a pair of leggins, *calzoneros*, they call them, of leopard skin, open at the bottom to show his big red or yellow boot tops turned down, and rows of buttons down the outside seam, and silver plates a good deal bigger than a dollar over the outside buttons of his spurs. Some came up afoot carrying their saddles on their backs with the girths and straps dragging, and others would ride up and unsaddle and throw their saddles down on the gallery around the house.

Col. Hunt was then on his horse, and rode up and shook hands with us and asked us about Uncle and Auntie. Then he called one of his bosses and told who we were and to take care of us. He said he would see us again tomorrow, and then he rode off on a gallop. He was riding a fine black horse as fat and sleek as a racer. Several of the men had come up round us and was talking about Comanche. They said he was one of the finest horses they had ever seen. One of them asked me where I got him, and I told him me and Nasho had roped him.

"Where, little one?" asked another one that had on calzoneros. I was going to tell him, but Mr. Kennedy said "wait till supper boys, I expect these young ones are tired. They have come from Kerrville, seventy-five miles above San Antonio, and are going to drive for the Colonel. Let them put up and get supper and then gas them as much as you like, only be easy with them. Capt. Dick, will you show them the ropes?"

"All right, Captain. I'll see to 'em."

Capt. Dick was the one with the "leopard skin" calzoneros. He was pretty tall and slender, with blue eyes and light hair and beard. He had a fancy worked overshirt and a buckskin jacket with flowers embroidered on the back. He told us to unsaddle and turn our horses loose with the rest, and one of the boys would drive them to the pasture. We was in a big pasture then, but there were smaller pastures kept for the horses that were used every day. I asked him if I couldn't get some corn for Comanche, and told him I was willing to pay for it. He showed me where to feed him, I took him to the stable and fed him, and then curried and brushed him. I always do this every night unless it is raining, and it does him nearly as much good as feeding him, and helps to keep him fat and sleek and supple. Then we went to the house and had supper. After supper most of them lit their pipes or made cigarettes. Some strolled out in the yard and some of them cleared off one end of the table and began playing cards.

Capt. Dick got a buffalo robe and, spreading it on the floor of the gallery, threw himself down on it and called me to come and tell him how I caught my horse. When I was telling him about his jumping into the Colorado with me he asked me how I felt when I was going over. I told him I was too busy thinking how I was going to feel when we went under and whether we would come up again or not. "I reckon you felt all over in spots," one of them said. Several had come up to us to hear my story.

"And the spots were as big as saddle blankets."

"Buffalo's you'd better say, with the hair in, and every hair sticking like a porcupine's feathers."

When I got through one of them said, "And the little greaser stuck to you and hunted you up?" I told them then something about Nasho, and asked them not to call him a greaser, for he didn't have any father or mother, or home of his own but Uncle's, and he was a real good boy, and would make a good hand.

"No boys," Capt. Dick said, "these boys ain't fair game. You all know I am as ready to take a joke as any of you, and I ain't going to ask for anything special for the little ones, but no imposition, remember. If anybody has anything against either of 'em, let him come to me and I'll make it good or give him satisfaction. Put that in your pipes and maybe it will save trouble."

He asked me then to take a walk with him to the stable, and on the way he told me that there were several bad hands that were always playing some trick on newcomers or anybody they could bully. They would slip a corncob, or cockle burs under a saddle blanket to make a horse pitch, or unfasten the girth and then ride up and strike the horse so he would lurch quick and jump from under the rider, or put powder in his pipe, and they had stampeded one man's horse.

He told me he was going as boss with a herd of beeves for Col. Hunt, and would start about the twentieth of April, and if I wanted to go with him he would get Col. Hunt to let him take us both. He said the beeves would need more watching at night, and would be apt to give more trouble about stampeding, but they wasn't really as hard to drive as mixed cattle. I told him I would be glad to go with him, and I thought he might count on me and Nasho making him good hands, for we had both driven cattle a good deal. When we went back to the house Capt. Dick gave us a bed in his room, and told us to keep our things in there while we stayed at the ranch. I was glad we were to have a room with him because I liked him better than any of the others I saw.

Cowboys are about the roughest people I have ever seen. They swear and use more dirty words, and they play so many mean tricks on each other. Because a man wears rough clothes and leads a rough life, don't seem to me to be any reason why he should curse and be dirty and mean. All cowboys ain't that way. Some of them are as quiet as anybody and as kind as they can be, always ready to lend a horse, or hunt for a lost horse, or to help another one about any work, and I have noticed that some of the quietest ones make the best hands. They don't say much about what they can do, or how many beeves they can rope or tie, but they are always ready to do anything that comes to hand.

HANDLING & ROAD-BRANDING BEEVES

The next day me and Nasho helped them finish road-branding. You see, when a man is going to drive cattle out of the county he has to put a road-brand on them, and have a bill of sale of every one he has, or he may be taken up for stealing them. Sometimes the road-brand is made of the initials of his name like R. S.; sometimes two letters will be put together like AL; sometimes it will be a figure like 6 or 70, or a churn-dasher, or a circle with a cross in it, or a hatchet. It is generally made of letters or figures, or something that won't cross lines, because where they cross they are apt to blotch and then it's hard to tell what the brand is and who the animal belongs to. They are not near as apt to blotch on grown cattle or horses or young calves, because the brand grows with their hides and spreads, and if there is any blotch it spreads too. A brand for horses is nearly always smaller than for cattle, because a big brand looks ugly on a horse. His hair is shorter and it shows a heap plainer than on cattle. Horses are 'most always branded on the left shoulder, and cattle on the left hip, but road-brands are put on the back above the ribs, or on the ribs.

You may be thinking, "I should think it would be a big job, Charley, to rope and throw down and brand a thousand beeves; it must take a long time."

They don't do it that way. They have a big pen that will hold five hundred or a thousand head, made high and strong so they can't jump over it or break it down, and in one corner they have a little narrow pen about twenty-five feet long and not more than five or six feet broad. This is made with posts and rails so that there won't be any corners, and is very high and strong. It is called a chute. It is fixed so where it opens into the big pen, it can be shut off from it by bars which are pulled out to one side when it is open. Several hands go into the pen and cut off ten or fifteen head and run them into the corner and then in the chute, and a man who stands outside ready, runs in the bars right quick and shuts it up. Other hands have the branding iron hot in little fires that they keep burning outside the pen and close to the chute, and the hands who are going to brand climb up on the sides of the chute and stick them to the cattle while they are hot. You see, the cattle crowd up so close together, and the chute is so narrow, that they can't get away, and just have to stand and take it. They can brand ten or fifteen head in this way in less than ten minutes, and if they have irons enough and keep them hot and ready they don't lose much time.

As soon as all in the chute are branded they draw the bars out and make them go back into the big pen the way they came in. This takes nearly as much time as branding them, because the pen is so narrow and they are so crowded they can hardly turn round, but as soon as one gets out the rest all try to follow him. If the cattle wasn't raised by the man who is going to brand them, but he has bought them, he and the man he buys from have somebody to take down the brands and marks while they are in the chute, and say what kind of cattle they are—beeves, cows, four, three or two year olds. If a brand ain't plain so they can see it well, they wet it, and that makes the hair lie down flat, and it is easier to make it out. In winter if an animal is poor and its hair is long sometimes, it looks so furry you can hardly see the brand. When they brand calves in the spring, if the iron is very hot and burns them, they often rub the place well with grease so it will cure up quick.

You may wonder: "So, Charley, suppose Mr. A. sells Mr. B. ten head of cattle, and Mr. B. don't want to drive them away, but just lets them stay in the range. Mr. B. puts his brand on them, don't he?"

"Yes, sir."

"Now suppose each of them has a thousand head of cattle, they can't recollect the particular looks of each one, and when they come to gather they find ten heads with the brands of both on them, how can their hands, who don't know anything about the trade, tell who they belong to?"

Why you see, the brands of Mr. B. would be the smallest and freshest, and would show it was put on last, and they were his cattle. But the right way is for Mr. A. to counterbrand the cattle when he sells them; that is, to put his brand on again. That shows they don't belong to him any longer. Then when Mr. B. puts his brand on it shows they belong to him.

"Then if Mr. A.'s brand is A and Mr. B.'s brand is B, and Mr. A. sells a beef to Mr. B., he would be branded this way: A. A. B."

Yes, sir, only all the brands may not be close together. The counterbrand ought to be close to the old brand, because that tells anybody that looks at the animal that he don't belong to the man who owns the first brand, and he will look then to see what other brand he has.

"But suppose two men have the same brand?"

That ain't allowed, sir. A man when he takes a brand and mark has to have it put down in a book of marks and brands at the courthouse, and that tells everybody that he has taken that brand for his cattle. If anybody else comes and takes the same brand, the man who took it first has a right to take all the cattle. These men have so many cattle they can't remember the flesh-marks, and it is very easy to cut the ear and change the mark, so the brand is the thing to go by.

"What do you mean by flesh-marks, Charley?"

The color and spots.

"All right, Charley, go ahead. I understand about the brands now."

We got through branding that day, and we was glad of it, for it was mean work. Running round the pen so much keeps the fine dust stirred up and it gets all over you and in your nose and eyes. Me and Nasho helped cut out and run into the chute some of the time, and the rest we heated irons and handed them to the men who staid on the chute to brand. Capt. Dick was busy on the chute all day taking down the marks and brands, for these were cattle Col. Hunt had bought. Col. Hunt was there too. Late in the evening when we got through he came to me and told me he was going to leave in a day or two and wouldn't see me any more until I got to Kansas. He asked me what kind of cattle I would rather drive, and I told him "beeves."

Then he said, "Suppose I send you with Capt. Dick next month?"

I told him I would like very much to go with him. He said I might then, and he wanted me to remember I was as much a hand as anybody else and not under anybody's orders but Capt. Dick's. When we were driving or herding or working with the cattle it would always be right for me to do as the older hands said, because they knew best, and there must be somebody to take charge, but no one had a right to order me or Nasho to do anything for them that wasn't any part of my duty as a hand. He said he had some rough, wild hands; that he couldn't be with them himself, and couldn't stop to ask questions about men when they wanted to hire, but that if anyone troubled me to let Capt. Dick know and he would see I was not imposed on. He said me and Nasho must be good boys and not get into trouble or learn what was bad from the bad men we might be with, and he would see us again when we got through to Kansas. I thanked him for his kindness, and he got on his horse and rode away on a gallop, for he didn't stay at the house where we did. He had just had a long talk with Capt. Dick before he came to me. All the men seem to like the Colonel, as they call him, when talking about him.

Capt. Dick told me that night that there wouldn't be anything for me and Nasho to do the next day, as he was going out west after cattle on the day after, and he had some chores to do about the ranch before he started. He said we had better take a rest day as we might have a hard trip gathering the cattle and would be gone three weeks at least, and as soon as we got back we would start to Kansas. I asked him if we mightn't go to the coast and take a look at the Gulf, for I never had seen it and I would like to now I was close to it. He said yes, that it was only about eight miles, and we could take the shotgun and maybe we might kill a goose or some ducks. He said there were plenty of deer, and panther, and turkeys, and cows, and wild hogs, and cattle, and some bear in the *busada*, but we had better not go there tomorrow. If we got time when we came back we would take a hunt before we started to Kansas.

"What is the *busada*, Charley?"

A big thicket miles long and wide so grown up with mesquite and chaparral and all kinds of thorny bushes that you can hardly get through it. Cattle and hogs get in it, and nobody can get to them, and they go wild and stay there and raise in it. There is plenty of grass and

young bushes and moss for them to live on, and water
to drink, and in winter it's one of the best shelters in the
country.

Adventure at the Gulf

The next morning me and Nasho started early, taking with us a double-barrel shotgun, loaded with buckshot, and plenty of buckshot and geeseshot. Capt. Dick shouted to me as we rode off, "Bring me a venison ham, Charley!"

"All right, Captain, I'll try."

I was riding Monkey, and the little rascal wouldn't keep still, but kept fretting and prancing about all the time. A cool norther was blowing, but as we had our backs to it, we didn't mind the cold.

We saw lots of geese and ducks, the geese flying about, or standing in bunches over the prairies where the grass was short, and in some places the prairie seemed almost spotted with the sandhill cranes, whose long necks stuck up through the weeds and tall grass where they were hunting their dinners. But neither the geese or the cranes would let us get close enough for a shot, and we didn't try very hard, because we thought we would have plenty of chances on our way back, and if we killed anything going we would have to carry it so much further. Wherever there was a pool of water, there was sure to be plenty of ducks, but ducks are as hard to creep up on as deer, and we didn't try much. We had several sloughs to cross, and one or two of them were boggy, but our horses were too smart to go in anywhere they couldn't get out. Sometimes we would have to go a good way round to find a place where we could cross.

About eleven o'clock we got to the sea. The first thing
I thought was how strange it was that so much water,
with no bank to hold it in, didn't run over. Nasho got off
his horse and knelt down and took a big mouthful, but
he spit it out pretty quick and sputtered, and wiped his
mouth and said, "Muy mala! Muy mala! Carley, what
for you no tell me water no good?"

I told him I wasn't thinking about his drinking it. I
thought he knew it was salt. Seems to me if I had never
read anything about the ocean I would have known
when I saw it that it wasn't fit to drink. I sat on my
horse a long time watching the water come tumbling in,
in long rolls, that would be smooth and even until they
got near the shore, and then rear up in a long line with
a white foamy top and fall all to pieces. I think I found
out what makes it do that way. It's because tho water
at the bottom strikes against the ground and can't go
on as fast as that on top, and so the top falls over the
bottom and breaks all to pieces.

Then I got down and walked along the shore looking
for shells, and found some pretty ones, though most
of them was large and white. It's curious that the star-
shaped ones should all be so near alike, and I'd like to
know where the fish stays—I couldn't see any place big
enough to hold him. The sea nettles look like lumps
of jelly or gristle floating in the water. I thought they
were some sort of vegetable that grew in the sea, but
Capt. Dick says they are live fish-like sponges, though
more like vegetables than fish, and that if anybody gets
against them in the water they can sting.

We picked up shells a while and then we stopped and
ate our dinner. We made a fire out of some sticks that
had been thrown up by the ocean sometime when the
water must have come up a great deal higher than it did
while we were there, and broiled our bacon. We hadn't

brought any coffee. After dinner, I walked up and down
along the water's edge for awhile and picked up a pocket full of the prettiest shells I could find. Nasho didn't
care anything about them, and stayed with the horses.

Sometimes there would be long heaps of sand as high
as a man's head back apiece from the water that seemed
to have been piled up by it when it was high, and then
the grass would come down almost to the water's edge.
Where there were level places that got covered by the
water nothing grew it was just bare sand. Wherever
there were any trees they all had their branches turned
to the north. Capt. Dick told me afterward it was because the south wind blew so much and strong that
they got turned that way while they were young and
tender.

I reckon it was nearly two o'clock when we started
back, going up a long narrow strip of water that seemed
to run from the sea back into the country. We didn't go
but a mile or so when we saw a bunch of deer on the
other side of a little hollow, and Nasho asked me to let
him take the gun and get a shot. I wanted to shoot them
myself, but I told him he might. He got off his horse and
bent down until he got into the hollow and I didn't see
any more of him until I saw the smoke and heard the
gun fire, both barrels, and saw two deer fall, one right
after the other. I hurried up as fast as I could with the
horses and found he had killed two. He had crawled up
in about fifteen steps of the bunch and made sure of
each shot. We just cut them open and washed them out,
and wiped them with grass, and put one on each of our
horses, and rode on up the bayou again.

It was getting cold with the wind in our faces all the
time. We went about a mile further and I saw two big
white birds a great deal bigger than geese swimming
about in a wide place in the bayou. We rode up as close

as we could and not scare them, and I got down and crept up in a few feet of the bank. They didn't see me, for I was behind some tall grass that grew along the edge, and kept swimming about just because it was so easy for them to swim I reckon. One lick with their big red feet would carry them a good way, and the least little turn of their feet would turn them round. Directly they came together and put their heads down right close together to something that was on the water, and I took good aim and fired. I was watching, ready to fire the other barrel if either go up, but they didn't, and I saw I had killed both.

Nasho came up with the horses, and we took the deer off and laid them on the ground. I loaded the barrel I had fired, and took out my knife to get the old cap off of the tube; it had got mashed down so tight I couldn't pull it off with my thumbnail. I laid my knife down on one of the deer, and then began to think about how I was going to get my swans. They was out in the middle of the bayou perfectly still, for there didn't seem to be any current. There wasn't but one way, because I was afraid to ride in for fear it might be boggy. I would have to swim in and get them. So I took off my clothes and laid them across the saddle to keep them off the wet ground—all but my hat, which I threw down on the deer by the gun. Then I jumped in and swam out to them and got them by the necks and brought them to shore.

The water was right cold, but I didn't mind that much. But when I got back and climbed up the bank again, Nasho and the horses was gone. I knew in a minute how it was. That rascally little Monkey had run off and Nasho was after him. Directly I saw them come out of a hollow going towards the ranch. They were half a mile off, but I could see my clothes were still sticking to the saddle. Monkey was ahead and Nasho didn't seem to be gaining on him much. I watched them till they got out of sight, and then began to think what I must do, for it was getting colder and I was shivering already.

I didn't stop to think long, because there didn't seem but one thing to do. I put on my boots which I had thrown down on the ground, and then took my knife and skinned the deer as fast as I could. I cut the skin off round the neck and legs, and just skinned the bodies, and it didn't take me very long because my knife was sharp and I worked fast, for I was cold and it was getting later all the time. Then I put one skin round each leg and fastened them with strings I cut off of the edges so as to make a pair of leggins, and run a string through holes along the top so I could fasten it round my waist and keep them up.

Now I wanted a coat. I pitched into the swans, and cut the skin round their necks, and then split them down the bellies, and found I could peel their skins, feathers and all, off just like the deer hides, only a heap easier. When I come to the wings I just cut them off. Then I took a narrow strip of the deerskin and fastened the bottom of one swan skin to the bottom of the other, and found it made me a pretty good cloak, plenty big enough to go round me and cover me from the neck down below my waist. The swan skins were nearly as tough as cloth, which was good luck for me. I cut some more strings off the deer legs, and fastened my feather cloak round me as close as I could so as to keep the wind off, and was ready to move, for I had no notion of staying there waiting for Nasho. I didn't believe he was going to catch Monkey until he got to the ranch, and then he wouldn't have any time to get back before night, and he couldn't see to travel after night, for it was cloudy and no moon, and he might get into a boggy slough.

I picked up the gun and stuck my knife in my waist belt so it would stay, and was going to start, when I remembered what Capt. Dick had said about bringing him a venison ham. In about a minute I had a ham off, and with that in one hand and the gun on my shoulder, I struck out pretty lively. I didn't go more than two miles before it began to get dark, and rain a little drizzle, and I knew I wouldn't be able to make the ranch that night because I couldn't see which way to travel after dark. If the stars would have come out it would have been easy enough. I think I could have managed it anyhow by the wind, taking care to keep it in the same place on my face all the time, but I was afraid I would strike some boggy slough that I couldn't get over, and have to lay out all night without fire. So I thought I would look for a camp while it was light.

My cloak did first-rate, but my leggins was rough and rubbed my legs and made it hard for me to travel. By good luck I soon saw a thicket of young live oaks and going to it found a big live oak tree that had been blown down by the wind. I commenced hunting for the finest, softest, driest grass I could find. I happened to think of the roots, and looking amongst them found an old nest of a rat or a rabbit, just the thing I wanted, dry as a powder house, and fine and soft as cotton. I drew the shot out of one barrel of my gun, and put the nest against some little branches and fired into it. It caught fire and I had some dry grass and little twigs ready and in a few minutes I had a good fire started.

I got some of the straightest limbs I could find and laid them from the top of the tree trunk to the ground, then covered them over with long grass like they do in thatching. This made me a snug place to lie down in and I got some more grass for my bed. It wasn't easy to get much, because it was nearly all wet. Then I got a big lot of branches and laid them so I could get them easy in the night, and was ready to go to bed, for it was dark. It was still raining a little, but not much.

I was hungry, and could have cooked some of the deer meat, but I didn't have any salt to eat it with, and I don't like meat without salt unless it is dried and even then it ain't good. I pulled off my leggins because I knew they would get hard and stiff, and sat under my shelter a while thinking about Uncle and Auntie, and wondering if Comanche had had his supper, and if Nasho caught Monkey, and wishing I was at the ranch. I was certain Monkey would go back to the ranch, so I wasn't uneasy about losing him. Then I put on some more wood, and laid down to sleep covering myself the best I could with the feather cloak and the dry grass I had got together. I put the gun close to me so I could lay my hand on it in a minute if I wanted to, but I wasn't afraid of anything, because I knew nothing would be out on the prairie such a night except the wolves, and they wouldn't trouble me.

I was fast asleep when I heard somebody shouting, and jumped up and looked out. You know I couldn't stand up in my shanty, and there was two somebodies on horseback.

"Who's there?" I said.

"Well, little one, you'll do!" Capt. Dick got off his horse and came to the fire leading his horse by the bridle. I crawled out and ran to him and shook hands with him, and Nasho came up and I just hugged him. I was mighty glad to see them.

They warmed a minute or two and then unsaddled their horses and fastened them to the tree. Then they came back to the fire with their saddle blankets, and saddles and things. Capt. Dick said, "Hello, Charley, what's this you've got on?" and I told him how I had made me a suit, and pulled off my leggins when I laid down, and about finding the rat's nest and making fire, and building me a bush arbor, and showed him I was fixed pretty well for the night.

"Well! Little one, you *will* do. You'll do to go to the Centennial, or the Rocky Mountains, or any other seaport. If I had known you was fixed so well I don't believe I would have come after you tonight but when I saw Nasho coming after your rascally little pony, and he told me he had left you stark naked six miles off, with no clothes or any way to make fire, I just crawled back into the saddle. As soon as Nasho could run in and get some coffee and grub, and a couple of oilcloths and blankets, we struck out lively, for it was getting dark fast. I brought my whiskey flask, thinking if we had the good luck to find you at all most likely you would be stiff and nearly froze; but I ain't going to waste my Robertson County on as lively a looking chap as you are. I am keeping that for stampedes and snake bites."

"I tell you, Charley, my little fellow,"—we was all sitting down by the fire, and he put his arm around me so I 'most felt like crying, for he seemed like an older brother, and you know I never had a brother—"I doubted mightily ever laying eyes on you again with life in you, and it hurt me terrible to think of coming upon your poor little body somewhere tomorrow stark and stiff, if the wolves hadn't happened to have lit on you and made a supper of you, and I would have started if I had ridden four hundred miles instead of forty, and it had been ten times as cold as it was, and ten times as little chance of finding you." And he drew me up in his arms on his breast, and I believe I cried a little. I do love Capt. Dick.

"Nasho said he was sure you would start for the ranch, and he knew he could go back to the place where he left you, so there was nothing to do but strike out in that direction and keep hollering, hoping you might hear us. I am as hoarse as a bullfrog, little one, yelling for you."

"We rode lively while we could see, and then we had to take it more coolly, and it was cool too, I needn't tell you. Thinking of you out alone in the prairie with that cold-hearted wind cutting around you, and going into your very blood, made mine run cold until the cold shivers run up and down my back like little water streaks from a house roof.

"Every few minutes we would stop, and I would holler my loudest, and you know I can raise the woods when I try, but never a note came back to us, and my heart kept getting weaker and weaker. Nasho kept saying, 'We no far enough, Capt. Dick,' and we would ride on again, but I was so afraid of passing or missing you that I would pull up again directly and yell out like a wildcat on the trail. I was beginning to think that it was all up, for it had been dark an hour, and the chances of missing you seemed about nine hundred and ninety-nine thousand, nine hundred and ninety-nine out of a million, when the sharp eyes of your little friend here caught the glint of fire way ahead, and to the left of the course we was going a long way, and we pushed for it and here we are, and damned glad to see you all right again, Charley my boy."

I think Capt. Dick was 'most crying too, for he pushed me away and said, "Get your duds on, little one, and we'll have some supper. I reckon you are hungry, ain't you?"

I told him I felt like I could eat a whole ham, and as soon as I could get my clothes on, I got the venison ham out.

"What was you carrying this for, Charley?" said he as he began to cut some slices off it to broil. "Afraid you would starve?"

"No, sir. You asked me to bring you a venison ham, and when I started after making my suit I thought about it and thought I'd try, and I got it this far."

"And you thought about me even then. Well, Charley, if ever I forget you or ain't ready to do a brother's part by you may I be everlastingly blowed into the middle of blue blazes. Excuse my swearing, little one, and don't take to it yourself, but I'm full tonight and bound to let off somehow."

We didn't talk much while we was eating, and then we stretched one of the rubber blankets they had brought, for a tent, and put down the other one and the dry grass I had and made a good bed with the saddle blankets, leaving the other ones to cover with.

We tied the horses close around the fire where it could help to keep them warm. While we were standing around the fire just before lying down, Nasho said "Me mighty glad we find Carley."

I just think Nasho is one of the best boys that ever lived.

We had to mend up the fire once or twice in the night, but got a good night's sleep, and was up early in the morning and rode to the ranch to breakfast.

I was going to leave my leggins and cloak, but Capt. Dick made me take them along, and said he would put them away in a safe place at the ranch, and maybe someday I would want them.

CAPT. DICK IN A TIGHT SPOT

It was a bright, clear day that day, but so cold that some of the hands wanted to put off starting until the next day, but Capt. Dick wouldn't listen to it. So we got ready and started. We took a light two-horse wagon to carry the provisions and bedding, and cooking things. There were seven white men and five Mexicans, and nearly all had three horses apiece. Capt. Dick told me and Nasho we might leave one of our horses apiece at the ranch in the pasture, and take one of Col. Hunt's, because we were going on the drive, and ought to have one fresh horse apiece to start with. I left Monkey because I intended to make him pay for the trick he served me in running away from me. Capt. Dick and me took two sacks of oats apiece to feed Milco and Beelzebub on, when we had harder work than common for them.

Beelzebub is his pet horse. He is as black as a black cat, with the prettiest curly mane and tail, and carries himself just as proud as can be, and can run like a streak. Capt. Dick never will let anybody ride him, and Beelzebub knows him as well as a dog does his master. I wouldn't give Comanche for him though.

We went about one hundred and fifty miles, nearly straight west, before we began gathering at all. Capt. Dick and me rode together most of the time, but sometimes he would call Nasho, who was 'most always behind, to ride up by us, and ask him questions about the Indians, and how he lived among them. Nasho don't like to talk to people much, but he was very willing to talk to Capt. Dick, and told him some things he had never even told me.

At last we got into the range of the cattle we were going to gather, and Capt. Dick said we would begin next day. The country was all prairie, but with a good deal of mesquite in it, and some chaparral. Chaparral is a thick thorny bush that grows over a good deal of the western country. On the Rio Grande it is so thick you can't get through it, but have to take the paths that have been made by cattle and horses, and when you get into a path it is often so narrow that you can't turn around, but have to just go ahead. Nasho told me this, for I never was there.

Next morning we began to gather. The cattle we wanted was all branded O M, and N U, and marked a square crop off of each ear, so it was easy to tell one when we saw it. We wasn't going to gather anything but beeves. Capt. Dick told the wagon driver where to meet him at dinner time, and all the rest of the hands left camp together. When we found a bunch of cattle we would ride round them easy so as not to scare them, and drive them all up close together. This is called "rounding up." Then we would pick out all the beeves in the brands we wanted, and keep them together, and let as many of the other cattle slip out as we could. Then seven men would be left with that bunch to drive them along slow the direction we were going, and the other five would ride on and make another "round," and drive the beeves we got, back to the first herd.

Capt. Dick always led the drivers and let me go with him, but left Nasho with the herd. Rounding up is harder work than herding, and a great deal harder on horses; often we would have to run a great deal to get the cattle together when they were much scattered but I had a heap rather do it than herd.

The herd is always hard to hold at first, until they get used to it, because they see the other cattle running away and they want to go too, and they keep dodging about trying to slip by the herders, or outrun them. Sometimes when any particular beef was very troublesome, and kept running out, and would make a break, one of the herders would start after him. Some of the others would holler "Go to him! Go to him!" and he would run by him, catch his tail and wrap it round the horn of his saddle and, with a quick jump of his horse past the beef, turn him a summersault. One or two of these falls nearly always made a beef willing to go back to the herd and stay there.

Cattle wasn't very plenty, because so many have been driven out of the country, but we gathered two hundred and fifty that day. That night we were lucky enough to have a pen to pen them in. Nobody lived there; it was just a pen that had been built to put cattle in when hunters were gathering to brand, or drive. We all slept round the pen with a horse apiece saddled and bridled, where we could jump on them in a minute if they tried to break the pen, and kept one man on guard all the time to watch them, but they were still enough all night.

The next night we had to stand guard round the cattle because there wasn't any pen. About sundown we rounded them up pretty close together, and put four men round them. Capt. Dick told the guards not to take stands, but to ride round the herd all the time, one behind the other, at equal distances apart, and in this way a beef could not slip out without someone seeing it, and the cattle would soon get used to them and would be easier to manage. Each relief stood three hours. I was on the second, with Nasho and Nueces Joe and three Mexicans. Next morning about sunup the cattle were let out to graze, the herders keeping round them so they couldn't scatter too much, or any of them run off, and the drivers started off to gather. Capt. Dick took Nasho with him that day.

That evening at camp Nasho went out a little way to see about one of his horses, and came back with an armadillo. It was a little animal not quite as big as a possum but covered with a thick shell divided into squares. His head didn't have any, but his tail did on the upper side. Under his belly his shell was most like a turtle, only harder, and he could draw his head in his shell like a turtle, and bring the shell over his back and the one under his belly together, and he looked like a curious ball, and you could kick him round without hurting him. One of the boys asked Nasho what he was going to do with him, and he said, "Me eat him—he heap good."

He let him be right quiet awhile until he put his head out, and then hit him a quick lick on the nose and killed him in a second. Then he cut him open and cleaned him and put him in the fire covered up in his own shell, and let him stay about an hour and a half. Nearly all of us tasted a little of it, and it was real good, very much like possum, but tenderer and sweeter. Capt. Dick always carried a six-shooter, but there was no time for hunting, or even shooting deer when we saw them.

The fourth day after we began gathering, Capt. Dick and myself had ridden off to a little bunch of cattle by themselves. There wasn't but one head in it that we wanted, but that was a large, fine one, and we started to drive him toward another bunch some of the other hands were going to round. He wouldn't drive a bit, but would dodge and turn and almost run against our horses when we tried to turn him.

"Well, old fellow, if you won't stop, there is a way to make you," Capt. Dick said, and threw his rope on

him. Then he got mad and began to fight. Capt. Dick
was riding a pony that wasn't very strong and didn't
understand roping well, and directly he got tangled in
the rope and when the beef made a run, he jerked him
down, and he fell on Capt. Dick's leg, so he couldn't get
up. The beef whirled round and, with his head down,
started at the horse as hard as he could go. I trembled
all over, because I was too far off to get to him in time
to stop him, and I expected in a minute to see him run
his horns into Capt. Dick.

I hollered and ran towards them as fast as I could go,
but Capt. Dick just reached round, drew his six-shooter,
and shot him through the head. He turned a summersault and fell so close to them that his heels were almost
against the pony's nose. I helped Capt. Dick up by pulling the pony off of him, and he fixed his saddle straight
again and we rode on to the crowd. His leg was a little
stiff that evening, but he rubbed it well with suet that
night, and was ready for work again next day.

Gathering cattle is the hardest work the cowboy has
to do, except branding, but it is a great deal harder in
the mountains than on the prairie, because the ground
is so rough and rocky, and there are so many rough trees
and bushes that brush and scratch one so in getting
through them. A cowboy has to go wherever the cattle
do. Sometimes when they get into a thicket one or two
have to get down and leave their horses, and go in afoot
and run them out, and then go back, catch their horses
and run as hard as they can go to catch up again. A pony
ought to be trained so you can get down and leave him
anywhere and he won't run off, but most of them are
tricky, and will leave you sometimes. A good cow pony
will follow cattle wherever they go, twisting and turning
to keep up with their dodges without being guided at
all.

Up in the mountains the cow hunters have to look out for Indians too. One night in Llano County some Indians slipped up and stole all the horses of some cow hunters, and they had to walk to the nearest settlement and carry their saddles. Mr. Hanscom was out cow hunting one day by himself and saw several men in blue Yankee overcoats riding about. He thought they were soldiers, but directly they got around him and he saw they were Indians, but his horse outran them and he got away.

In a week we had gathered about fifteen hundred head, which was as many as Capt. Dick wanted, so we was ready to start back. First, though, we had to cut out the cattle we didn't want—beeves in other brands, and cows and young cattle.

"I thought you said, Charley, that you let them get away in first rounding up."

So we did, whenever we could, but sometimes some of them wouldn't try to get out, and we wouldn't ride into the bunch to get them out, because that makes the cattle wild and hard to hold.

"What do you mean by holding cattle?"

Keeping them close together, and not letting any get away. I tell you it's hard to do sometimes, because a half a dozen will be trying to get away at the same time, and all going different ways, and you have to keep running your horse as hard as he can go first after one and then another to keep them in. It ain't half as hard in the prairie as it is in the brush.

There are two ways to cut cattle out of a herd. One is to round the herd up and let several good hands go in and pick out the cattle they don't want, and work them out one at a time, or two or three if they can get them together. By being easy they can generally work one out close to the edge of the herd, and then by dashing at him right quick run him out and away before he knows what they are after. The easier they can do it the better, because if they run in the herd much, it makes the cattle wild and hard to manage.

The other way, and the best one, is when the cattle are grazing, for several good hands to go in and work out what they don't want. The cattle are scattered then and busy feeding, and don't notice the riders much, and you don't have to run your horse much to get them out.

The day that we started back to the ranch at dinner, Capt. Dick, and me and Nasho and one other hand, went into the herd while they were feeding, and cut out about a hundred head. There was one big fellow we had to rope and lead out, and tie down to get the ropes off. When he got up he took after Nasho and ran him about three hundred yards, but Nasho's horse was fast enough to keep out of the way.

That night we killed a maverick for fresh meat.

"What is a maverick, Charley?"

A yearling or big calf that ain't either marked or branded. They have 'most always quit following their mothers, and nobody can tell who they belong to, so whenever cow hunters want fresh meat they kill a maverick.

We got back to the ranch in ten days and had splendid luck. The weather was good and we didn't have a stampede, or lose a single head. We put the cattle in the big pasture, with about five hundred more that Capt. Dick was going to drive, and kept four hands with them to keep them together and get them used to being under herd before starting. Then we had a week's hard work road-branding. Col. Hunt's road-brand was S. We got through Saturday night, and Monday morning we were to start.

Life on the Cattle Trail

Sunday was a general getting-ready day. Some had washing to be done, and others saddle-rigging to be fixed and bridles to be mended, and there were horses to be got up out of the big pasture, and the wagon to be loaded with the provisions, and two of the hands that lived a few miles off went home to spend the day.

Monday morning early the gate of the big pasture was opened and some of the ranch hands turned the herd out. It wasn't opened wide just so that only two or three could come out at once, and Capt. Dick and Col. Hunt's head boss sat on their horses on each side of the gate and counted the cattle as they came through. They kept one hand inside to hold them up a little when they crowded too much. They both made two thousand and eleven head. As the beeves came through they would trot off pretty lively, but the hands kept about them and didn't let them go ahead until they was all out. They kept hollering and singing to them to keep them quiet, for they were restless and wanted to keep moving, as cattle 'most always are when they are turned out of a pen. When they was all out we let them string out and take the direction of the trail. They were a good deal of trouble, because some of them wanted to stop all the time and feed, and some wanted to go ahead too fast, and some was lazy and had to be pushed up all the time to make them keep up with the rest of the herd.

About twelve o'clock we stopped to let them feed, but we didn't get to rest much, because they wasn't used to being herded and wanted to scatter too much, and we had to keep riding all the time to keep them together. When cattle first start they don't like to feed so close to each other, but they get over that pretty soon. The wagon had kept up with us, and by two at a time we went to it to get dinner. Capt. Dick and Highover and Whistling Bill didn't stop to get dinner, but just drank a cup of coffee and took some meat and bread in their hands and rode off again. Me and Nasho did that way too.

About half-past one we started again. They didn't know which way to go, and it took some time to get them strung out the right way, but when a few moved off right the rest soon followed. Some bosses always have one man to go ahead as a leader, and the cattle soon learn to follow him, but Capt. Dick said that was just throwing one hand away, for they would learn themselves which way to go in two or three days.

When the sun was about an hour high we stopped again and let the cattle feed until sundown. Capt. Dick showed the wagon where to stop, and sent me and Nasho to drive the loose horses to it. They had been in the herd all day, 'most always back at the tail end of it, for they kept stopping to pick grass. They all kept together very well, and hadn't made us any trouble about driving. When we brought them up to the wagon Capt. Dick and Mose Baker had tied long ropes to the hind wheels and each of them went out as far as the ropes would go, and stretched them out straight about as high as a man's waist, making a sort of pen with them and the wagon.

We drove them into it, and I jumped down and went in to catch them while Nasho minded the open end to keep them from getting out. Capt. Dick and Mose Baker came closer together and held their ropes tight, and the horses didn't try much to get away. I took ropes in with me, and as fast as I caught two I took them out and tied them to the wagon wheels. When I had enough for every man to have a change I took neck ropes and necked some of them together two and two, and hobbled those that had hobbles on their necks.

There were two mean ones that didn't have any hobbles, and Capt. Dick made the cook get him a piece of new rope out of the wagon and cut off about three feet of it and untwisted it and made a hobble for them. We necked them together and hobbled one besides. I necked mine and Nasho's together two and two and let them loose, for they were used to camp and we wasn't afraid of their running away.

As soon as I had got through with the others all of us that was at the wagon unsaddled the horses we had been riding and turned them loose or hobbled them, and saddled fresh ones. Capt. Dick took Beelzebub and I saddled Comanche, for I intended to ride him at night, because he was the fastest horse I had and everybody wants his best if there is a stampede. Then we rode out to the herd and Capt. Dick sent the other hands in three at a time to change their horses and get supper.

"What did you do with the loose horses at night, Charley?"

We let them feed. That is the best time for them to graze, for the horses that are ridden during the day don't get much chance to eat, and would get poor if they couldn't feed at night.

"But won't they run off?"

No, sir; they ain't apt to. Whistling Bill had an old gotch-eared, flea-bitten gray horse that was a good camp horse, and we put a bell on him at night, and the

rest soon learned to stay with him. We could always tell
by the bell where they were, and if they was getting off
too far a hand would be sent to drive them back closer.
It is always the business of the guard that is on herd at
night to keep a look out for the horses too, and not let
them stray off. They ain't apt to try unless the grass is
very poor or they are thirsty. Old Gray was one of the
best camp horses we had. Whistling Bill said he was
the "Old Gray Horse that came a'tearin' out of the wil-
derness, and he was so glad to get into a prairie again,
that there wasn't any danger of his taking to the woods
anymore."

About sundown we began rounding up the herd for
the night. As soon as we got them close together and
they were still, Capt. Dick sent Highover and Whistling
Bill and one of the negroes to the wagon to get their
supper. There was three hands already there. As soon as
they got through they came back, and we who had been
herding went to get ours. As it was the first night, Capt.
Dick said he would have to keep half of the hands on
guard at a time, until the cattle got more used to being
kept so close together.

As we were going to have the first watch we didn't
make down our pallets, but just got out our blankets
and put them where we could get at them easy when
we came off watch. Then we went back to the herd and
let those that was herding go to the wagon to sleep until
half-past twelve.

It was moonlight and no trouble to see the cattle, and
no trees or bushes in the way, and we just kept riding
around them, and driving back any that tried to stray
out. They flurried once or twice while we were on guard,
but didn't try to run, and at half-past twelve Capt. Dick
rode to the wagon and waked up the second relief, and
when they came out we went to the wagon and laid

down. We didn't undress at all, but just lay down on our blankets, and tied our horses to the wagon wheels so we could jump on them in a minute if the beeves ran.

At the first peep of day, Capt. Dick sent me and Nasho out again to drive up the loose horses. We caught them just like the night before, and tied up those that would be wanted and turned the ones we had rode at night loose to feed. By the time we got through this the cook had breakfast ready, and we ate and went out to the herd, and let the other watch come to breakfast and change their horses. The cattle had already been turned loose to feed, and we had to keep riding pretty steady to keep them from scattering too much. About nine o'clock we started again, and about twelve came to a creek where we stopped to water and let them feed, and get our dinners. That evening we got to the road and camped on it that night. We made about twelve miles that day.

"How many hands did you have, Charley?"

There were twelve besides the cook. Drovers generally allow about six hands to the thousand head. The cook don't herd or have anything to do with the cattle, but drives the wagon and does the cooking. As quick as the herd stops at night, the boss shows him where to camp, and he unharnesses the mules and begins to get supper. When that is over and his dishes are washed up, he can lie down and sleep, and don't have to get up in the night, but at the first crack of day he has to get up and make his fire and get breakfast.

The mules are driven up with the loose horses and tied for him, and as soon as the last hands have eaten breakfast, he harnesses up and starts behind the herd. If the country is prairie and there is very little wood, he has to stop whenever he comes to wood and put enough into the wagon to last to the next wood, and he has a ten-gallon keg that he keeps water in for the hands to drink, and to cook with. Very often we made dry camps, that is, we camped where there was no water. If the cattle and horses were watered along in the evening they didn't need any more, and the grass was often better away from the creeks and branches. The cook don't have such an easy time if he don't have to stand guard at night, because he has to be up very early in the morning, and it keeps him busy to get enough cooked for the hungry hands.

"What provisions did you have?"

We had corn meal and flour, and bacon and coffee, and sugar, and rice, and molasses and dried fruit, and, when we could get them, Irish potatoes and onions. There are stores all along the trail that keep just what drovers want, and Capt. Dick bought what he needed at the towns we went by so as not to have so much to haul at once. We had fresh beef most of the time. There were herds ahead of us of mixed cattle, and every two or three days a stray yearling from some other herd would get into ours, and when we wanted fresh meat we would kill one. All the herds do this. Sometimes we would pick up a bunch of five or ten at a time that had strayed out in the night, or got away in a stampede. We would always put them in the herd and drive them on, and then when we got to Kansas the owner could come and get them.

Capt. Dick was our boss, and a good one too. It is the business of the boss to take charge of the herds, and divide out the watches, and pick the camps, and have control of everything just like the owner would if he was along. He ought to know all about how to manage cattle, and the best way to drive them. Some bosses start the herd on the trail the first thing in the morning, and then stop about nine o'clock and let them feed until about two, and some start about nine o'clock and don't make but one drive a day. Most of them though make two. Fifteen miles a day is a pretty fair drive, because it won't do to hurry cattle; they would get poor on the road. Beeves can travel faster than mixed cattle.

"Well, there were Capt. Dick and you and Nasho. What other hands did your herd have, Charley?"

There was Mose Baker—'most everybody when they wanted to speak to him would begin "Mr. B-a-ba-kr, Bakery?" And Black Jack, he was the one that always looked so rough and dirty. Whistling Bill said he hadn't washed his face since the time he got caught in the night by a rise in the creek, and lost his saddle and blankets, and had to swim out. Nobody liked Black Jack much because he was so crusty, and never seemed to feel pleasant toward anybody.

I don't know what Highover's name was. They called him Highover because two men found him on the prairie once stretched out where his horse had fallen down with him, and asked him if he was much hurt, and he said "No, but he had got the awfulest highoverest fall ever they saw." He was hurt so bad they had to carry him home, and it was a month before he could get on a horse again. He was a first-rate hand, but nobody liked him. Capt. Dick used to leave him in charge of the herd nearly always if he had to go ahead for anything or to some place to buy provisions, but nobody seemed like talking much when he was in camp.

There were two negro men named Scip and Hannibal, but the second night out Whistling Bill said he was going to do like Adam in the garden—he was going to call up the two-legged livestock of that herd and name them. He said them darkey's names had to be changed, for he wasn't going to have any fighting on the road except what he did himself, and they'd be sure to fight if they kept their names, so he called Hannibal General Foot, because he had such a long foot. He said his arithmetic said three feet made a yard, but three of that nigger's feet would come nearer making a mile and two or three barrels of beef thrown in. One of the Mexicans was named Manuel, and he called him Wellman, and Antonio he nicknamed Aunt Tony. Another was named Jesus. He was in camp at the time, and Whistling Bill made Nasho tell him in Mexican that among the Americans it was a sin to call anybody Jesus, and they would have to give him another name, that they would call him Señor Schezeredicks. He said that was a big name among the Americans. The Mexican laughed when he heard his new name, but didn't say anything. Whistling Bill called me Carley, like Nasho does, but he said he couldn't make Nasho's name any better if he tried, so he would let him go. They all called each other by their nicknames so much that anybody might have been in camp a month without knowing what a man's real name was.

CROSSING THE GUADALUPE

The second night we had to stand guard again half the night, but the third one we had three watches with four men in each, and got to sleep more. I was glad of that, for the second day, before we stopped for dinner, I was so tired and sleepy I could scarcely sit on my horse or keep my eyes open. I went to sleep a dozen times riding along, and could hardly see the cattle right under my eyes.

Capt. Dick put Highover, and Mose Baker, and Scip and Wellman on the first watch, and Whistling Bill, and Black Jack, and Aunt Tony and Gen. Foot on the second, and took the third with me and Nasho and Señor Schezeredicks.

We didn't have any trouble till we got to the Guadalupe River. We had to drive through the river bottom apiece, and had to watch the cattle close to keep from leaving any of them in the bushes. At the crossing place the bank had been beat down by so many cattle crossing before that they could get down to the water easy, but they wouldn't go in. Some of them would stand in water halfway up to their sides, and now and then when they would get to turning around some of them would get into swimming water, but they wouldn't strike out for the other bank. We would crowd them as close as we could, and holler at them and throw sticks, but we couldn't crowd them in. We worked at them two hours. Some got down and tried it afoot. Every now and then some of them would break out and run off through the bottom, but somebody would be after them in a minute and bring them back.

At last we got them as close together as they could be and kept pressing in on them, and crowding them closer until some of the front ones got pushed off into swimming water, and in a minute there were two hundred of them heading for the other bank. As soon as they were fairly started, Nasho and Señor Schezeredicks started in a little above them and swum their horses across, so as to gather them up on the other side, and keep them from straying off. There were some boys on the other side with a little boat, and they came over and Capt. Dick and Whistling Bill and one of the Mexicans got in and pulled over, holding their horses by the bridle reins.

The other hands crossed the same way. The wagon went round to a bridge about a mile and a half below. As soon as all the hands were over we drove the herd round the town on to the prairie, about two miles the other side, and stopped for dinner. Capt. Dick told Nasho and Señor Schezeredicks to make a fire and dry themselves. He went to town to buy some things we wanted, and when he came back he gave them a dram of whiskey to keep them from catching cold.

We didn't go but three or four miles further that day, because there was a belt of timber ahead of us about fifteen miles through, and it would take all day to drive through it.

"Why couldn't you camp in the timber, Charley?"

Because it is so much harder to herd cattle in woods. You can't see them like you can on the prairie, and some of them will slip off and get away. They are more apt to stampede in the timber. If an old dead limb were to fall it might start them to running, and it's a heap more dangerous running them in the woods at night, because you cannot see the limbs and bushes, and dead trees, and a horse is more certain to fall down or run against a tree.

We started early the next morning and by driving hard all day, except about an hour at dinner, we got through to the prairie again. But I tell you it was hard work. In some places the young post oaks and hickories were so close you could hardly get through, and they rubbed and scratched our necks and arms and legs, in crowding by them. And the cattle would keep stopping to pick the young buds and leaves that were coming out, and straying out to one side, and kept us dodging backward and forward and running and hollering all day. I was so hoarse that night I could hardly speak, and my arm was so tired swinging my rope to drive them along with I could scarcely raise it. I was glad I wasn't on first watch.

"Why don't you use whips to drive with?"

Because the noise they make cracking might stampede the herd. Some of the hands got long sticks, and some took their quirts or ropes. I let about ten feet of my rope hang with a hard knot in the end, and when I wanted to make one move I would give the rope a jerk so the knot would hit him, and he would move quick. It hurts them worse than a lick with a stick, and you can ride up behind one easy and jerk him a hard rap before he knows it is coming.

One day's work like that is harder than three days' driving on the prairie.

About sixty miles from the Guadalupe we came to the Colorado River, but we didn't have much trouble crossing that because the river was shallow a good way out, and the cattle got into swimming water before they knew it. There was a ferry boat close by, and the hands crossed on that. Two of them had gone over on it before the cattle was put in the river. When we got 'most to the railroad track a train come along, and the cattle got scared and whirled back, and milled for half an hour before we could get them started again.

"What is milling, Charley?"

It's turning round and round. They crowd as close together as they can and hold their heads up, and just keep going round and round. They are so close together you could walk on their backs easy, and their horns look like a piece of brushwood. It's the hardest kind of work sometimes to get them started when they get to milling. You can ride in among them and holler as much as you please, but they just keep turning round, each one following the one in front of him. Sometimes if they are just let alone they will get quiet themselves and then some of them will start off, and the rest will follow. The horses generally all get close together and stand perfectly still. They look like a little island, with the cattle moving round them all the time, but the cattle never hurt them.

We crossed the river right at the City of Austin. Austin is the capital of Texas. Capt. Dick took me to town with him, and I went up to the Capitol. It's the biggest house I ever saw. You go up twenty or thirty long stone steps, and right in front before the doors is a little monument to the men that fell at the Alamo. It is made of rock taken from the old Alamo fort, and has the names of all the men that were killed there on its sides. Uncle Charley's name is there too, though two or three of the letters have got broken so you can hardly read it. It is painted a sort of dark green, and don't look much like rock, and it has a little iron picket fence around it to keep it from getting rubbed and the edges broken by people passing.

In the Capitol there were some pictures, one of them was Genl. Sam Houston. I had seen pictures of him before, and knew him as I saw it. He was the first President of Texas when she was a Republic. Uncle used know him well. He hasn't been dead many years. I didn't have time to stay at the Capitol long. Some day I want to go there again and take a good look at the rooms and pictures.

THUNDERING HERD

Two or three trails come together at Austin and make a big one. From there on we had prairie almost all the way. There wasn't anything particular happened to us going through Texas. We had some bad weather, and several times the cattle flurried a little, but we had first-rate luck and not much trouble. There was a big red steer that always took the lead and kept it, and the others learned to follow him. As soon as the head was started he would strike out north, for he was always near the head of the herd, and if he didn't happen to be first he would soon get there, for he was the fastest walker in the herd.

After we left Gonzales the country was nearly all rolling, and we always rounded up at night on top of a rise. It's more level, and drier, and the cattle will lie more quietly, and it is easier to see them. If they was on the side of a hill, a horse would be more apt to stumble downhill, and that might scare the cattle. They are as easily frightened as mice. I believe sometimes one of them dreams and jumps in his dream and scares the others.

I was watching them one morning, just as day was beginning to break. I could just see them, and all of a sudden every one that was down was up and ready to run, but I couldn't see anything to frighten them. It's curious how what frightens one way over on one side of the herd will run clear through it and scare all, though the rest haven't seen it, and don't know what they are scared at. They don't scare that way in the daytime.

I liked the trip first-rate. Sometimes when I would be waked up to go on guard, I would be so sleepy I could hardly see, but it wouldn't last long, and I would get to sleep a little at dinner and catch up. It was right hot a heap of times, and all day in the sun without any shade except the shadow of the wagon at dinner, or maybe when the cattle were lying down at dinner, and you could sit down in the shadow of your horse and watch them. The country was a good deal alike, and the trail kept out of the settlements so as not to be bothered by the cattle breaking into any fields. One day was just about like another. Get up in the morning, catch the loose horses, get breakfast, drive and herd all day, except an hour and a half at dinner, change your horse again at night, and sleep and stand guard most nights. We didn't get to see much of each other, because in the daytime we were scattered about the cattle, and at dinner, when half of us were together, some would nearly always be asleep when they wasn't eating, and at night it was the same way.

I tell you driving cattle don't give a man much time for anything else if he sticks to them. We travelled Sunday just the same as any other day, because it was just about as much work to herd as to drive. Sometimes a beef would get stuck in the mud and two or three would have to put their ropes on him and drag him out by wrapping the ropes round the horns of their saddles, and making their horses pull. A horse can pull a great deal that way.

We crossed the Brazos River at Fort Graham, but it was fordable. We lost one beef there. He got down too low into swimming water, and washed against a log and turned over in the water and strangled, I reckon, for he didn't try to swim afterwards.

The grass was better and better as we went farther, and the cattle fattened all the time. Our horses held up well too. Comanche and Monkey got fatter, though I rode Monkey every other day, and Milco every night.

Red River was the last stream in Texas. The water of Red River is a deep, thick red. It gets colored by the kind of clay it flows through in Indian Nation. It is a little brackish, and not good to drink, but there was a good spring close by where we got plenty of drinking water. The cattle seemed like they couldn't get enough of it. There was a high bank on this side without any timber, but on the other it was low and sandy, and there were a few cottonwoods and chickasaw plums just like what we had at Uncle's. It looked curious at first to see them growing out here wild. As it was after dinner when we crossed Red River, we made a dry camp that night. I forgot to tell you that Red River is the boundary between Texas and Indian Territory, and when we got over we were in the Nation.

The country was all prairie, in great long swells. It would be from two to three miles from the top of one swell to the top of the next. There was a creek about a mile and a half to the right, and we drove the horses there and watered them. The cattle didn't need any water. Indian Territory looked a good deal like one of the pictures of it in my geography. The grass was high and thick and coarse, and there was hardly any timber. There is plenty though in the eastern part of the Nation, where the Choctaws and Creeks and other tame Indians live. You know Indian Territory was given to the Indians for home, and a great many of them live in it. The part where we were going through was where the Comanches, and Keorias, and Kickapoos lived, but we

didn't see any of them. They were all west of us. They
don't have any regular houses, but live in tents, wandering round where they can find game, and going to the
reservation to get their rations every month. Fort Sell
was the place where they got their rations. I would like
to have gone there to have seen some of the Indians,
but it would have taken two days to go and come, and
I couldn't leave the herd that long. If one man goes off
the rest have to do his work, and everyone has enough
of his own without taking part of somebody else's.

We didn't see any roads except the trail. That is nearly
a hundred yards wide, a great big plain road with little
paths on each side winding in and out and twisting into
each other, and little lanes of grass between. The grass
grows fresh and high right up to the edge of the trail, so
that in ten steps of it there was good grazing.

There was a heavy thunderstorm came up that evening about sundown, but we were just in the edge of it
and didn't get wet. About a mile ahead of us there was
a herd camped, and another behind us. The herds don't
come close together for fear the cattle will get mixed.

When we got up next morning it was showering a
little, and kept it up all day. Sometimes it would rain
right hard for a little while. The third night in the Nation we camped close to some rocky hills with piles of
rocks on top here and there, but I don't know who piled
them up, or what for. The Indians, I reckon, for drovers
wouldn't stop for that.

It had been showering nearly all the time since we
crossed Red River, and the ground was pretty wet. It
wasn't raining when we lay down, but looked like it
would, and we didn't take off any of our clothes, but just
threw down a blanket and lay down. Capt. Dick held his
horse by the bridle reins. I thought we would have time
if we was called, and tied mine to the wagon wheel.

We hadn't been asleep but two or three hours when Whistling Bill waked us up and said he thought it was going to storm, and we had better come out to the herd. We jumped up and got our horses and started. Capt. Dick told the cook to be sure to keep the lantern burning, and to keep the fire covered up with the skillet lids so the boys could have some hot coffee whenever they come to the fire.

"What was the lantern for, Charley?"

So we could tell where the wagon was. Whenever it was at all dark a lantern was always kept swinging from the front bow of the wagon, so we could tell how to find the way to it, and then if the cattle ran we would know which way to turn them back.

It was so dark we could scarcely see, and raining a little and thundering. The cattle looked like a big dark spot. You could hardly tell the white ones, it was so dark. Directly after we got to the herd it commenced raining hard, and thundering and lightning terribly. It was so black I couldn't see my hand before me, or my horse. I tried it lots of times. We had to be very careful in riding about the cattle not to ride so close as to make any of them move.

It was raining hard, and the big peals of thunder would seem like they shook the very ground. It was almost like somebody had hit you. You would dodge and crush down 'a the saddle, and in a minute, there would come another one, and the lightning flashed so it almost blinded us. One second you could see the herd, and the men scattered about it—some riding, but most of them sitting drawn in their saddle with their backs to the rain the best they could—and the wagon, and the hills, and the creek, and the next second when you opened your eyes after the flash it would be as black as pitch, and by the time you could begin to make out the herd a little there would come another. The wind was from the south, and I was on the south side of the herd. The cattle all had their heads turned north. All of a sudden it whipped round and blew harder than ever from the north, and the cattle all turned round with their heads to the south.

Whistling Bill was on one side of me, and one of the Mexicans on the other. Capt. Dick came round and told us to keep moving in front of the cattle and singing and hollering, that they were frightened and would run unless we kept up a noise. Everybody was singing or hollering, but you couldn't understand what anybody said. The cattle all had their heads down close to the ground, and their eyes looked wild and frightened. When a flash would come, the foremost ones that I could see would shut their eyes and turn their heads, as if it hurt them.

It kept on storming for about three hours, and then commenced slacking up. It wasn't raining much, and the lightning didn't come so fast, or the thunder, and it wasn't as loud either as before. I was tired, but I hadn't got wet, only my feet a little. I had my soldier coat on, and that kept my body dry, and my leggins kept my legs from getting wet. When it was blowing so hard the raindrops stung our hands and faces, almost like we had been hit with pebbles.

But the wind had slacked up now and everything was stiller. The hands were all tired and had quit singing and hollering, and were gathered about the herd two or three together for company. I could see that by the lightning, for it was too dark to see any other way. Whistling Bill rode up to me and said he thought the storm was about over now, and we wouldn't have any more trouble with the cattle, but just then there came a flash that blinded us and a terrible thunderclap, and here they came. It sounded like the whole herd had started at once. They were so quick that they were almost around us before our horses jumped off.

We were separated in a minute, running to keep in front of the cattle, and hollering and yelling at them to try and keep them back. They wouldn't stop though, and I kept riding in front of them until by a turn I got out of sight of the lantern. I couldn't see the ground, but I knew by the feeling of my horse that we were going up hill. The ground was so wet that my horse would sink 'most to his knees sometimes. By the time the foremost got on top of the hill they were tired enough to stop, and they had got scattered a good deal too, and they never run as bad when they get scattered. Each one seems to keep the others scared when they are together.

I got the foremost stopped, and began riding round in the dark rounding up all I could find, and driving them together. When I would find a bunch moving, I would ride the way they were going until I couldn't see or hear any more, and then stop and turn them back, and drive them to the others. In this way I got together a pretty good bunch, and it wasn't any use to ride off far because I couldn't see which way to go, or where the cattle were unless I got right close to them, and I might lose what I already had, so I just stayed with them until they began to lie down. I knew then there wasn't any danger of their moving away until daylight, and I was cold and thought I would try and find my way to the wagon and get a blanket, and come back. They were right on top of a hill, and the wind was strong enough to be real chilly.

In riding about I came to the trail, and followed that south until I caught sight of the lantern, and then went to the wagon. I found two other hands there that had come in to get coffee and blankets. I just took a cup and my blanket and hurried back and, as it was getting lighter found my bunch, and lay down close to them holding Comanche by the bridle reins. The ground was soaking wet, and I didn't have any pillow but my arm, so you may know I didn't have a very good bed. I don't think I slept an hour when something waked me up, and I found day was just breaking.

I got on my horse, and about a quarter of a mile off saw another bunch of cattle, and two saddled horses, and when I got to them I found it was Whistling Bill and Aunt Tony. They were lying down asleep, holding their bridle reins. I woke them up and we drove their bunch to mine, and then took them all to the bed-ground. We had together about five hundred head. We found two of the hands at the wagon that had followed a bunch until they stopped, and then left them and come to the wagon, and hadn't gone back. Whistling Bill started right away with them to find their bunch, and left me and Aunt Tony to herd what we had. There were a few straggling lots in sight, about a hundred in all, and we got them together, and drove the horses up near the wagon. One would herd while the other ran out and drove up. The bed-ground looked like a mortar bed, it was all trod up so.

In about half an hour Nasho and Señor Schezeredicks came up with about two hundred and, directly after, Highover and Gen. Foot brought in about a hundred and fifty, and Black Jack and Mose Baker and Whistling Bill came back with three hundred, and Scip came in by himself with a hundred, so that everybody was in but Capt. Dick, and we had about thirteen hundred head, and were out about seven hundred. Scip said Capt. Dick had been with him, but had sent him into camp and told him to tell Highover to take charge of the herd. He had gone to two other herds to see if any of our cattle had got into theirs.

We caught the horses, changed, tied up one for Capt. Dick, and then let the herd leave the bed-ground. Everything was wet, and we knew it would take the cook a good while to get breakfast, so Highover put half the hands on herd, and sent the others out to follow up tracks and try and find more cattle. They came back in an hour with a hundred and fifty, and got breakfast and came out to herd while we ate. Highover took Wellman with him and started off again to hunt up cattle. While we were eating, Capt. Dick came up with about fifty head. That made fifteen hundred, and we were still out five hundred.

Capt. Dick said he had been to three herds near us and they had all had stampedes. One herd of three thousand didn't have but five hundred left, and another herd of a thousand had next morning about twenty-five hundred. They had kept their own cattle together, and part of the big herd had run into theirs. They had all agreed to stay there that day and hunt, and take up any cattle of each other's they could find, the next day they would cut out. Capt. Dick said he had found about a hundred of ours in another herd, but he would let them stay there until tomorrow.

As quick as we got through eating Capt. Dick sent the other hands to the herd and told them to tell Black Jack and Mose Baker and Señor Schezeredicks and Gen. Foot to stay with the herd, and for Whistling Bill and two hands to hunt, and Highover and Wellman to keep on hunting. He said he knew it would be hard work for four hands to herd, but he wanted to find all the cattle today, and get away from there for fear we should have another storm and stampede, for the weather wasn't clearing up much.

He took me and Nasho and started off hunting. There were cattle tracks going 'most every way, but directly

we struck the trail of a good big bunch and followed it.
They had kept it right straight on without stopping, and
I reckon we followed them six miles before we came
up with them. There were about three hundred head
scattered about feeding. They were ours. I tell you we
were glad to see them. The country we had ridden over
was very rough and broken, full of great, deep gullies in
the red clay where you could have hidden a house. We
saw a good many turkeys and deer, and one bear track.
It must be a good game country to hunt in. Riding was
hard work on our horses, and us too. The ground was
slippery, and the gully banks hard to climb, and every
little branch full and sometimes boggy.

Capt. Dick said, as we were following the track out,
that at one of the herds some of the hands thought the
Indians had stampeded the cattle, for we were in the
Comanche reservation. One poor fellow got separated
from the rest and so badly scared that when his horse
got bogged in a little branch he just left him and kept on
afoot. He thought the Indians had shot his horse with
an arrow, and were after him. He carried his six-shooter
in his hand all the time. In crossing a branch he lost it,
but stopped and fished it out again with his feet, taking
his shoes off so he could feel better for it. He didn't wait
to put them on again but started running, and thought
all the time he could hear the Indians following close
to him. At last he broke plum down and lay down, and
next morning when one of the hands found him in sight
of the wagon, he was nearly crazy from fright. He said
he had seen the lantern at the wagon, but thought it
was the Indians' fire, and he could hardly persuade the
poor fellow to go with him to the wagon.

Capt. Dick said he knew the Indians didn't have anything to do with it, that they could sweep the whole
trail any time if they wanted to, for there wasn't enough

drovers to whip them off and watch their cattle too, but they were afraid to, lest the United States government should get after them about it. I thought about the Indians when I was lying down with my bunch of cattle, but I didn't believe they were about, and I knew if they wanted to they could kill us all any time, and I intended to stick to the cattle till I saw them anyhow.

We got back with our bunch about two o'clock, and found all the other hands there. One bunch of about fifty had come back themselves. Highover said he had counted them as close as he could, and he didn't think we were out more than a hundred. As quick as we got some dinner we went to the herd, and strung them out so we could count them, and Capt. Dick and Highover counted. They made nineteen hundred and ten head.

Capt. Dick sent the wagon on about two miles to a better camping place, out of the low grounds, and that evening we drove the herd there. The moon came out pretty that evening, and we was glad to see it, for we was all tired, and wanted to sleep some to make up for what we had lost. After the herd was rounded up Capt. Dick rode over to the herd where our missing cattle were, and they agreed if he would come back next morning before they let the herd off the bed-ground, they would hold them up and let him cut out.

Parched & Plum Tired

The next morning we were up by the first peep of day, and before sunup drove the herd over in about a quarter of a mile of the herd that had our cattle. Capt. Dick took me and Whistling Bill with him to cut out. It was hard work, because the ground was so wet our horses kept slipping, and we were afraid they would fall down with us. It took us nearly two hours to cut out all our cattle, because they were scattered all through the herd. While we were cutting out, two hands from that herd rode all through ours to see if they could find any of their cattle in ours, but they didn't. When we finished cutting out we drove back near the wagon, and half the hands herded while the other half ate breakfast, and when all had eaten we took the trail again, glad to get away from a place where we had had so much trouble. We was real lucky, though, not to lose any cattle in such a stampede. The herd we had cut out from had two hundred and fifty head gone when we left them.

That night was drizzly again, and the wind blew chilly. I was in front of the cattle with my back to the wind listening, for it was dark, and I couldn't see, and they had walked off from the bed-ground when it began to drizzle. I thought the wind was going to change, and sure enough in 'most a second it turned right round and began blowing the other way. The cattle all turned their heads and started off. I was afraid to start behind them for fear I might ride into them without knowing it, for it was so dark I couldn't see anything, and waited a few minutes for them to get on a little and then started to ride clear round and get ahead of them again. Cattle are apt to get scared if you come riding up behind them in the dark when they can't see. But somehow I got turned round and couldn't find the herd at all, and didn't know which way to go. I felt pretty sheepish to think I had to let a whole herd walk right off under my nose and lose them. I hollered several times but didn't hear any answer, and then started to find the wagon, thinking maybe I would find somebody there that could tell me where they was.

As I got up on top of the hill I saw the lantern, and hadn't been at the wagon but a few minutes when Mose Baker come up and said he had lost the herd too. He said maybe the herd had gone back to the bed-ground, and we rode out there and sure enough there they were. The hands said they had come back of their own accord. We didn't have any more trouble with them that night.

Some of the boys laughed at me a good deal for losing a whole herd, and said I must have been asleep, but Capt. Dick said I would come out all right yet, that he lost a herd himself once the same way. The next night was rainy again, and the herd kept running and moving all night. They didn't make a big stampede, but they would all start and run a few hundred yards and then stop, but wouldn't be still. It was pitch dark, and we lost the wagon directly, and didn't know where we were. All hands were up and in the saddle. Sometimes they would keep still for half an hour, and Capt. Dick would ride round and tell every other man to lie down close enough to the herd so that he wouldn't lose them if they ran, but we could hardly get to sleep before they would be off again, and we would jump into our saddles and be after them. We laid down in our overcoats, hats, boots, and spurs.

Next morning we were clear out of sight of the wagon. It was raining so hard that we knew the cook couldn't cook anything, so Capt. Dick sent Highover and three other hands back to find the wagon, get up the loose horses, catch the ones we wanted, and tell the cook to drive on. Then he started off to find the trail.

When he found it we drove to it and let the cattle feed along it until the wagon came up. Then we changed horses and started again. There was a little cold bread and meat at the wagon, but hardly a mouthful apiece.

We didn't get anything to eat that day, for it kept raining, and the cook had let his wood get wet and couldn't get a fire started, and there was only one green tree in sight, and no dry wood. That night we had to be up until about three o'clock again, and then when the cattle did get still, it was our turn to go on guard, and we didn't get to sleep any, only little catnaps we caught in the saddle.

But it cleared off pretty, and the sun come out bright and warm, and when we were relieved and went to the wagon, old Jose had a good breakfast and plenty of strong, hot coffee for us, and we felt a heap better. Herding is hard work when you have to be up nearly all night two or three nights at a time, and don't get anything to eat for twenty-four hours besides. I went to sleep riding along beside the herd a dozen times that day—I just couldn't keep awake. When I would be trying my hardest I would go to sleep before I knew it. Several of the men went to sleep on guard that night. Some horses will keep right on around the herd all the same, but some of them just as soon as they find their riders is asleep will come to the wagon, or go feeding about. It's the funniest thing to watch a man on horseback asleep and see him riding zigzag anywhere his horse wants to go, and he bobbing about first one side and then the other like he was going to fall off all the time. And if his horse goes to the wagon and stops and he wakes up and finds himself there, he looks so foolish.

One night when I was riding Monkey on herd I went to sleep, and the little rascal went to the wagon with me, and when he stopped I woke up and saw where I was; but I just got down and went to the water bucket and got a drink as if I had come there for that, and I don't believe any of them knew I had been asleep. I think cowboys are very faithful to stick to their cattle as they do, when it would be so easy to ride off a piece and lie down and go to sleep, and say next day they had lost the herd and couldn't find it. They don't get much pay and have to work real hard.

We had good weather again now and get rested up some. The country was all rolling prairie, with hardly any timber at all except on the rivers and creeks, and not much there. There was water every ten or fifteen miles, so the cattle did not suffer any, though it was right mean for drinking sometimes.

The day we crossed the Washita the wind blew hard from the north all day, and kept up such a cloud we could hardly see, and sometimes it would get into our mouths and almost strangle us. At dinner time the cook piled up everything he could get on the north side of his fire, but everything was full of dirt. There was a little old bark shanty near the trail at the Washita, where the Indians used to keep a man to take toll from every herd that passed. They made the boss give them a beef for every thousand head. They said it was their grass and their water, and ought to be their beef too. But they haven't done it for several years now. I believe the United States made them quit it.

We made a dry camp that night, and next day we didn't get water until about three o'clock, and the cattle and horses were very thirsty. The front ones kept travelling fast to get to water, until the herd was strung out about two miles. Some of them kept up a lowing all the time. When they got to water it was a little narrow creek, where only a few could get in at a time and when the hindmost got to it, it was so muddy they could hardly drink it. Capt. Dick said once when he was driving out to the Pecos there wasn't any water for thirty miles. They let the cattle feed and water until near sundown, and then drive all night, and it was late in the evening the next day before they got to the water.

He said some of the cattle got so thirsty that they seemed to be 'most crazy, and a few of them fought them for five miles before they got there. The men too were nearly choked for water. They chewed bullets, and pieces of rawhide, and two of them got so hot and mad and thirsty that one of them shot one beef that kept fighting them, and cut his throat, and they pulled off their boots and caught the blood in them and drank it. They were 'most ready to fight each other for it. He said there were some pools of alkali water not far from the road, and they had the hardest kind of work to keep the cattle out of them, but they knew that every one that got a big drink of alkali water would die.

When they got within a mile of the river the cattle smelt the water, and, tired as they was, they started for it in a trot. Two or three killed themselves drinking, and several more got washed away by the river, crowding each other in so. He said it was the most mournful thing he had ever heard, the way the poor things kept up lowing before they got to the river.

All along the trail we would see ashes where other herds had camped. A burnt place shows a long time.

Some of them were two or three years old, but they still showed plain. The ashes was all washed away, but the bare place is there. Wood is so scarce that the cook don't use any more than he can help, and you could nearly always cover it with a broad-brimmed Mexican hat. It looked curious to me that such a little thing should be all there was to tell where so many cattle, and the horses and men and wagon, had staid all night, and we knew just as well that a herd had been as if we had seen them.

"But, Charley, might not some of the fires have been made by men who were not travelling with cattle?"

Yes, sir, but they nearly always went farther from the trail so as not to be in the way of any cattle that might pass. If you wanted to know for certain, you could tell by finding the bed-ground. You couldn't see it from the trail maybe, but if you rode out and hunted for it you could always find it, and if there wasn't any, you could know it hadn't been a herd. A bed-ground won't show more than two or three years, and sometimes you can hardly find it the next year.

At the Canadian River there was a little supply store where a man kept goods to sell drovers, and trade with the Indians for buffalo robes and other skins. His house had a dirt floor, and the roof was made of poles covered with dirt or clay, and he had a big chain with a heavy lock to stretch across the door at night to keep anybody from getting in and stealing his horses. He had two, and the stable was next to his room, just a little partition between. He had some fine robes hanging up in his store. Some of the men bought some tobacco there. I wouldn't like to live in such a place, because the Indians might come any time and kill him and take all he had. He had a few cattle that he had got from drovers for supplies. Sometimes a beef gets foot-sore so he can't keep up with the herd, and then they trade him off the first store they get to. I used to feel real sorry for the poor things limping along behind the herd, and getting poorer all the time. Most of them get well though.

We crossed the Canadian without any trouble, for it wasn't very deep. I remembered that was the river where Washington Irving had the buffalo chase, and the young Swiss Count got lost, though I don't reckon it was at the place where we crossed it. I read about in a book called *Crayon Miscellany,* that Miss Masover lent me. But there wasn't game like when he and the Rangers was there. I expect there is game away from the trail, but we never saw a single deer or turkey. Sometimes in herding we would scare up a prairie chicken, and once I found a nest with ten good eggs in it.

It was at Turkey Creek we saw the first prairie dogs. These don't look like dogs at all, but like squirrels. They stand up on their hind feet and hold the grass roots between their forepaws just like squirrels, and they are 'most the color of a fox squirrel, but a little bigger, and chunkier, and they only have a little squatty tail about four inches long. They live on the roots of the buffalo grass. We never saw any only where there was buffalo grass. They have holes in the ground with the dirt thrown up around them like an ant heap. We would see them sitting on top of the little mounds barking at us like squirrels when they think they are safe in a big tree, but just start towards one and he would give a little yelp, his heels would fly up, and down he would get into his hole.

We travelled through a dog-town five miles that day, and the boys shot at them a heap but nobody killed one or, if he did he, got into his hole and he didn't get him. There are little screech owls that seem to stay in the same holes with the prairie dogs, though maybe they only take holes the dogs have left. You nearly always find rattlesnakes in their towns too, and if you get after one he will always run into one of the holes. But I should think they would eat up the little prairie dogs if they lived in the same holes.

Capt. Dick said he thought the prairie dogs could keep the rattlesnakes out of their holes by biting them, but he expected sometimes they slipped in when the old ones were out and made a meal off of the little ones. One night when we had camped in a dog-town, two of the boys took the bucket and filled a hole with water and made the prairie dog come out and caught him. It took nearly three buckets of water. There wasn't but one dog in that hole. They tied him to a stake, but next morning he was gone. He had cut the string with his teeth.

Sometimes you catch one by a slip noose in the wagon whip, and putting it over the hole, and lying down right quiet. When the prairie dog puts his head up through the noose you must jerk it tight right quick, and you can snatch him away from his hole. They can't run very fast, but there are so many holes and so close together that they can always get into one before you can catch them. They are good to eat, though nobody likes much to eat them because they are called dogs.

Capt. Dick killed two one day with his pistol, and I ate some and thought it was real good. They are too tough to fry, unless you boil them first. Capt. Dick said he asked an Indian once if they ate them, and he said, "No, no good; there come a time when there come the hair all off." Nasho said the Indians he was with used to eat them if they couldn't get anything else. Several of the boys tried them, but all gave it up except Capt. Dick and me. They laughed at us a good deal about eating dog.

That evening we saw the first bunch of antelope we had seen, and away off two or three miles were some tents. They were a party of surveyors or Indians, we couldn't tell which. I thought it looked like Indian country, for there wasn't a house or tree in sight, and no tame animals except ours, and no herd in sight, just us out in the big prairie.

MUTINY ON THE TRAIL

We were camped on Nine Mile Creek about a short drive from Salt Fork. Something had waked me up very early in the night and I thought I would go out and stake Comanche in a fresh place. There was a little hollow close to the wagon, big enough to hide a horse in, and I staked him down in that. When I started back I heard a fuss at the wagon like two men fighting and cursing, so I crawled up the hill to see what was the matter. I thought first it was Indians, because the Indian Reservation for the Osages was on the sight of the trail, and the Cheyennes and Rapahoes on the left, but the noise I heard wasn't made by Indians. It was American.

When I got where I could see, the moon was shining bright. Highover and Black Jack and the three Mexicans were at the wagon. They had Capt. Dick and Whistling Bill tied, and was talking to Mose Baker. He was begging them not to hurt him. Black Jack wanted to tie him too, but at last Highover said if he would get on his knees and swear not to leave them, and to help drive the cattle, they would let him loose, and he done it. Highover said Col. Hunt owed him and Black Jack a good deal of money, and wouldn't pay them, and they were just going to take the cattle to Wichita and sell them, and pay themselves, and leave the rest of the money there for Col. Hunt, and that they wouldn't hurt Capt. Dick and Whistling Bill, but they would have to keep them tied and out of the way until they had sold the cattle, and then they would let them loose.

Highover asked whereabouts that little Charley was, but nobody knew, for nobody was awake when I had left the wagon. He waked up the cook and asked him, but he didn't know either. Highover said if they didn't get hold of me he would come back and let Dick and Bill loose, but Black Jack said they would fix that by leaving Wellman on guard at the wagon with a pistol, and when I came up he would make me lay down and keep still until they came off herd. Highover said that would do, and told Wellman to stay at the wagon and keep a good watch, and if Dick or Bill tried to get loose to shoot them, and when they sold their cattle they would give him two hundred dollars besides his wages, and to be sure and not go to sleep. Then he said they would go and see about their herd; maybe them blamed Africans had let them get away. They rode off, but directly Highover came back and staked out his horse, and got on Beelzebub and rode away to the herd.

I didn't know what to do. I was sure Highover and Black Jack intended to steal the herd, and the Mexicans was going to help them drive it, and they would make Mose Baker and the negroes help too. I was afraid they would get tired of keeping Capt. Dick and Whistling Bill tied and watching them, and kill them to keep them from ever telling on them. I thought first I would go to some other herd and tell them and get the hands to come and let Capt. Dick and Whistling Bill loose, and then I thought if Highover found I didn't come back he would think I had gotten away, and would leave the trail and maybe get away with the cattle before we could find them, and kill Capt. Dick and Whistling Bill.

While I was studying what to do, and afraid all the time they would come back and I would have to run off without doing anything, Nasho got up and walked out in a few steps of me. Wellman looked up, but when he saw it was Nasho, he didn't say anything or watch him. I called to Nasho right low, and he looked up quick and then went on like he hadn't heard anything. But he kept moving about and stretching like he was sleepy, and getting closer to me, and then dropped down in the grass and crawled up to me. I told him quick what had happened, and he said. "Yes, me hear all. That what for me come out here; me tout you was here somewhere."

I told him I wanted to get Capt. Dick and Whistling Bill loose and I didn't know how to do it before Highover and Black Jack come back.

"Give me pistol, Carley. Me crawl up and shoot Wellman."

I told him no, because Highover and Black Jack and the other Mexicans would be back when they heard the shooting, and Capt. Dick or Whistling Bill or maybe both of them would be sure to be killed.

"Well, Carley," he said, "me get horse and slip up hollow and stampede herd, and while dey run, Wellman jump up to see what matter, den you cut Capt. Dick and oder fellow loose. If Wellman come, you shoot him. It light, cattle no run far, me go wid 'em and we get 'em again."

I told him that was a good way to do, but be sure and keep out of the way of Highover and Black Jack, or they would shoot him.

"Dey not catch Nasho, you no be 'fraid."

He went back to the wagon like he had come, and put on his blanket. Then I saw him go to the fire and light a cigarette, and slip the bread pan under his blanket. Then he got up and started to his horse. Wellman raised up and asked him where he was going. He said it was 'most time for him to go on guard, and he would go and see about the horses, that he hadn't heard the bell since he waked up.

He got on his horse and rode off in such a way as to get into the hollow where he wouldn't be seen. I couldn't watch him any further and just lay still and listened. I took out my knife and kept it in my right hand, and had mine and Nasho's pistol in my other one. I tell you my heart beat fast.

It seemed to me a half hour before I heard a horse's feet running, and somebody yelling like an Indian. I was so excited I jumped up and saw Nasho running toward the herd as hard as he could go, beating the tin pan with one hand, and swinging his blanket with the other. The hands were all in a bunch on the other side of the herd. The cattle all broke, but I didn't wait for anything. I just ran to Capt. Dick and cut him loose and handed him my pistol, and told him there was a horse in the hollow, that Highover had his horse. I heard him muttering, "Curse their thieving souls!" and he was gone. It didn't take a second hardly, and in another second I had cut Whistling Bill loose. We started for the horses, but the whole herd was coming toward us like a streak, and Whistling Bill broke back again for the wagon.

I thought I could get to a horse before they would catch me and kept on. I had just got to a pony that was saddled and put my foot in the stirrup when a steer hit him and knocked him down and sent me heels over head in the air. I crawled back to the pony and laid down just as close to his back as I could get. A beef stumbled and fell over us and broke his neck. He lay dead almost against me. As the first cattle came to us they had to jump, for they were so thick they couldn't go round, but directly they began to thin out and then they dodged to the right and left. I reckon though at least twenty jumped right over me and the pony. I tell you it was a scary place. They raised so much noise you couldn't have heard thunder.

As they began to get pretty thin I heard pistol shots at the wagon. I knew something was wrong, and jumped up. A bullet whistled close to my head. I saw Whistling Bill fire and a man on horseback fall. His horse ran back. In a second Highover and Aunt Tony came up horseback and began shooting and Whistling Bill fell. They rode on then after the herd, as hard as they could go. I ran up to Whistling Bill and asked him if he was hurt much. He said no, not very much, and told me to watch Wellman under the wagon, but I saw he was lying still and didn't go to him.

Whistling Bill didn't say anything else, and when I asked him anything he didn't answer me. I was afraid he was dying, and there was nobody in sight, and I had to watch Wellman too. I picked up the pistol Whistling Bill had dropped. It was Wellman's. I knew he must have snatched it away from Wellman, and either shot him or knocked him down, he lay so still. There wasn't but one load in it.

Every minute seemed like an hour. I didn't know what to do. I couldn't go off for help, and I didn't know what to do for poor Whistling Bill. He was shot in the side, and was bleeding a little, but not much. Now and then he would moan as if in pain, but he never answered anything I asked him.

I could tell from the sound that the herd had stopped running, and knew the hands had got round them and had them in hand again. I was listening for them to come back when I heard two pistol shots so close together they seemed almost like one. That made me more anxious then ever, for I knew those shots meant fighting, and I was afraid Capt. Dick might be killed. I wanted to jump on a horse and run over there, but I couldn't leave Whistling Bill. I got a blanket and spread it over him to keep the dew off him. I thought I heard him say "water," and ran and got him a drink out of the bucket, and raised up his head so he could drink. He drank the whole cupful, and looked at me and said, "Carley, is that you? The herd's stampeded...go for 'em. Blast that Highover! the..." and then he fell back again and didn't know anything. I would have given everything in the world I had, and promised to turn back home for a doctor, or somebody that could do something for him. I thought every minute he would die, and I couldn't do anything for him. I didn't know what to do.

I know it wasn't long, though it seemed like a month, before I saw the herd coming back. When they got closer I could see Capt. Dick riding round and stopping a minute with each hand. Then he left the herd and came galloping up to the wagon. How my heart thumped, I was so glad to see him! I ran out to meet him and told him Whistling Bill was shot, and didn't know nothing, and I thought was dying. He only muttered "Serve him right!" as he jumped off his horse, caught me in his arms a second and hugged me so I almost hollered, and kept on to Whistling Bill. He knelt down by him and felt of his arm. Then he saw where the blood came from and loosened his clothes so he could get to the place. I stood by him. He raised him up a little so he could pull his shirt up from his back, and I saw another bloody hole in his side behind. Capt. Dick's face lightened up a little, and he said to me low, "He's pretty badly hurt, Charley, but I don't think he'll die. The ball's come out again. Get on my horse and go to the herd, and tell Gen. Foot to come here, and the other boys to watch the cattle close, and for none of them to leave the herd."

"Wellman's lying there under the wagon, Capt. Dick. Watch him."

I sent Gen. Foot in and told the boys Capt. Dick said they must watch the cattle close and none of them leave the herd. I didn't have time to tell them anything except that Whistling Bill was badly shot, but Capt. Dick didn't think he would die, or to ask them any questions, because some of the cattle was restless and scary and we had to keep riding round and talking to them to keep them still. It wasn't but a little while till Gen. Foot came back and said Capt. Dick wanted me. I rode to the wagon and got down and went to him. Whistling Bill was lying on a nice pallet under the wagon, but his eyes was shut and I could tell he didn't know nothing. Capt. Dick was sitting by him, Wellman was lying near the wagon wheel with his head all bloody. Capt. Dick got up and came to me and said low, "Charley, I want you to go to Ellis and get a doctor. It's a long ride, and you must go day and night till you get there. If you get too tired you can lie down on the road and sleep an hour, and then go on again. Whistling Bill's going to be very sick, and I am afraid he'll die if we don't get a doctor pretty quick, I'll—"

"Ain't there a doctor at Caldwell, Capt. Dick?"

"Yes but I am afraid to trust the old pill-peddler. You must go to Ellis. There's a good one there. I will write you a couple of notes, and you get a cup of coffee and some bread before you start. Put some bread and meat in your saddle pockets too, and take your rubber blanket and overcoat. It may rain before you get back."

"I ain't a bit hungry, Capt. Dick."

"But you will be before you are gone an hour. Try and eat something, Charley, before you go."

I started up the fire and put on the coffee pot and got out some cold bread and meat and ate a snack. I wasn't hungry and didn't eat much When I got through, Capt. Dick had his notes ready.

"Stop at the first herd ahead of you, Charley, and ask for the boss. It's one of Capt. Littlefield's, and the boss knows me. Tell him what a fix we are in and ask him if he can't spare me a hand for a few days. He'll send him, I know. Then go on to the next one, that's one of Major Mabry's, and ask the boss if he can't spare me a hand. Tell them both I'll get hands just as soon as you can get to Ellis and they come from there. If they don't send them stop at every herd you come to until you do get them. Tell them, too, if they have got any wine or anything nice to eat in camp to send it for poor Bill. Then you hurry on to Ellis, go to the Railroad House, and ask for Capt. Millet or Major Mabry, or Capt. Littlefield, or Col. King or any Texas cattleman. Some of 'em's sure to be there, and give whoever you find this note. He will send the doctor and two or three hands. You stay at the hotel and get something to eat and take a good rest. Rest as long as you want to, and you needn't be in such a hurry about coming back, though I know you won't waste any time on the road."

"That I won't, Capt. Dick."

"Stop at dinner time and at night with herds on the road, and get something to eat and a blanket to sleep on. If your horse gets tired going, stop at some herd and give the boss this note, and he will let you have a fresh horse. Leave your horse until you come back. If you can't get a horse from one, try another. 'Most all of them know me, and I know some of them will let you have a horse to save a man's life. It's a long, hard ride, Charley, and I hate to send you, but I would rather have you go than anybody else. I know I can depend on you."

I girted my saddle tighter, and Capt. Dick helped me to tie on my overcoat and rubber. Then I got into the saddle and reached out my hand to bid Capt. Dick goodbye.

"Tell whoever you find at Ellis to send some good wine and nice things for a sick man with the doctor. I know you won't let grass grow under your feet. Goodbye and God bless you, Charley!" I couldn't say a word. I was 'most crying, so I just popped the spurs to Comanche and was off in a long gallop. Comanche wanted to go too fast, but I knew he would need all his bottom before he got there, and pulled him up until he settled down steadily to his work.

Day was just breaking as I rode up to the first herd. The boss was on herd, and I rode out there and found him and told him my errand. He broke out with a pro-longed whistle when I got through. "I've been on the trail five years, and never heard the like before. All right. Tell Capt. Dick I'll send him a hand right off. He can go back with you now."

He started to the wagon with me, but I told him I was going on to Ellis.

"Then a hard long ride you've got, little one. Reckon you'll give out on the road. All right, I'll send the hand right off. Goodbye. Keep up your pluck, and good luck to you."

When I told my story at the next herd I thought the boss wasn't going to send any help. "Mighty short-handed we are. Don't know how we would manage if there should come a storm. Whose herd is it anyhow?"

"Col. Hunt's."

"Who's your boss?"

"Capt. Dick."

"All right. Capt. Dick can get anything I've got. Helped me out of a quicksand in the Platte River, he did wonst, and lent me three hands to help gather the bulls in Idaho arter the wust run ever I seed, and that ain't been a few I tell you." He called one of the hands, but I told him I was going on to Ellis.

"All right. I'll send him in less'n no time. Capt. Dick can get anything I've got, he kin. Get down, young one, and have some breakfast. It ain't no pleasure trip you're going on."

I thanked him but told him I had had breakfast, and struck out for the trail again.

"Just be easy about that hand," I heard him holler after me. "Capt. Dick can get anything I've got, he kin, you bet."

Every few miles I would come to a herd and have to turn out and go round, and two or three times I had to stop a minute or two with a drover to tell my errand. Comanche couldn't travel as fast over the grass when we had to turn out as he could on the beaten trail, but he never slacked his gait, and I felt pretty sure we were making eight miles an hour, and I thought more. It wasn't much if any after ten o'clock when I got to Bluff Creek. That was the line between The Nation and Kansas. About twelve by the sun I stopped on a little branch the other side of the Shawocaspah River to let Comanche rest and pick a little, and get a little rest myself, for I was getting tired. A mile or two gallop is mighty pleasant riding, but just try fifty of 'em on a stretch, and see if you don't get more riding than you bargained for.

I ate a cold snack and went to sleep before I knew it, but I didn't sleep more than half an hour, and when I woke up all of a sudden, I was so scared to think I had gone to sleep when maybe Whistling Bill was dying for want of a doctor, that I jumped up, tightened Comanche's girth, climbed into the saddle and struck out again. I would like to have had some coffee, but the next herd I came to was ten miles ahead and had had dinner and was moving on.

Comanche kept up his long smooth lope just as steady as when he began in the morning, but I began to get mighty tired, and the sun seemed to me to go down mighty slow. I shifted about in the saddle but that didn't do any good, and I began to be afraid I would never get through, and I felt like I would almost rather die than not get through. I didn't pay any attention to the country I was going over, only I remember I had left the tall grass behind and most of it now was sedge and short buffalo grass. I remember, too, going through a dog-town, but I was too tired to watch the little barkers.

As the sun got low, every minute was like an hour. It seemed like I just must fall off my horse and go to sleep, but I managed somehow to keep on and at dark I galloped up to a herd camped on Rattlesnake Creek, a hundred miles from our camp on Nine Mile Creek. I was just able to tell the men where I was going and what for, and ask the boss if he wouldn't be sure and have me waked up in an hour, and then dropped down and went to sleep.

Rescue Ride

Iknew by the shining of the moon that it was past twelve o'clock when I was waked up, but the man who had called me said it wasn't no use to wake me up any sooner as I was 'most dead for sleep, and if I got to Ellis in the night I would have been too tired to have gone round and hunted up anybody I wanted to see. Everybody would be in bed of course. He had some supper ready for me and some good hot coffee, and while I was eating he brought Comanche up and saddled him. He had been grazing and seemed almost as fresh as when I started.

"One of us would have went on for you, youngster, but you didn't tell us who you wanted and seemed so dead for sleep we thought we had better let you alone. I'll go now if you'll stay and drive for me till I come back."

I thanked him, but told him I was ready to go on now for I was rested, and climbed into the saddle again, shook goodbye with him and struck out again. The sleep and the coffee had done me so much good that I felt nearly as fresh as when I started, only a little stiff and sore. The Arkansas was down so I crossed it without any trouble. There were no herds on the trail and nothing to bother me, and Comanche kept on as steady as a clock. It was just sunup as I rode into Ellis. I went to the hotel, hitched Comanche, walked in and asked the man behind the counter if Capt. Millet was at the hotel.

"Yes, he's in, but he ain't up yet."

I told him I wanted to see him quick, that I wanted a doctor for a man who was shot, and he sent a boy with me to show me his room. Capt. Millet was in bed, but I gave him Capt. Dick's note and told him what I had come for. As soon as he read it he jumped up and began dressing, talking to me all the time, asking me when I left camp, what had been the trouble, how many hands Capt. Dick had and where he was camped. As soon as he was dressed he told me to stay at his room until he came back, and he would go out and send the doctor off. I got tired of staying in the room, and went downstairs. It wasn't long until he came back, and said the doctor would start in a few minutes.

He came up directly, a tall man with black eyes and hair, riding a fine bay horse, with little saddlebags on his saddle. He asked me a few questions about where Whistling Bill was shot, and where the camp was, and then rode off on a gallop.

As soon as he was gone, Capt. Millet said, "Well, little one, I reckon you are about tired out. I will send an ambulance with a good bed in it and everything he needs for your sick man, and three hands to drive. I'll have your horse put up, and you get some breakfast—it'll be ready directly—and then go to bed. You've had a hard ride and must be tired out."

I told him I wasn't tired and wanted to start back, but he said that wouldn't do, that if I wasn't tired now I would be, that I couldn't do anything if I went back, and that Capt. Dick had written him not to let me start back under twenty-four hours anyhow. He said he should be surprised if my ride didn't lay me up for a week. I wanted to go back mighty bad, but Capt. Millet had been so kind in sending everything off, that I thought I ought to do as he said, and when I began to feel stupid after breakfast I went up to his room and laid down. When I woke up a gong was beating and Capt. Millet was just starting to leave the room, but seeing me awake, he stopped.

"Well, little one, you've had a good sleep. Feel like breakfast don't you? Sort of stiff and sore ain't you?"

I told him I wasn't sore at all, but as rested and fresh as I had ever been.

"Well, dress and come downstairs and we'll have some breakfast. I'll wait for you in the barroom."

After breakfast I told Capt. Millet I wanted to start back to camp, but he said he had telegraphed to Col. Hunt and he would be here on the ten o'clock train, and I had better stop and see him. He might want to go to camp himself.

I went to the stable to look after Comanche, but the old fellow was looking better than when I started. He had been rubbed off clean and nice, and was picking at some hay as if he didn't know what else to do with himself.

"That 'ar hoss yours?" a man asked me who came up with a curry-comb in one hand and a brush in the other, and his shirt sleeves rolled up to his elbows.

"Yes."

"Had a powerful long ride, didn't you?"

"Yes. I have come nearly a hundred and fifty miles."

"Whew! Wonder it didn't kill you. You're a little one for that sort of work. But I tell you that hoss of yourn is clear grit and no mistake. He's ready for another hundred mile gallop."

I started away, but he came up and said, "I say, boss, you oughter give me a dollar for tending to your hoss. I worked mighty hard rubbin' him down, for I seed he hed a powerful long gallop, and would be stiff if I didn't."

I happened to have a little money in my pocket, and gave him a dollar and went back to the hotel. There wasn't anything to do but wait for the train. There were some well-dressed nice looking men lounging round the hotel, reading papers, smoking, and talking, or walking up and down the gallery. Now and then a rough looking fellow would come along with his pants in his boots, a slouch hat on his head, big spurs, and pistol in his belt and if he had "bull whacker" written on him you couldn't have read it any plainer.

We went down to the depot when we heard the train coming and met Col. Hunt. He asked me a good many questions about what had happened at camp, and then left us to look for some hands he wanted to send back with me to take the place of those Capt. Dick had borrowed and the others. He came to the hotel about noon and said, "Charley, if I understand you, you are short six hands."

"Yes, sir. Wellman, and the other two Mexicans, and Highover, and Black Jack, and Whistling Bill."

"Well, I have got six hands with eight horses. You don't know whether any of the horses were run off or not?"

"No, sir; though I don't think they were, because I heard the bell north of the herd, and the stampede went to the south."

"Then they'll have horses enough. You had better start back this evening with these hands and get there as soon as you can, though you needn't hurry particularly. I have no instructions to send. Capt. Dick knows just as well what to do as I would if I were there. I'll settle your bill here and remember you when you get through. Do you want anything now?"

"No, sir."

"You had better take this anyhow. You may want something before you go out," and he handed me five dollars. I didn't spend it though, because I wanted to save all my money to go to the Centennial on. The gong beat just then and we all went in to dinner.

Cowboy Justice

When we got to camp we found the herd right where I had left it. Whistling Bill had been too sick to move, but was over his fever now and the doctor was going to start to Ellis with him the next morning in the ambulance. He said he would be well in a couple of weeks, but would have to be quiet so as to keep fever from setting in. He was lying under the wagon, and the sheet had been stretched round it so as to keep the sun off of him. I went to see him, and he was right glad to see me. We got to talking about the night of the stampede, and I asked him how he came to be at the wagon.

"Why you, Carley, I saw I couldn't make it to a horse before they would be on me, and I just cut back to the wagon to get out of their way. First time I ever was afraid of cattle in my life, but Nasho had give 'em the devil of a scare, and the mad bulls was comin' like an avalanche. They would have run square over the wagon if I hadn't got in front of it with a blanket and hollered and cavorted about worse'n half a dozen Injins. Between Nasho and his thundering old tin ration-bag, and me and the blanket, I don't think the whole herd of bulls had sense enough left to have stocked a skunk for breakfast. By George! if it had been at Austin we would have corralled the whole lot of 'em in the crazy-folks' hotel there. They was greater looneys than any of the two-legged naturals.

"You bet, Carley, when I thought about you I didn't feel like I was at a weddin'. I thought they had made hash of you sure. There was one good thing: their eyes was so big they would think you was ten feet high, an' I thought they might dodge you. As the tail end of the bulls began to pass, I remember seeing Old Coly and Lame Spot—never a bit lame was he then, with his tail up going like a scared wolf. I'll salt his hide for him the next time I catch him behind. Señor Schezeredicks came up on horseback and shot at me. I shot back, an' he went over backwards like a bullfrog when a chunk of mud takes him in the belly. Then Highover and Aunt Tony came up an' took a hand, and Highover throw'd the ace an' I flung up my hand an' that's the last I remember about it. I tell you, Carley, if it hadn't been for you, me an' Capt. Dick woulda went up I reckon, for I believe them ar' scoundrels would have cut our throats, or else took us off in some hollow and left us to starve to death an' be eat up by the coyotes. You bet, my boy, I ain't goin' to forget you."

I told him I hoped he would get well soon so he could come back to us, for we would all miss him a heap.

"You bet I'll come back as soon as I can. I'm like an' old black sheep in a flock I herded when I was a boy. He was more trouble than all the rest. Many a mile I've run after the blamed old rascal, but when the wolves had chops for supper one night off him, I missed him more'n any sheep of the lot. I reckon you won't have much devilment goin' on till I get back but I'll wake you up then, for I'll be good rested like a stabled colt. Better laugh than cry, Carley, any time. It's fattenin'. Come back when you can. It's sorter lonesome here. I'd a heap rather be after the bulls, you bet."

I didn't get to see Capt. Dick to talk to him until night, he was so busy, but we were on guard together then, and while the cattle were still we got on a little knoll where we could watch them, and he told me what had happened while I was gone.

"I had got to the herd after leaving you and stopped them and was rounding them up when I saw Highover coming with his pistol in his hand. I felt for mine, but it was gone. The mean villains had taken it when they tied me. I had to run and leave the herd and all of you, or take the chance of dashing at Highover and jerking him off his horse before he could hit me. I tell you, Charley, I felt rather ticklish, for I thought my time had about come. Just then I saw Nasho coming up behind him full tilt swinging his rope. You bet, he was in good time, for Highover would have got me the next shot. But before he could cock his pistol again Nasho's rope fell over his head and he was jerked a higher damned summersault than when he got his damned name. Charley, my boy," and he put his arm around me, "I have tried to stop this blamed swearing on your account, but I can't think about that night without feeling like I could stand on my head and swear my boots off. Don't get into the way of it, Charley. It's a bad practice, and sticks to you worse than mesquite gum, once you get into it.

"I jumped off my horse, snatched the hobbles from his neck, tied Highover's hands behind his back, got Nasho's hobbles and tied his feet, so I knew he'd stay there till judgment day, if somebody didn't cut him loose, and away me and Nasho went after the herd which had broke and run again when Highover shot at me. The moon had gone down by that time and we had only starlight to go by, but we caught up with them directly and was rounding them in and getting them quiet when..."

I just wish you could have seen, how quick that herd was gone. More'n half of them was lying down, but they bounced up and was off in a second, and nothing in the world to get scared at, unless it was a sneeze Beelzebub give just then. We was after 'em in a second, and with the other hands who was in front and had kept 'em well checked up, we brought 'em all back to the bed-ground again in a few minutes. We rode around them until they got quiet again, and then Capt. Dick and me went back to our old place.

"That's just the way the damned cattle have been doing ever since that night. We won't get no more rest till we get through, and I'll be glad when they're sold and off our hands. I hope to the Lord we won't have a bad storm before we are done with them, for they'll scatter so bad if we do. The devil himself couldn't hold them. Col. Hunt ain't a-going to sell these bulls to be delivered in Wyoming or Dakota, not if I know anything about it.

"Well, as I was saying, we had started them back again when we heard galloping feet and two more pistol shots, and off went the mad bulls again right over the ground we had just come. I had forgot about Highover till I heard two awful screams—o-o-gh—I hear them now, and my hair 'most stands on end, and I knew in a second it was all up with him. We gathered them up again and got them back to the bed-ground this time, and the boys managed to keep them there the rest of the night. You know it was nearly day then.

"The next day, or that morning rather, while the bulls were feeding, I found that the last shots me and Nasho had heard was between Black Jack and Gen. Foot. Mose Baker and the General was rounding up some cattle when Black Jack rode up and shot at Mose. Gen. Foot out with his old horse-pistol and shot at him but missed, but before Black Jack could fire again he ran up to him and brought him a lick over the head with the barrel that stretched him out; the pluckiest thing I ever knew a darkey to do. Mose had the good sense to get down and take his pistol away, and then they struck out after the herd again.

"The next morning when the cattle were grazing and everything was quieted down a little, I rode to the nearest herds and asked the bosses to come over to our herd with me. When they got there I told them what had happened, and that I had one of the Mexicans tied, that I was satisfied Highover was dead and I reckoned Black Jack had got away. They said we must find out, and we started to look for them. We found Highover first, what was left of him. The cattle had just trod him into a jelly, and one had evidently caught its foot in the rope that tied his feet and dragged him apiece. There was hardly enough left of him to bury. I've seen men pretty badly torn up by cannon balls and shells, Charley, but I never saw anything to equal that corpse that had been run over by a stampeded herd. It was just horrible. That evening they sent me some hands, and we wrapped what was left of him in his blankets and laid him under a little bank where a wolf had had a den, and caved the earth in on him, for we didn't have anything to dig with, and just left the grave so without anything to show what it was. We didn't have anything to make a headboard of, and if we had, when you can't say anything more for a man than we could a' said for him, I think the least said the better, and none at all best.

"Then we went to the place where Gen. Foot said he had knocked Black Jack off his horse. He wasn't there, but his trail showed he had crawled off, and we didn't go far till we found him sitting under a little bank by a little hole of water, washing his bloody head. He started to draw his pistol when he saw us coming, but he saw in a second that wasn't no use, and just sat still. We put him on a horse and took him to camp, the man whose horse he was riding walking by him to keep him from falling off. He didn't have anything to say, but after he got to camp and had some breakfast and hot coffee he was ready enough to talk. He denied most positively shooting at Mose Baker, said he was just trying to round up the cattle when he felt a tremendous lick on his head and fell off his horse, and didn't know anything more until he felt the sun shining in his face. We asked him why he didn't start towards camp, and he said he didn't know which way camp was, but knew from the lay of the land that the way he went was the nearest to water, and that was what he wanted worst.

"I asked the men what ought to be done with 'em, and they said there wasn't but one thing to be done, and that was to swing 'em to the first tree. I told 'em I didn't like that way of doing, and at least the fellows was entitled to a fair trial, and the jury oughtn't all to be bosses either. There was another herd come up about that time, and they said there was another one about a mile and a half behind them, so we went back and got that boss to come up. After talking the matter over, we agreed to get twelve hands and give the fellows a regular trial, and whatever the jury said we would do. They all come in about two o'clock that evening, and we got to work, for there wasn't no time to lose. One of the bosses was made Judge, and Nasho and me and Gen. Foot was the witnesses, for you was gone and poor Bill couldn't speak for himself. We brought up the prisoners, but Wellman wouldn't say nothing, and Black Jack only swore he didn't know anything about any plan to steal the herd.

"The jury wan't many minutes in concluding that there wasn't but one thing to do, and that was to swing 'em.

They had tried to kill me and Mose Baker, and maybe had killed poor Bill, and they ought to have what they was trying to bring on honest men. We took 'em down to the branch where you see that dead cottonwood, put 'em on horses, tied ropes round their necks—one of the boys climbed the tree and fastened 'em to a limb—and at the word, two quick cuts made the horses jump from under 'em and left 'em swinging.

"Black Jack begged like a dog to the last, but Wellman never said a word. We just waited long enough to be sure that the life was clean gone out of 'em, and then took 'em down, laid 'em under the bank, throwed some old brush over them and shoved the bank down on 'em and left 'em, an' I reckon they'll stay there till Gabriel blows his horn. When we got back to camp dinner was ready, and after that I treated 'em all to some whiskey I had brought for chills or snake bites, and the crowd broke up."

"What became of Aunt Tony and Schezeredicks?" I asked.

"The last one is lying out there in the prairie, what the wolves have left of him. Whistling Bill had laid him out cold enough. That other yeller rascal must have scooted when he seen how things was going, for nobody has ever seen anything of him since."

"And the horses?"

"Saved 'em all. When Nasho snatched Highover off Beelzebub, the damned scoundrel—it's a shame to cuss a dead man, but I can't help it when I think about him a ridin' old Beelzebub—he just cut out from there and went to camp a-flying, and next mornin' we found Black Jack's horse saddled with the rest of 'em. We ain't lost no cattle 'cept one that broke his neck out there close to the wagon, though we've got several lame ones that it'll be a tight shave for to get through, and one lame horse that won't be fit to back for a month, but we are just a goin' to catch fits with these bulls the rest of the way. They'll stampede from here to Ellis. Did Col. Hunt say anything about when he would be back to Ellis?"

"Yes, he said he would be there when you got in, and before if he could get through with his business in Kansas City."

"You bet I'm glad to hear that, for I'm powerful hot to get rid of this herd, and if the Col. don't sell the first chance, he'll have to get another boss for this outfit, that's all."

The cattle began to get restless and we had to quit talking and ride around them to keep them quiet. The next morning early the doctor started for Ellis with Whistling Bill in the ambulance, and by nine o'clock we were on the trail again.

When we got to the Arkansas it was up some, and we had to ferry the wagon over on a little scow there was there. We put two ropes to it, for there wasn't any ferry rope, and two of the boys hitched them to the horns of their saddles and started across with it. About two-thirds of the way over it stuck on a sandbar and they couldn't drag it off. A few feet the other side the water was swimming, and the horses couldn't get a foothold to pull. The river was rising and it was nearly sundown, and things looked pretty squally for the wagon. I galloped up to the herd, got a couple of hands and come back, and we stripped and went in and fairly lifted the heavy old scow out of her bed in the sand. That night we had a thunderstorm, and the cattle kept us busy all night. A herd nearby ran into ours, and we were kept in the hills nearly all next day to give them a chance to cut out. Five more days brought us in sight of Ellis.

ROPING ANTELOPE & BUFFALO

W e didn't stay there more than a month before Col. Hunt sold the herd. Herding was a heap easier than driving. I caught two prairie dogs and made a cage for them out of a box, but I had to get tin to line it with, for their teeth are so sharp and strong they would cut through the wood. I bought a book that told me all about trapping animals and skinning them, and dressing their skins and stuffing them. I caught three prairie chickens in snares, and trapped two badgers. They are just like coons, only they are a little heavier and have longer claws, and live in holes in the ground. I reckon if coons were brought here they would have to learn to live in holes, for there ain't any trees.

It's the worst country to get lost in I ever saw. It's all exactly alike, covered with, thick, short buffalo grass about four inches high, and often not a tree or bush for twenty miles. One time we had to use buffalo manure to cook with for several days, because there wasn't a stick of timber on the trail. They call the manure "chips," and sometimes when you ask a man "how's wood ahead?" he will say "plenty of buffalo chips."

When you get a mile away from camp there ain't a thing to tell you where it is. The prairie is all alike, and the wagon being down near the creek you can't see that, and it's pretty much guesswork whether you hit camp or not.

There were plenty of antelope around and sometimes they would get into the herd. Nearly everybody said they were the fastest animals in the world, and a horse couldn't catch them. But one day when I wasn't on herd I saw a little bunch out on a level part of the prairie, and saddled Comanche and started towards them. Before they began to notice me I got off my horse and, getting behind him, drove him along letting him stop every two or three steps as if he was only feeding. I got up in about two hundred yards and then, as they began to be scary, I got into the saddle and started for them. They didn't run fast at first, and I let Comanche out and was within a hundred yards of them before they knew it. How they did clip it then! You could have most covered the bunch with a blanket. They seemed to be almost flying, but the ground was good and Comanche kept crawling on to them. When we got within fifty yards the bunch broke. I picked out the biggest buck, touched Comanche with my heels, clucked to him, and I tell you he just let himself out.

In less'n half a mile I was close enough to swing my rope, and the first throw dropped squarely over his head. When I checked up the antelope turned a double summersault and never got up again. His neck was broken. I petted Comanche a little and then took the bridle off so he could graze. I knew then he was fast, for there ain't many horses can catch an antelope. The boys call them "goats" sometimes, because they are chunky like goats and have little short, two-pronged horns, but they don't run like goats. Me and Comanche could swear to that.

Then I began to skin my buck, and was as careful as I could be. I left the feet and head on. It took me three hours, for his feet and head were a heap of trouble.

When I got to camp I washed the skin out clean inside, cleaned the head out, took the eyes out, sewed it up again and stuffed it. I filled the legs and neck with oats I had bought for Comanche, and made a frame to keep the body tight, and filled the frame with dry grass. Then I propped it up and put a blanket over it to keep off the dew and sun. It cured first-rate and looked very natural only it didn't have any eyes. The first time the wagon went to town I sent it in, and the merchant where Capt. Dick bought our supplies put it away for me.

I caught two big rattlesnakes and shut them up in a box. I didn't have much trouble catching them, because I chloroformed them, but they were a heap of trouble until I could get a box for them. I tied them together head and tail until my box came, because if I had staked them out separately they would have choked themselves to death or bitten themselves. I found out where their poison is. It is in a little bag at the root of their fangs. Their fangs are curved, and each one has a little groove on the underside from the root to the point, and if you pry one's mouth open wide you can see the poison come out of the bag and run down the groove in the fang. For fear my snakes might bite somebody sometime I gave them chloroform and pulled their fangs out with a pair of bullet moulds. I fed them on bugs, and frogs and meat.

One night two Englishmen staid at our camp that were fitting out for a hunt on the plains. They had splendid horses and the finest kind of rifles and pistols, and two men to take care of their horses and dogs, and another one to cook. Next morning I was out early looking after the horses and saw a buffalo bull not a half mile from camp. When I told it in camp the Englishmen wanted to go and kill him right off, but I told them he was my meat, and I had a great mind to rope him. One of the

Englishmen said I couldn't do it. Capt. Dick offered to bet him fifty, dollars that me and Nasho could rope and tie him. The Englishman took him up.

After breakfast we started and found him directly feeding along down a dry hollow. We got into another hollow that the one he was feeding in ran into, and waited for him. He didn't see us until he was in about a hundred and fifty yards of us, when we went for him. I was to rope his head and Nasho his feet, and the rest of the party promised to stay behind and not get in the way.

We caught him before he had run more than half a mile, but I missed the first throw because his horns were so short, and his hair so long and thick that the noose fell off. I made my noose smaller next time and caught him round the throat and one horn. He was so big and heavy I 'most dreaded to check up and stop him, but when I drew my reins Comanche dropped back on his haunches, set himself hard, and turned him a summer-sault. He was up like a flash and after me before Nasho could get a chance, and I had to get away from there lively. I reckon he ran me half a mile.

I kept thinking I would have to turn my rope loose, but I didn't want to do that with those Englishmen watching us, and managed to stick to it, though the old bull come in an ace of catching me two or three times. I reckon if Comanche had put his foot in a hole it would have been all up with us. I began to think he wasn't going to stop running me, and I would have to throw down my rope and get away from him anyhow, when Nasho came up behind, wrapped his tail round the horn of his saddle and gave him a terrible fall. Up he came in a second and went for Nasho this time, but Comanche was ready and made him change ends again, and this time Nasho had his rope round his hind legs before he could get fairly on his feet, and we stretched him. He was so strong and quick that we had hard work to keep him down, but our horses set to him faithfully. When he got pretty well choked and worried, down Nasho slipped off his horse, ran up to him easy, drew his tail between his hind legs and set to him. He surged once or twice but couldn't get up. Then Nasho managed to get the rope round his hind feet round his fore ones too, and drew them close together and tied them hard and fast.

The rest of the party had come up and were watching us. Nasho let go the tail and got on his horse, and I threw down my rope and told Capt. Dick there was his bull. He asked the Englishman what he wanted to do with him. He said he didn't know that he couldn't kill him now that he was tied, and he couldn't do anything with him if we let him up; he guessed we would have to turn him loose. Capt. Dick said he would mark him anyhow, and cut a slit out of each ear, and bobbed his tail. Nasho untied his forefeet and then ran to his horse and stretched his hind ones out again. I rode up to his head and reached down and took the rope off, and drew off out of the way a little. Nasho unfastened his rope from the saddle and gave it a twirl that made it rap the bull on the side. He bounced up and took after the Englishman, but he had a good horse and soon left him. The rope dropped off his feet and Nasho watched where it fell and picked it up.

The Englishman paid his bet, and then gave me and Nasho ten dollars apiece. We didn't want to take it, but he said we must for he wouldn't have missed seeing it for five hundred dollars.

When Col. Hunt sold out we all went in to Ellis to settle and be paid off. Whistling Bill was getting well fast, and was staying at a house where he was taken good care of. Capt. Dick said he wouldn't have left him

if he hadn't been sure he would be taken care of. Col.
Hunt paid all his expenses and his wages just the same
as if he had been on herd all the time.

Col. Hunt took mine and Nasho's horses, all except
Comanche and Nasho's pack pony he had traded from
some Indians that came to camp while I was gone to
Ellis, at the same price we paid for them. Then he gave
us each a fine Mexican saddle with all the ironwork
about it, the rings and buckles, heavy silver plate, and
housings of the finest leopard skin, and a fine saddle
blanket and bridle apiece to go with them. He also gave
us a fine suit of embroidered buckskin apiece, worked
with silk thread. He told us he knew most of the railroad agents clear on to New York, and he had procured
tickets for us to Chicago, and would give us a letter to
the agent there, and he thought he would take us on
to Philadelphia without charging us anything. He said
for us to leave our horses and saddles with him and he
would take care of them for us until we wanted them.
He said if I would take my stuffed antelope and my pets
to the Centennial he had no doubt I could sell them
for a good price. He went with us to the depot and introduced us to the agent, and told us to write to him at
Ellis if we wanted anything any time, and then bade us
goodbye because he was going to Denver. We thanked
him for his presents and being so good to us, but he
said we had saved him a great deal more than he had
given us.

That evening we went with Capt. Dick and stayed
with Whistling Bill. We hated to leave him, but knew he
was in good hands, and that it wouldn't be long before
he could go home himself. Next morning Capt. Dick
started back for Texas in a wagon. Mose Baker and the
negroes went with him and drove the loose horses. The
cook went too. When we came to tell them all goodbye

we felt like we would like to start home with them too, and yet we was glad we wasn't going. Capt. Dick told us we must be sure and come and see him when we came back to Texas, and he hoped we would go over the trail with him next year. We all shook goodbye, they rolled out for Texas, and in an hour me and Nasho was whirling along toward St. Louis.

Everybody was good to us on the road. The conductors passed us free on Col. Hunt's letter, and at the hotel where we stopped at Chicago they didn't charge us any board. We got through to Philadelphia without any trouble, and my pets was all right.

CHARLEY & NASHO AT THE CENTENNIAL

I think I must take Charley's story out of his hands here. My readers will remember that I met him at the Centennial and, though I have not told them so, knew what he was doing there up to the time I left. There was scarcely a day that I did not meet him, and sometimes have long talks with him and, without his knowing it, I think I helped him some by writing to the papers about the two young Texas rancheros and their exhibition. For Charley was not there ten days before he thought he might make some money as well as pay his way and see all the exhibition too. Somebody who met and took an interest in him—and somebody was doing that every day, for he was so manly and straightforward and independent and yet a genuine boy without a particle of that impertinent fastness which marks and makes so unpleasant so many boys who are brought forward earlier than boys usually are—took him to Gen. Hawley to find a place for him. Gen. Hawley most kindly, for he had a dozen men's work to do, gave him a note to the superintendent of the stock department, who at once gave Charley and Nasho employment in the stockyard.

Their work was not heavy—to help feed, water and look after the stock on exhibition—and being mostly to be done early and late left them plenty of time for sight-seeing. One day while looking at some of the rough whips and quirts and saddles and other things made by the natives of South Africa, it occurred to him that he and Nasho might make some money by making pretty bridle reins out of white and black horse hair, and quirts plaited from different colored leathers, and lassoes of rawhide, and cabrasses of horse hair.

I think Charley would rather have spent all his time looking at the million things on exhibition, and reading papers and books about them, but he was anxious to have some money to buy some things for his Uncle and Aunt when he went back to them. So he and Nasho set to work when he had spare time, for he made it a point to spend several hours every day, except during the time the cattle were on exhibition in the ring when they had to be with them all the time, in the exhibition, and they had very good success selling what they made. Then Nasho suggested that he could do better making wax figures, and Charley bought wax and the little tools he wanted, and secured a corner in one of the stalls of the Main Building where he could put their products on exhibition. He also fitted up a table for his pets in the stall, and put his stuffed antelope in one corner, and in a day or two they had more orders than they could fill at good prices.

Not unfrequently a gentleman would come to them and get Nasho to make for him in wax an exact copy of some article on exhibition on the grounds, and would always pay well for it. Although they were so successful with their work and had more orders than they could fill, they did not give up their places in the stockyard, because the work was not hard and was a change from their other work of which they often grew very tired.

One day a gentleman who had bought some things from them became interested in Charley's narrative of their life on the trail, and said he would give ten dollars to see them ride and rope something on horseback. Charley told him they would be glad to show him how it was done if they had their horses there, and a place to rope in. That led to telling about Comanche, and the gentleman became so much interested that he told them if one of them would go to Ellis and bring their horses to Philadelphia, he would arrange for a place where they could ride, and guarantee them enough money to pay for their expenses in bringing and keeping them there. So Charley started to Ellis leaving Nasho to look after their corner stall and his pets.

The gentleman succeeded in obtaining permission for them to exhibit in one of the lots of the stockyard, and let it be known that an exhibition of skill in riding would be given by two young boys from Texas on such a day and hour. Quite a crowd gathered at the time appointed, and when Charley and Nasho rode into the ring in their buckskin suits, their beautiful horses well set off by the fine saddles and the picturesque riding suits of their young masters, the interest of the onlookers became very great. Their style of riding, so much more easy, natural and graceful than that which is taught at riding schools, and is so general among people who have not learned to ride by constant practice, gave great satisfaction, and when Charley swept by at full speed and, bending low in his saddle, picked from the ground a silver dollar which someone had thrown there as a test, the applause was loud and hearty.

It was arranged then that they should give such an exhibition once a week, and they always had a crowd and, better still, the hat which was passed around for them always came back with a good many dollars and halves, and quarters and dimes in it. They had only given four or five of these exhibitions when they were offered one hundred and twenty-five dollars a week to go to New York and Boston and Long Branch and other places, and give their exhibitions there. All their expenses were to be paid, and all the arrangements made for them, so they would have nothing to do but ride. Charley did not like to leave the exhibition, but that was more money than they were making there, and as they did not intend being away more than a month, he consented. They were well received everywhere and cleared over five hundred dollars on the trip.

Charley and I used often to visit different portions of the grounds together and talk about what we saw. I noticed he was very much interested in the people of different countries, the style of houses of other nations, of which there were a number, and everything belonging to them, and particularly in the weapons and other things used by uncivilized people.

Collections of the cured heads and skins of the wild animals of different countries were made to be photographed, and he took a great deal of interest in them, particularly those from Africa. He used often to say to me how much he would like to make a hunting trip through South Africa, and kill some of the many kinds of antelope that are found there, and the hyenas, and lions, and giraffes, and hippopotami, and elephants, and ostriches. I have very little doubt that he will go there some day. If he does, I hope he will write a book and tell us about his adventures, for I am certain it would be very interesting, for there are more wild animals, and of more different kinds, in South Africa than in any other part of the world, and I believe all boys like to read about hunting adventures. I did when I was a boy, and do yet as much as ever.

Two or three of the photographers at the exhibition were very anxious to get pictures of Charley and Nasho in their riding suits on their horses, but Charley would never consent, for he knew they wanted to sell them, and he did not want to be up everywhere for sale. I wanted a picture of them myself, and having found a photographer I knew I could depend upon, Charley agreed to be taken. The artist succeeded in getting a very good picture, and then took one of each of them separately without his horse. Charley sent one of each home to his Uncle and Aunt, and one to Capt. Dick. I kept one of each, and the rest were given to Charley except one which he allowed the artist to keep. Then the negative was destroyed so that it might not get into any other hands, and other pictures be taken from it.

There is one other thing that I do not like to speak of, and yet it ought to be told, because it may have a good deal to do with Charley's life. Although his life has been rather a rough one, his grammar not as correct as it should and will be, and although he gave exhibitions of his skill in riding for money, there is nothing of the rough about him in appearance or manners. Naturally polite and full of good feeling, he has learned rapidly from those about him, and though there is a certain wildness of manner and freedom of action about him that tells at once he was not reared in a city, his courtesy is so genuine that almost everyone that meets him likes him.

One day a gentleman and his wife were strolling along one side of the stockyard stopping frequently to look at some of the fine animals on exhibition therein. A little girl about eight years old was with them, but she had become so much interested in a cute, shaggy little Shetland pony from the rough, iceclad hills of Ireland, that she had fallen far behind her companions. Through carelessness on the part of some attendant a gate had been left open, and a huge, white, shaggy yak, a Tartar ox, which had been put into the yard for a day or two until he could be transferred to the zoological grounds, came out and, catching sight of the child's red cloak, dashed at her. She was too much alarmed to run, but began to scream.

The gentleman was too far ahead to have been able to reach her, but by good fortune Charley was sitting on the fence nearby, and attracted by her cries. Springing from the fence he snatched up a blanket which was lying near, and interposing in front of the charging animal, threw it over his head in such a way as to blind him. In his furious efforts to rid himself of it the yak thrust his horns through it, but instead of relieving him, that only fastened it the more firmly over his eyes and kept him blinded. Seeing there was little danger from that source, Charley ran to the little girl and, picking her up, carried her to the gentleman who was coming towards him as rapidly as possible, and showed them to a gate inside of which they would be safe. Then he ran back to the struggling and furious animal whose hoarse roars of rage were attracting a crowd, though none dared approach very nearly. A policeman who came up was on the point of shooting the bewildered animal which was whirling wildly about and tangling its feet in the folds of the blanket, falling and rolling on the ground, but Charley succeeded in checking him. Getting a rope from an attendant, he soon had the animal safely fastened to a stout post. Another rope was thrown over his horns and, several stout men holding firmly the ends, the yak was soon reconducted to the small pen out of which he had escaped.

The next day the gentleman called at Charley's stall to thank him for his prompt exposure of himself to danger, and became so much interested in him that he insisted upon his visiting them at their hotel and making the acquaintance of the lady and her little niece whom he had rescued. When he came Mrs. Lenton was no less interested than her husband had been, and little Marion was soon as glad to welcome him as the older members of the party when he made his weekly visit during their stay. He gave her some of the finest figures that Nasho's cunning fingers could fashion, encased in handsome glass stands, and when at his parting visit previous to their departure the gentleman asked what little token of friendship he could leave him, I think Charley astonished himself not less than the others by asking for her picture. It was promptly given by the fair hands of little Miss Marion herself, and with a cordial invitation to visit them at their beautiful country home in distant Minnesota.

Are you ready to ask what has all this to do with Charley's future life? Wait and see. Time solves many a mystery.

Soon after that event, about the middle of September, I left the exhibition and started to Texas, and I leave Charley to tell how he got back to Texas across the plains in winter.

A Stranger's Burial

I always like to see the last of anything that I have enough to do with to get interested in. I have often when cow hunting been the last one to leave camp, because I felt like I wanted the last look. And I was real glad to have a chance to see the last of the Centennial. I won't try to tell you anything about it. You know there was a crowd, and it rained, and the umbrellas made the crowd look like a lake full of turtles, and then it seemed a race for who could get away soonest.

I was all ready to go when it closed, for we had been getting ready for a week or two beforehand. I had sold my pets before I started on that trip to New York, and we had boxed up and sent to Kansas City some things we wanted to take home, for fear at the end there would be such a jam of freight that we wouldn't be able to get them there in time, so we sent them ahead. Nasho had gone there a week before with the horses, and was to wait for me. I stayed one day after it closed to see what the grounds looked like without the people, and then started. I wouldn't have missed being at the Centennial and seeing the wind up for anything in the world.

At Kansas City I found Nasho with the horses and our things, and we began to get ready for the trip home. We were going to Fort Dodge on the Atchison, Topeka

and Sante Fe Railroad, and from there start home in a
wagon over the trail. For fear something might happen
to us on the way we had sent Uncle a draft on San
Antonio for six hundred dollars, and took six hundred
with us to buy our outfit and to have money with us
on the road. I have found out already that with money
a traveller can go anywhere and get well taken care of
when without it he would be like a bogged wagon.

We bought a span of young, stout, well-matched
mules; these short, chunky fellows that look like half-
breeds can live on grass and stand anything. They cost
us three hundred dollars, but they were well worth the
money and in good order for the road. Then we bought
a two-horse wagon with a stout duck cover, a small tent,
blankets, some cooking utensils, and coffee, flour, sugar,
bacon, rice, dried fruit, peas, potatoes, onions, molasses and tea and chocolate, for Nasho and me both like
chocolate and he can make it real good. We had some
condensed milk too, and some vegetables already dried
to make soup of.

We had a real nice oil stove that I was taking to Auntie
to use when she only wanted to make some coffee or
tea or cook an egg—it is so much easier than to go to
the trouble of making a fire in the wood stove—that was
boxed up but I bought also a small one just to make tea
or coffee on or cook some soup when we were in a hurry.
On the prairie, when the wind blows, it blows away the
heat of your fire so much that it takes a long time to
cook anything, and then sometimes it ain't half done.
We could cook two things at once on our oil stove, and
had a can of oil to heat it with. I tell you we were fixed
up nice for cowboys or any other sort of boys. I know the
boys here would say we was citified, but we had worked
and earned everything we had, and I don't know what
money is good for if it ain't to buy what you want.

The reason why the horses and cattle and hogs up North look so much better, and get so much larger than ours, is because they are taken so much better care of, have more and better food, and stables to keep them out of the weather. I believe the better people take care of themselves the longer they will last, and the better able to work they will be. I believe I am as ready as anybody to work hard, and stand guard all night if it rains, but when it is over I do like to have a warm tent to come to, and a dry bed and something good to eat that makes you feel ready to go out again if you have to. We couldn't have such things on the trail, but I was going to have them on the trip back.

We got blankets for the mules and horses to put on them at night, and ropes and halters, and a feed trough for Comanche and Spot, as Nasho called his Indian pony. I bought an Evans repeating rifle that carried twenty-five cartridges, and can be fired as fast as a six-shooter, and Nasho got a breechloading shotgun and we both had our belt revolvers. I had a little five-shooting, breechloading revolver that I could carry in my pocket. I never carry it except when I am on the prairie or in the woods, but I like to have it then because it is so handy, and shoots nearly as far and hard as a big pistol. I had bought at the Centennial a fine field-glass that I could make out cattle or horses with from three miles off.

We got to Fort Dodge too late in the evening to make a start, and I wasn't much sorry, for it was snowing. We left our things at the depot, put our stock in the livery stable, and went to the hotel. Then I went out to buy some oats and corn to take with us for the horses and mules, for we couldn't get any on the road until we got into Texas, and I didn't want to depend on the grass in winter. I wanted to travel, and to do that our stock would need feeding. I had bought the feed and a couple of good buffalo robes for bedding, and was on my way back to the hotel when under a little bunch of thin bushes I came across a man lying down in the snow. His clothing was all ragged and dirty, his boots full of holes, and his hat was in pieces. I thought first he was drunk, but when I stooped down over him there was no smell of whiskey about him, and I knew from his face he was sick. He was getting old, for his hair and beard were grizzled, and his face was full of wrinkles and pinched up like when one has been sick a long time. He didn't answer when I spoke to him, and I couldn't rouse him up by shaking him. I hurried off to a wagon standing before a store and got the driver to come with another man and put him in and take him to the hotel.

There was a doctor boarding there who came up to the room and examined him. He gave him a big dose of hot brandy, and we undressed him and began to rub his arms and legs and feet. After a little he began to come to, and in a couple of hours he was strong enough talk a little. He said he had been mining out west and was trying to make his way to Illinois where he had a brother living, but had no money. Lying out in the hard weather had made him sick. The doctor gave him a warm sponge bath in bed and I brought him some flannel underclothes. Then the doctor ordered some hot soup for him, and left me to sit with him.

The poor man seemed to feel a great deal better, but he was so thin and pale and weak that I didn't believe he would ever get up again. He slept tolerably well that night, seemed better next morning, but he soon began to get worse. The doctor told me he was too far gone to ever live. I asked him if he would like to send a message anywhere, and he gave me one to send to Wm. J. Lenton, Bloomington, Illinois. That was the name of the gentleman I had met in Philadelphia, but I thought there might be two of the same name and didn't say anything. It was two hours before I got an answer, and the operator at Bloomington only said there was no such man living there. I told the poor sick man then that I knew such a gentleman who lived at St. Paul's, Minnesota. He asked me a few questions about him and his wife and the little girl, who he said was his niece, but he hadn't seen her for five years. I was going out to telegraph to him, but he stopped me, and said it was too late, he would be gone before his brother-in-law could get there.

He said he was worn out and couldn't last long, and asked for a lawyer to make his will. Then he motioned for all the others to leave, and when they had gone told me that he had left gold where he had been mining, and told me to rip open his coat and I would find a paper that would tell me just where it was, so that I could find it. I got the paper and he told me then that he was going to leave his gold to his niece and me, and asked me to promise him on the Bible that I would go and look for it, and if I found it would divide with her fairly. I promised him, and he seemed a great deal better satisfied.

The lawyer came in a few minutes, and drew up his will as he told him, and the landlord and the minister, who had heard of the sick man and had come in, signed it as witnesses. I was to keep his will and do what he wanted done after he was gone. I paid the lawyer and he left. The minister talked to him a while and went away. I asked him if he would like to be buried at Bloomington, but he said no, it didn't make any difference with him where he was buried, that one place was as near heaven as another. He began to grow weak so fast that I went for the doctor, but he couldn't do anything to rouse him. We sat with him until nearly twelve o'clock that night. Then he roused up a little and beckoned me to come to him. I bent, down close to his ear and he put his arm around my neck and said brokenly, "Charley be sure divide fair with little—"

Then he dropped back again. The doctor came up and put his hand on his arm and in a minute he said, "Poor fellow, he's gone."

We laid him out and took turns sitting with the corpse the rest of the night. Next evening we buried him in the town graveyard. There were scarcely enough there to lower the coffin into the grave and fill it up. The ground was all covered with snow, and the sky was cloudy and dark, and oh, it looked so lonesome! He was so far away from those that cared anything for him. Before the snow was gone he would be forgotten here and nobody would ever come to put flowers on his grave or plant a tree at its head. It seemed so hard to leave him there all alone, but just as we turned away, the sun burst out bright and clear and I thought of that passage in the Bible I had heard Parson Theglin read at funerals at Kerrville: "I am the resurrection and the life: he that believeth in me, though he were dead, yet shall he live. And whosoever liveth and believeth in me shall never die. Believest thou this?"

And I believed it.

A headboard giving the name and day of death was put in the grave, and I got a carpenter to put up a neat fence around it. I wrote a letter to Mr. Lenton at St. Paul's, telling him that I had happened to find his brother-in-law sick there and had staid with him until he died and seen him buried. I did not tell him how I had found him, nor say anything about the will, except that he had left no property. The lawyer told me that was best. No one knew anything about his buried gold, for he had said nothing about it in his will. The fence was finished that morning and everything settled up.

That evening we loaded up and started for Texas and home.

Robbed by Indians

We were almost due north of Kerrville and had nothing to do but keep the trail. Nasho drove the wagon and I rode ahead leading Spot. The weather was cold, but we had warm clothing and didn't mind it much. We would stop half an hour at dinner to make some coffee and get a snack, and then again at sundown for the night. Most of our cooking was done at night so that we could get an early start next morning. When we stopped we would unharness the mules and turn them loose to graze. We staked the horses out, putting our picket pins down close to the wagon. We wasn't afraid of their running away, but it is always a good plan to have at least one horse tied, for then if a stampede should take place you won't be left entirely afoot. Then we pitched our tent and got supper.

As soon as it began to get pretty dark we brought in the mules and horses, fed them with corn and oats, and rubbed them down. We always tied them to the wagon wheels, for that kept them so near us that it would be hard for anybody to take them away without waking us up, and if they should happen to get scared they couldn't get loose, for the wagon would give a little when they pulled back. I always enjoyed seeing the horses and mules eat their supper, and they liked to have us about feeding and rubbing them. Comanche knows me as well as Nasho does. I believe if I was to slip up in the night when he was asleep and touch him he would know it was me. Sometimes at dinner time he will stop grazing and come to me for a handful of oats, or a lump of sugar. He likes sugar as much as I do, and I often give him a lump. I like to treat him well because he is always ready to carry me, and don't need whip or spurs—just a word and he will strike out as hard as he can go.

It was so pleasant the first three or four days that we had a real nice time. I found Spot would follow the wagon so that I didn't have to lead him, and could ride off to either side hunting. I killed a deer, three rabbits and several prairie chickens, so that we had some fresh meat. We had a good lantern, and after we were done feeding the horses and had made all ready for the night, I used to read, for I had brought some books with me. I had several books about hunting on the plains and in the Rocky Mountains and in Africa, and a natural history, and books about birds and fish, and two or three histories and some others. The nights were so long that sometimes I would read two or three hours before going to sleep. Nasho nearly always went to sleep right off. He didn't care about reading, though sometimes he would look over the pictures about the animals and birds, and ask me questions about them. How I did like to read about hunting! I would rather go to Africa than anywhere else, because there is so much more game there, and so many different kinds.

One night while I was reading I happened to look out and saw a pair of eyes shining only a few yards off. I lay down my book and got my rifle and tried to shoot, but at first I couldn't see the sights. After a little I held it so that the light would fall on the front sight, and taking the best aim I could between the eyes, fired. Nasho was up in a second. "What matter, Carley?"

"Only a wolf," I said, and ran out to see. Sure enough it was a wolf. I had shot him square between the eyes. The horses and mules jumped a little when I shot, but didn't try to break loose. Almost every night we would hear a pack of wolves howling and sometimes close to our camp, but we knew they wouldn't trouble our horses and wasn't afraid of them. I like to hear wolves howl at night.

That same night about half an hour afterwards I thought I heard something snuffle, and looking up saw a polecat's head poking under the tent. I was afraid he would come in and scent everything up. You know how they smell, so I got my little pistol easy, and when he stuck it in again took good aim and fired. Nasho popped up in a second—I believe he was a little scared, because I shot right over him, and a pistol makes a loud noise in a house or tent, but I told him what it was, and we went out and looked at him. His head was all torn to pieces by the ball. Polecats are dangerous little vermin. I have heard of several men being bitten by them in Texas and killed. They come into camp in the night when everybody is asleep, and 'most always bite in the nose. We didn't skin either the wolf or the polecat because we had finer skins of both at home.

After that I wished we had a dog to let us know when anything came about. A dog may be sound asleep, but if any animal or person comes about he is sure to wake up.

Just six days after we left Fort Dodge we camped on the south side of the Red Fork, in Indian Territory. The next morning when we woke up—we always got up at the first crack of day—everything was covered with snow, and it was snowing hard. I was sorry for the horses and mules, because the nights hadn't been very cold and we hadn't put their blankets on them. We gave them a

good feed and after breakfast we started. The trail was
so covered with snow that we couldn't tell where it was,
but we thought we could travel pretty well by compass.
About eleven o'clock I unsaddled Comanche and left
him with Spot to follow, and rode in the wagon with
Nasho. That night when we camped we couldn't tell
whether we were near the trail or not. The next morning it was still snowing, but not very hard. I was more
than half a mind to lay up until the snow cleared away,
because I was afraid we would drive into some gully or
hole and break something; but I wanted to get home,
and we started.

About eleven o'clock all of a sudden an Indian rode
in front of our mules and stopped them. We looked out
and there were half a dozen around the wagon. The
Indians were all supposed to be friendly, but friendly
or not we had to make out like we thought they was,
for they had slipped up on us too well to give us any
chance to fight if we had wanted to.

One ugly looking rascal, with a dirty red blanket
around him and some feathers stuck in his long black
hair, came up to us and said "Injin's wagon, Injin's
mules, Injin's horses, all Injin's. Ugh!"

"No!" I said. "Our horses and wagon. We buy 'em in
Kansas."

He motioned us to get out, and Nasho said, "Day got
us, Carley. Must get out."

We got out, though I didn't like to, because if they
intended to kill us, our guns were in the wagon and
that was our only chance for our lives. But I thought it
wasn't any use to show fight. Four of them had guns
and pistols, and the other two bows and arrows and
lances. We wouldn't have stood any show in a fight.
When we got out the dirty old rascal pointed to Comanche and Spot, and said, "Dem Injin horses, you steal

dam heap. Now Injin get back—take mules, wagon too. You no like, take scalp too," and the ugly villain made a motion as if he was lifting a scalp, and his black eyes shone like a snake's. The rest all laughed.

Nasho commenced talking to them in Indian. I couldn't tell what they said, but I knew from their motions and looks that they pretended not to believe what he told them, and from the way the old rascal who acted as leader tapped his gun, that they intended to take everything we had. Directly Nasho turned to me and said, "It no use, Carley. Day got us. Day take mules, wagon, horses, all; we no can help. No can fight now."

One of them got off his horse, gave his bridle rein to another, and got in the wagon and took the reins, laughing like a baboon. It would have done me good to have made a hole through his ugly head. They started off laughing, and bowing to us, and two or three of them hollered out as they rode off, "Goodbye! Heap walk now."

I had my little revolver in my pocket, but it would have been foolish to have thought of shooting. It was enough to make anybody mad to have a good outfit taken right from under them and be left in the middle of a prairie in a snowstorm, with nothing to eat, and no arms but a little revolver but it was better than to have our scalps taken. I was looking after them and feeling like crying about Comanche when I heard Nasho say, "Nodder rascal coming!"

I looked up and saw another one coming on a lope. He was riding a fine spotted horse, and as he got closer I saw he was dressed in a good suit of fringed buckskin and had a fine blanket lying across his Mexican saddle. He had a lance in his hand and his bow and arrows slung to his back. He came up as if he was going to ride right over us, but we never moved. Nasho had told me that was the way they always came and when he was in a jump of us he pulled up so quick that it almost threw his horse on his haunches.

He was a young fellow not much bigger than Nasho, and cleaner and better looking every way than the rest. He had a fine head rig of eagle feathers and bear claws round his neck, and silver buttons on his buckskin shirt. As quick as he got a look at Nasho's face he called out to him in Indian, and jumped off his horse, and caught both his hands and fairly hugged him. Nasho seemed as glad to see him as he was to see Nasho, and for two or three minutes they talked as fast as two schoolgirls. Then I could tell by Nasho's gestures that he was telling the Indian about our being robbed. The young Indian scowled and looked on the ground a second, and then said something to Nasho and jumped on his horse and started after the others who had got out of sight under a hill.

"Dat Co-shel-to," Nasho said. "He heap friend me when me with Kickapoos. He try get wagon, horses, all back again. He chief."

I thought from his dress he must be a chief's son. How I did watch to see if they were coming back! It reminded me of the time I was in the tree watching the horse when I caught Comanche. I didn't much believe he could make them give us back our outfit if he was a chief, because he was hardly anything but a boy, and they didn't have hardly anything and wouldn't like to let their prize go. Directly we saw Co-shel-to coming back with the wagon and horses; the same Indian was driving and another one leading his horse. When they came up the one in the wagon got out, and Co-shel-to motioned to the wagon and horses with a sweep of his hand, and said something to Nasho. Nasho bowed and said something to him, but I couldn't make out anything about it, only I was sure Co-shel-to intended for us to keep everything.

Wasn't I glad to get Comanche back again! I couldn't help walking up to him and patting him. Co-shel-to noticed me, and said in Spanish, "Muy hermoso caballo, señor!"

I answered. Then I went to the wagon, got my best pistol with the belt and cartridges, and walking up to him said, "Haga me el favor señor, acceptar este pistol."

"Muchas gracias, señor."

He took it with a proud bow and buckled it around his waist, and I could see he was glad to have it. Nasho said something to him, and he turned and spoke to one of the Indians, and he started off on a gallop.

Nasho told me then he had asked the young chief to send for the others to come back and drink coffee with us. He told me not to seem to be afraid of them, or act as if I did not like them, but to be friendly. When we saw them coming back he said, "You drive, Carley. We go to water."

I got in and drove and he walked along by the side of Co-shel-to. It was only a little ways to a running branch, where I stopped. I was sorry and almost mad with Nasho for sending back for the thieving rascals, for I was afraid they might rob us again and for good this time, but there was nothing for it but to put a good face on the matter, and I determined none of 'em should see how I hated them. By good luck we had some deer meat and a ham. We got that out and our meat-pot to make coffee in, and started a fire. They didn't seem to care for the bread, but they ate all the meat and drank the pot twice full of coffee. We didn't have but two cups, so they had to take it time about. As soon as the last one had drank his coffee they got on their horses to leave. I got out some of the tobacco I was taking to Uncle and

Parson Theglin. I divided it among them and gave them some matches, and they rode off.

Wasn't I glad to see them go though! I could tell from their looks that they hated to leave without our outfit, but they didn't want to take it as bad as I wanted to keep it.

Then Nasho and Co-shel-to talked a little, and I knew from their gestures that he was telling Nasho which way to go. When they were through Nasho went to the wagon and got his shotgun and belt, and a box of cartridges, and gave them to Co-shel-to. He put the cartridges in a buckskin bag that hung at his side. Then he took off his bow and arrow, and handed them to Nasho with his lance. He shook hands with me, said "Adios, Señor," shook hands with Nasho, saying something to him in Indian, jumped on his horse and rode off at a gallop in the direction the others had gone.

I saddled Comanche, took my rifle and mounted, and Nasho got in the wagon and we started, bearing more to the left than we had been travelling.

That evening I kept a sharp lookout with my field-glass, but didn't see any more Indians. I was riding ahead nearly at sundown when I saw something like a wolf lying down right ahead of us. I thought first it was a wolf, but in a minute I saw it was a dog, and riding up to it found it was a dog so poor and crippled that it could not walk. It was a fine, large dog that looked like a cross between a bulldog and a greyhound. It must have been stolen from some army post by the Indians, got crippled by some animal, and left by them when it couldn't keep up. I was sorry for the poor dog, and when Nasho came up we put him in the wagon and took him with us. When we camped I made him a pot of hot soup, and he ate as if famished. Then I put some liniment on his sore feet and tied them up, and on a place in his side where a deer or a buffalo had hooked him. After supper I covered him up well with a saddle blanket.

Nasho told me that night that Co-shel-to was a young Blackfoot Indian that had been captured by the tribe of Kickapoos he lived with, and that he and Co-shel-to had been great friends. They had each cut a little vein on his arm and drank some of each other's blood. That meant that they were to be as dear to each other as brothers. Since he had left them Co-shel-to had become chief, although he was so young. Old Kee-watch-ie, who was chief when Nasho left them had been killed in a fight, and Co-shel-to chosen in his place because he was the bravest warrior in the tribe.

Co-shel-to told him that the trail was miles away to our left. He said the Comanches were going to their winter quarters ahead of us, and we must look out and not fall in their way or they would be sure to rob and perhaps kill us. He said we must hurry and cross the prairie as fast as we could, and get into the red mountains, where we could travel without being so apt to be seen, and that the sooner we got through the Nation into Texas the better for us. There was nobody travelling through the Nation in winter, and nobody would know if we were robbed and killed. He said it would take us four days more to get through, and we would have some rough roads in the mountains.

Nasho said we would sleep until twelve o'clock, when the moon rose, and then get up and travel. You may be sure I didn't read any that night. It was a good thing for us that Co-shel-to came along. We would have had a hard time if we had been left in the prairie without anything. I didn't feel as easy and good that night as I had been doing, and I believe if I had been back at Kansas City I would have come home by rail. But we were in for it now and had to go through. So I went to sleep.

Desolate Prairie—Home, Sweet, Home

It seemed to me I had not been asleep an hour when I heard somebody stirring, and raising up found Nasho getting ready to start. The moon was up, but it didn't shine very brightly. We hadn't stretched the tent, so it didn't take us long to harness up and start. We put the poor dog in the wagon. I rode Comanche, and Spot was tied behind the wagon already saddled, so that if the Indians should come on us we could leave the wagon and get away on horseback. We had on our overcoats, and a good blanket apiece strapped on to our saddles, and plenty of ammunition, and some provision, mostly bacon and coffee, and a coffee pot and our cups. We didn't intend to be set afoot again without anything unless the Indians outran us.

I rode ahead to pick the way and keep a good lookout. It wasn't snowing, but the ground was covered with snow, four inches deep, and it was very cold. It was scarcely light enough to see well, and I had to be very careful to keep out of gullies, and find places where the wagon could cross. The prairie was pretty smooth, and we kept ahead steadily, but about daylight I got so sleepy I could hardly keep my eyes open.

At sunup we stopped, fed the mules and horses without unharnessing or taking the saddles off, made a fire, and had some breakfast. The hot coffee did us a heap of good, for we were both real cold. I gave the dog a good breakfast too, and was glad to see him looking better already.

As quick as breakfast was over we hitched up and started again. Was you ever on the prairie in winter?

If not, then you don't know how much difference there is between it in spring and winter. Everything looked so barren and desolate. Just one great mass of white all around as far as you could see, with hardly a tree, and overhead the sky was cloudy. Now and then the sun would break out for a minute and light up the snow so it would almost dazzle us, and the few bushes would sparkle and glisten, but it would only last a minute, and everything would turn a chilly gray again. It seemed like Nature was dead. Not a sound was to be heard except the horses' feet and the crunching of the wheels through the snow. And it seemed like we would never get anywhere. It was just snow, snow, snow; and when we got to the top of a rise hoping to see timber ahead, it would only be snow again as far as we could see.

About twelve o'clock we struck a gang of buffalo. There must have been ten thousand of them. They were not moving, but scattered about, feeding. They didn't pay much attention to us, and we could have killed lots of them if we had wanted, but I didn't feel like shooting them and leaving the poor things to die in the cold, and Nasho didn't want to stop either. I killed one fat cow when we stopped for dinner, and we took the hump, and some ribs, and the tongue, and some steaks, for we were out of fresh meat. It seemed like a pity to kill as large an animal as that for so little meat. There are hundreds of men that make a regular business of killing them for their hides. I was pretty nearly tired out when we stopped, but a good buffalo steak, a slice of bacon and some hot coffee freshened me up heap, and in less than an hour we were moving again.

We were in sight of buffalo nearly all the evening, and the snow was broken in thousands of places where they had pawed it away to get at the grass. I didn't like to see so many buffalo, for I was afraid the Indians were about somewhere, but as long as they were there I liked to watch them as I rode along. Very often I would ride in thirty yards of them without scaring them.

About the middle of the evening I began to get cold and sleepy—oh, so sleepy. It seemed to me I must get down and go to sleep on the snow. I thought if I could only sleep ten minutes I would feel a great deal better. I could hardly keep from going to the wagon and getting in to take a nap, but I thought Nasho must be as sleepy as I was, and one of us ought to stay on horseback to keep up a watch and pick out the road. I don't know how I managed to keep at all straight that evening. I had the compass, but don't remember looking at it. I know I must have been half asleep most of the time. I have a recollection of the snowy prairie, and now and then gangs of buffalo, and turning round every little while to see if the wagon was coming on, and if I was getting too far ahead, and of it getting darker, and then the next thing I remember is feeling something hot about me. When I got fairly awake I looked around and saw the wagon standing nearby but the mules wasn't unhitched, and there was a big fire burning. I remember drinking something hot, and getting warm and feeling good—oh, so good—and then I must have dropped asleep again.

I didn't wake up until daylight, and then I jumped up quick thinking I must help Nasho unharness and get ready for night, but I found myself undressed and in the tent. I dressed myself and stepped out. The mules and horses were hitched to the wagon with their blankets on, and the ashes showed there had been a big fire. I hardly knew what to make of it, but I looked to the east and saw it was day, and I knew then I had been asleep all night. Nasho hadn't waked up and, as he had done everything the night before, I knew he must be tired out, so I didn't wake him, but fed the horses and mules and got breakfast. I cooked some rice and made some strong tea, for Nasho is very fond of tea, put some bacon and buffalo steak on to broil, and then went and called him. He got up and came out, but he seemed almost asleep, and hardly to know what I said to him. He said he was cold, and didn't eat much, but the tea stirred him up a little.

"You 'most froze when me drive up here last night, Carley. You was lying on ground and me couldn't wake you up. Me hurry and make fire and heat pot of water. Den me stretch tent and take off your clothes and dip blanket in hot water, and wrap you up in him. Me didn't know if you come to any more. Me pour whiskey and chile down you and you open you eyes and look round little, but you no know nothin. Me feel you arms and me know you was coming to, and me soon take off wet blanket and wrap you up good in heap blanket. Me say Carley be all right in morning. Den me feed horses and mules and sit by fire while dey eat. Me too tired and cold to eat. When dey done, me tie em up and go to bed. Me feed dog first, and me feel you arm. Carley all right in mornin'. Den me go to sleep. Me ain't warm yet—need sweat heap, den me feel well."

He went and lay down again. I knew then that I had fallen off my horse and didn't know anything when he came up, and he had taken care of me and tended to everything, though he was half-frozen himself. It was my time now.

Camp was in a good place in a hollow well sheltered from the north, and plenty of grass and water. I made up a big fire, and put in a lot of big smooth rocks that I found in the branch. Then I hobbled the mules and staked out the horses. I cut some long, slim poles and, sticking one end in the ground, bent them over and fastened the other end, making a framework like a big beehive, or a large pot. I covered this well with blankets and a buffalo robe. Then I woke Nasho up and at last got him to understand that he must undress and get in. I helped him, for he was more than half asleep. I had put the hot rocks, so hot I had to handle them with two sticks, on each side of the shanty so he wouldn't get on them and burn himself and, setting a bucket of water inside, crunched down in the door, drew a blanket over me to keep out the air, and began pouring the cold water on the hot rocks. It make such a steam it almost stifled me. In a couple of minutes Nasho roused up and said, "Me all right now, Carley. Give me cup an' you git out, no good for you. Me all right now."

I saw he was waked up good and left him. In three or four minutes he came out and ran into the tent. I rubbed him dry, covered him up well with blankets, gave him some hot tea, and left him. I went to him two or three times during the morning, but he was sleeping well and I didn't trouble him. About twelve o'clock he waked up, dressed and came out, and said he was all right. There wasn't anything the matter with either of us except getting chilled through riding so long in the cold but if I had been by myself I don't know whether I could ever have waked up again or not. It was a good thing for me that Nasho wasn't as cold and tired as I was.

We had a good dinner that day of hot buffalo soup with rice and peas in it, roasted Irish potatoes and stewed peaches. Our stock was looking a little thin from not having time enough on the road to graze, so we stayed there that evening to let them feed.

The next morning we were off again early. The country was hilly and rough and we couldn't travel as fast as we had been doing. We had to zigzag about a good deal to dodge steep hills, and find places where we could cross the gullies. It was that way for two days, and kept getting worse instead of better. More than once we had to unhitch the mules and let the wagon down a steep bank by a rope running round a tree to keep it from slipping too fast. Then we would hitch up, fasten a rope to the tongue and I would wrap it around the horn of my saddle, and by the hardest kind of work we would drag it up the other bank. I told Nasho we had better turn off almost square to the left and find the Trail, for we wouldn't be any more apt to be troubled by the Indians there than wandering around through the woods where we were likely to run into a camp at any time.

We saw plenty of game but didn't like to shoot for fear of being heard by Indians. That evening directly after we stopped a bear came close to camp and we killed him. Anybody can't be careful always, and a chance to kill a bear don't come every day. Although it was winter he was in pretty good order, and gave us some good meat.

Rover, that was the name I gave the dog we picked up on the prairie, had got so much better he could keep up very well, though he was still a little lame. I had rather trust him and Comanche to let me know if anything or anybody was coming than soldiers.

The next morning while Nasho was driving along slowly, for the ground was rough, we came to a piece of smooth prairie with a hill and woods on the other side. I rode ahead, crossed a deep ravine and climbed the hill, but I dodged back out of sight quick, for there were a party of Indians riding through the woods almost exactly in our direction. They were nearly a mile off, and were not coming in Indian file like they nearly always ride, but scattered along over two hundred yards. There were about twenty. I ran back to Nasho and told him what I had seen, and to hurry up and get into the ravine and maybe they wouldn't see us. He drove up quick. The ground wasn't rocky and the wagon didn't make much noise, and we struck the ravine where the bank sloped so he could get down into it. As soon as he stopped he jumped out, locked the wheel, untied Spot, brought him up in front of the mules and stood by his head with his bow strung and an arrow ready. I didn't get off my horse, but had my rifle so I could shoot in a second.

"No shoot, Carley, if can help it. All hear gun. Arrow make no noise."

I didn't need that to tell me that shooting was the last thing to be done. The ravine we were in ran nearly due north and south, but just below us turned almost square east, ran a few yards that way and then turned south again. We sat waiting almost breathless. Directly we heard a horse coming down the bank below us. Comanche pricked up his ears, but I patted his neck and told him to keep still. Rover raised his head but didn't growl, and I spoke to him low. Nasho raised his bow. We could hear the Indian coming up the ravine. In a second he turned the bank, saw us and pulled up but before he could do anything, I saw him throw up his hands and fall.

Nasho ran up and caught his horse. I was worse scared than when the Indians had us, for fear a horse or mule might make a noise, or another Indian happen to stumble on us, and I knew if they did there was nothing for it but to cut and run. I could hear their horses' feet through the woods, but they got fainter and fainter until they died away. Nasho beckoned me to come to him. We took the dead Indian and dragged him out of the way so the wagon wouldn't roll over him. He was shot right through the heart. The arrow was in too deep to pull out. Nasho said he was a Comanche. We waited nearly half an hour for them to get clear out of reach of hearing. We wasn't afraid of their coming back to hunt for the dead one, at least until next morning, because one often leaves the party that way to scout or hunt, and they didn't know what had happened to him. They were not going in a direction that would be likely to bring them across our trail, though we were very much afraid one might straggle out to one side as this one had done, and find it, and if he did they would be sure to follow it up.

When we thought it was safe we drove on, and a quarter of a mile down the ravine came to a place where we could get out. I tied the Indian horse in the ravine and helped pull the wagon out. Nasho went back with his bow and arrows, unsaddled him and, stepping off a few feet, whizzed an arrow into him. He reared up, fell back, kicked a little and was dead. Then Nasho took the halter off—he didn't have any bridle—carried them away a few steps and threw them into some bushes, I asked him why he didn't put them in the wagon, but he said if any other Indians got us and found the saddle, they would think we had killed an Indian and then kill us. I knew why he had killed the horse. He was afraid if he let him go he might go on and overtake the party, or go back to their village, and when they saw him they would know something was wrong and go out to look for him. It wouldn't do to tie him up to starve, so there was nothing to do but kill him.

That night we camped by the trail again and I felt better satisfied, though I knew I would hardly draw a

safe breath until we were out of the Nation. I wouldn't
have been a bit uneasy in summer, but there is nobody
travels there in winter, and we had had trouble enough
to make us scary.

"Charley, might not those have been friendly Indians?
It looks very cruel to shoot a man down without a word,
and without knowing whether he intends hurting you
or not."

I know it, but Nasho was right. Indians are not like
white men. They don't give you any chance when they
get the advantage of you. As to being friendly, none of
the wild tribes will do to trust if they have a chance
to rob or kill without being found. Nasho knew in a
second from his dress he was a Comanche, and they are
one of the worst tribes in the Nation. Some of them raid
down into Texas almost every moon, and steal and kill
whenever they get a chance. If we could have captured
him I would rather have it, but when I saw him pull up
I knew it was our lives or his—whoever was the quick-
est. In another second he would have whirled his horse
behind the bank, and they would all have been on us
and been almost certain to have caught us. We would
never have got out of that ravine unless they took us out
to torture us, or carried us away prisoners, and we were
too old for that. I was sorry for him, but I had a heap
rather that Indian was there than me and Nasho.

Next morning we were off by daylight, and it was much
travel and little sleep until we put Red River between us
and the Indian's country. I thought when we started we
would have a good time hunting in the Nation, but you
may be sure we didn't stop to hunt. We were only too
glad to find the rivers all fordable so that we could cross
them. We kept the trail to Fort Griffin in Texas, and then
took the country roads and reached home, just in time
for Christmas. Wasn't I glad to get back and see Uncle

and Auntie again! As the Indians say, as long as grass
grows and water runs, I shall never forget how we went
to the Centennial.